PRAISE FOR
NO GUN INTENDED

"In *No Gun Intended*, Mario Rutledge brilliantly manages a nearly insurmountable task: a timely anatomy of the tragic and nuanced interplay of school violence, guns, and human isolation. He does so with great sensitivity and an unflinching but empathetic eye. Readers will be captivated by the multidimensional characters, psychological insights, and dynamic plot. This novel should be a must-read for students, parents, and educators."

—Thomas H. Carry, Author of *Privilege*

No Gun Intended

by Mario Rutledge

© Copyright 2023 Mario Rutledge

ISBN 978-1-64663-897-0

Published by

 köehlerbooks™

3705 Shore Drive
Virginia Beach, VA 23455
800-435-4811
www.koehlerbooks.com

NO GUN INTENDED

NOVEL

MARIO RUTLEDGE

VIRGINIA BEACH
CAPE CHARLES

For Mom—my biggest cheerleader.

PROLOGUE

It's a typical summer day in Lakehurst, Indiana—or so it seems. A quaint suburban town that sits in the northwest end of the Hoosier State between Chicago and Detroit, it's a twenty-minute drive to the town's biggest attraction, Lake Michigan, which they only get a small piece of, considering the neighboring cityscape giants of Chicago, Milwaukee, and Grand Rapids. It's the middle of June. The thick and humid air covers the quintessentially uneventful neighborhood of Fox Trail, which sits in the middle of Lakehurst. All the houses look basically the same, with marginal differences in color. Even the shrubbery bordering each house looks similar. The grass is just as green from one house to the next. There is one house that stands out from the crowd of dittos, though—only because of the '84 Cutlass Supreme Oldsmobile that sits in the driveway. The car is clean and in mint condition; the owner obviously takes care of it. Inside this house, in an upstairs bedroom is Ian Moss, a bright-eyed five-year-old with strawberry blond hair. Most don't notice the faint freckles dotting his face. He's sprawled on the floor of his small, boxy room, coloring in a scrapbook atop a vibrant rug that takes up most of the space in the room. Toys are scattered about—Legos, Hot Wheels, and a G.I. Joe action figure that looks worn down. Even an original Slinky slumps in the corner. Ian is the type of kid that can have fun by himself for hours, as long as he has the tools to occupy his busy mind, which comes in handy since he is an only child. And here, he looks to be in his element.

Ian is adding color to a picture he drew in a scrapbook, highlighting a pair of blue pants worn by a child in the drawing, who stands holding hands with two adults. It's a picture of his mother, his father, and himself, standing off-center from a house he drew. His mother to his right, and his father to his left. The portrait is no work of Picasso but given Ian's creative efforts, still shows it's deserving of being pinned to the fridge. He finally scribbles *Love you* at the bottom of the landscape page, an artist's signature to a worthy creation. The anticipation of showing his father has Ian excited. Not for accolades, but in using this as an incentive to persuade his father to let him indulge in some ice cream he knows is in the freezer.

"Daddy!" Ian yells, as he makes his way downstairs. Much of the décor of this house is compliments of Ian's mother, Katherine. She has a knack for these kinds of things. Growing up on a farm most of her life, she misses the remote countryside, but appeases her reminiscent taste with photos of sunflowers framed on the walls, as well as antique farming memorabilia littered throughout the home. Ian runs down the stairs passing framed photos of his father, Ray, his mother, and himself. He jets past the kitchen, which is beautifully sunlit. White linoleum and kitchen appliances accent the wooden kitchen table and chairs. He opens the door to his parents' bedroom to find his father seated on the edge of the bed. Ray looks disheveled. His graying brown hair is stringy. His shirt is sloppily buttoned and wrinkled. Heavy black bags under his eyes would indicate he's been on a two-day bender, but he's as sober as a nun. Beads of sweat stream from his forehead, dripping from his stubbled chin. Holding a 9-milimeter in his hand, he's distracted once Ian enters the bedroom. Ian rushes in holding up the prized portrait of his family.

"Look what I made, Dad!" he says excitedly. Ray looks at Ian, forcing a crooked smile.

"Hey, buddy. Sorry you have to see this," he says casually. Ray slides the gun into his mouth and pulls the trigger. The loud bang startles Ian as he stays frozen in place. Blood and brain tissue project on the bedroom furniture, the ceiling, and the thick yellow window curtains hanging behind Ray. Flecks of blood pepper Ian's clothes and splatter his portrait. Ray falls back on the bed, gun still in hand. The blood flow oozes from the exit wound, absorbed by the fine bed linen. Ian stands in shock, eyes bulging in the dead silence.

Ian faintly replies, "Dad?" But no answer. A constant drip can be heard hitting the carpet. It's not blood, but Ray's urine dripping from the cuff of his soaked jeans.

A couple hours later, Katherine pulls into the driveway. She is medium height with long brown hair and a soft midsection but is mostly in shape. The sun stubbornly continues to set as she exits her silver Honda, a brown paper bag of groceries in hand. She opens the front door to the house, hanging her purse on a wobbly coat rack that leans over, hitting a picture frame on the wall. The frame falls to the ground, in it a photo of Ray holding Ian in his arms as they both smile.

"Oh shit!" She picks up the frame and notices a crack in the glass that's split over Ian's face. She glances over to see Ian sitting on the living room couch in silence, his portrait on his lap. "Hey sweetie, I didn't see you there." Katherine places the cracked frame on an end table in the living area. She walks over to Ian, who has his head down. "Honey, are you okay?" she gently rubs his shoulder.

Ian doesn't answer. Katherine picks up his portrait and gets a good look. She thinks the picture is wonderful, aside from the red droplets plastering the page.

"Wow! This is a great picture, Ian," she says enthusiastically.

"Thanks," Ian says softly.

"I'll put it on the fridge."

"Can I have some ice cream?" Ian asks, looking up at his mother.

"Not now sweetie, I'm about to cook—what's all over your face?" Katherine swipes Ian's face with her thumb, realizing it's blood. She's struck with an uneasy feeling of paranoia. "Where's your father?" she asks, sounding concerned. Ian points to the bedroom.

Katherine sets the portrait and bag of groceries down on the living room coffee table. Dusk is now creeping through the sky. Slowly walking to the bedroom, she calls out Ray's name. No answer. Walking in, she sees Ray's lifeless body lying on the bed, a grotesque scene that would make the bloodiest of horror films pale in comparison. Katherine notices the gun in Ray's hand. She screams in shock as she rushes over. His leaking wound has eased its flow drastically. The entire bed is saturated with blood. She cradles him in her arms and rocks back and forth as she cries out in agony, asking why, and praying this is all a bad dream. She is soon covered in Ray's blood. Katherine's voice begins to strain from her shrieking cries. Ian stands in the doorway of the bedroom watching the tragedy unfold. Although too young to fully grasp the severity of the situation, this is a numbing feeling for Ian. But deep down he knows his life will never be the same.

SENIOR YEAR

CHAPTER 1

Ian wakes up in his bed, a bit startled. A bad dream? Possibly, but he can't remember it. He looks over at the clock on his nightstand. 8:20 a.m. Next to his clock is the photo of him and his father, this time in a better frame. He sits up and stretches to the sound of birds chirping in the summer air. A light tap is heard at his window above his bed. Again, another tap, then another, then another. He opens his blinds, flooding his room with sunlight. Squinting toward the brightness, he spots the culprit, a bumble bee repeatedly flying into his window as if trying to come inside. Ian rubs his eyes and hops out of bed.

It's been eleven years since his father's suicide. His bedroom has changed with his age. It now consists of blue walls and a plain wooden furniture set, including a matching bedframe, dresser, and nightstand. His walls are bare and not much stands out about his room, personality wise, except that the room is completely spotless. Not a speck of dust or anything out of place. This room is clean and organized from the closet to the entrance. He walks out, making his way to the bathroom. He hears voices coming from downstairs and recognizes one of them as belonging to his mother. *Who is she talking to this early in the morning?* he thinks.

Ian steps into a spotless bathroom. He spies a single strand of hair left on the sink. Ian picks it up, dropping it into the trash. He looks at himself in the mirror. Obvious bedhead and in need of a shower. He opens his medicine cabinet and sees a tube of Crest sitting next to a medicine bottle with his name on it. Ian smirks as he closes the cabinet door and begins to brush his teeth. He spits the residue into the sink and washes his mouth out. Placing the toothpaste back into the medicine cabinet, he grabs the medicine bottle and shakes out a pill. He grabs a small cup off the sink and fills it with water, washing down the pill with precision. He's done this many a time. Closing the cabinet, he's startled by laughter coming from downstairs. He casually walks down the steps to the living area where he sees his mother and a salt-and-pepper-haired man sitting across from one another. He is Dr. Andrew Price, Ian's psychotherapist. A young gentleman who looks to be in his mid thirties, Dr. Price is dressed in an expensive button-down shirt and a pair of gray slacks. He looks up, noticing Ian as he sets his mug on the table in front of him. Katherine greets Ian with a welcoming smile, daintily holding her coffee.

"Good morning, Ian." She pats the cushion on the couch next to her, signaling Ian to sit. He is a bit confused. Dr. Price usually doesn't do house calls, and Ian's next appointment is not until next week. "Come sit with us for a second," she says eagerly. Still a bit confused, Ian walks over and takes a seat next to his mother.

"Hello Ian. How are you this morning?" Dr. Price says, crossing one leg over the other to present himself in a more professional manner. Ian takes notice of his expensive shoes, which look like they must have cost hundreds of bucks. Eyebrow raised like the morning sun, Ian responds to Dr. Price.

"I'm doing good. Why are you—? Ian stops himself as he takes note of Katherine and Dr. Price smiling at each other. *They look like they're up to something. What is this about?*

"Bet you're wondering why I'm here, huh?" Dr. Price says in a light manner.

Ian nods his head. "I am." He looks at his mother, who's trying to hide a guilty expression on her face with a half-assed smile.

Katherine sets down her coffee cup and places her hand on Ian's knee. She looks over at him. Her expression is mild, as if she's holding onto a secret she's dying to let out. "Well, Dr. Price and I have been talking a lot about your health and—" Ian now feels this is an ambush. He tenses up a little, thinking this must be about the medication he's taking, or that they want to increase his therapy sessions from once every two weeks to two or three times a week. He gets a bit defensive.

"I'm doing good. Mom, you know it's been a while since I had an episode."

"We know, sweetie, that is why we wanted to talk with you," Katherine assures with the upmost grace. Dr. Price leans forward a bit, interlocking his fingers.

"Ian, you have been a fantastic example of what therapy and treatment can do to benefit someone with your condition. Not only have you been exceeding in your academics, but we both have noticed through the years at how mature and responsible you have become." Katherine nods her head, looking toward Ian, giddy and gleeful. "That is why we have a proposal for you." Dr. Price grabs his coffee cup and takes a sip as he leans back on the couch. Katherine scoots a little bit closer toward Ian. She grabs hold of his hand.

"Up to this point, homeschooling has been great, and next year you'll be graduating and living as an adult. Which is why I want to ask—how would you like to spend your senior year in public school? And whatever you decide to do, Dr. Price and I are going to support you one hundred percent," Katherine says, gently patting the top of Ian's hand with her own.

"Public school?" Ian asks, just to be clear what they are asking of him because this sounds farfetched at best.

"This will give you an opportunity to be more independent, prep you for college, and gain a ton of social skills along the way," Dr. Price assures.

"You'll get to make friends, experience prom . . . maybe even find a girlfriend—" Katherine is interrupted by laughter from Dr. Price. He disguises his outburst as coughing after Katherine gives him a withering look.

He slightly pounds his chest. "Sorry."

"This is unbelievable!" Ian shouts. Katherine and Dr. Price look to one another nervously, thinking they may have offended Ian in some way. Katherine begins second guessing this idea. She puts full blame on Dr. Price. She knew Ian was not going to be ready for this.

"Yes . . . YES! I'd love to go to public school!" Ian's grin is suggestive of a kid on Christmas morning. He's on the verge of jumping out of his skin, he's so excited.

Katherine yelps joyously, giving one good clap.

"This is amazing! Thank you. Thank you both!" Ian rushes upstairs to his room.

Dr. Price stands with Katherine, following her lead. He brushes his shirt off a bit to knock out a few of the wrinkles that accumulated from sitting down. He knows Katherine thinks that is a pretentious act on his behalf but given their long history since Ray's suicide, she should be used to his quirks by now. He bends over and picks up his expensive-looking, leather-bound briefcase.

Katherine smiles. Looking down, she sees the glitter-covered figurine of a unicorn on her coffee table is off kilter. As much as she wants to straighten it, she's afraid Dr. Price will call her out on her slight OCD behavior and start booking her for therapy sessions. Although she is not opposed, she'd rather focus her time on more important matters than her slight case of obsessive-compulsion.

"I think this is going to work out great for Ian," says Dr. Price, looking down at his flashy watch and noticing that not much time has passed during this visit. He thinks now he has enough time to swing by the dry cleaners and pick up one of his favorite suits before his next session begins.

"I agree. And thank you for suggesting that, Doctor. I 'm very proud of Ian, and thanks to you and your . . . expertise, I'm confident that he can finally start to live the life he deserves."

Katherine wants to give Dr. Price a hug but thinks that may be a bit inappropriate. Especially since he's been flashing his wedding band throughout the visit and she is unsure whether he did so subconsciously or not. Like picking up his coffee with the hand his ring sits on. Or scratching his head with the same hand. Even casually twisting his ring at points during the conversation. Maybe she's reading into it a bit more than she should. After all, he is the type to brush wrinkles out of his shirt. He must think every woman wants to be with him.

So instead she gracefully floats to the front door and opens it for him with ease. Dr. Price feels as though she is now acting a bit nervous around him. He thinks, *Maybe she is flirting with me. Nothing wrong with having a harmless little crush, right? Just be professional, Andrew.* He ignores her subtle girlish flirtations, but simultaneously sympathizes, knowing her traumatic history.

"I couldn't agree more," he says with a smile. "So, I will call sometime next week to follow up and we can schedule another meeting within the coming weeks."

"Sounds good. Again, thank you for everything, Doctor." Katherine holds the door open for him.

"My pleasure. Have a nice day." Dr. Price walks out onto the porch. The heavy clunks from the soles of his shoes echo with every step he takes. Katherine watches as his oppressive footsteps fade to the sounds of summer mornings in Lakehurst. She waves goodbye, but he doesn't notice. He beelines to his freshly waxed BMW. The sun reflects a blinding glare off of the vehicle directly into Katherine's eyes. Her squinted eyes admire the whole package that is Dr. Price.

"You do the same," she shouts, walking back into her home and softly closing her outdated and paint-peeled front door. She walks over to the coffee table, clearing off dishware and again noticing her off-balance unicorn. She turns it forty-five degrees to mirror the unicorn opposite it on the table. Katherine smiles, giving a reassuring head nod and walks to the kitchen.

CHAPTER 2

ater that evening, Katherine is in the kitchen stirring a thick red sauce in a pot. One by one she carefully places meatballs into the pot and continues to stir. Ian walks into the kitchen immediately knowing what's for dinner.

"Spaghetti again?" he says unenthusiastically. Katherine looks over toward Ian with a bewildered look on her face.

"Hey, easy there, buddy. Just be glad you have food on the table and a mother who cares enough to cook for you," she says in a condescending way. She figures today's kids don't know how good they really have it. She remembers as a little girl she would have to collect chicken eggs from her farm just to have something to eat for breakfast. An easy task most of the time, but then there were other times where the chickens would act less than cordial, or she'd have to fight off snakes from eating the eggs entirely. She learned how to have tough skin from her father. Ian harbors a sensitive personality trait, but that still doesn't give him right to complain about the food she makes.

Ian rolls his eyes as he pulls the kitchen chair from under the table and takes a seat. "Besides, this spaghetti is different. It's healthier and tastes better." Katherine pulls two plates from out of the cabinet and sets them down. She grabs a spoon and begins scooping noodles onto the plate. Ian sits at the table with his arm supporting the weight of his head.

"What's so different about it?" he says, even more unenthusiastically. Katherine scoops the meatballs out the pot, placing them gently on the pile of noodles.

"These meatballs are made from ground turkey and veal," Katherine says with a big smile. Ian doesn't look impressed. He figures if it looks like regular spaghetti, then it most likely tastes like regular spaghetti. "Try it!" she utters in a high-pitched tone. She and Ian both know that she is not the best cook in the world. Far from the worst, but definitely not the best. At times Ian feels as though his mom just experiments with foods that don't—and shouldn't—go together, like the raisin-sprinkled beef stroganoff she made just two weeks prior. He grabs his fork and takes a stab at one of the meatballs. He spins the fork to catch some of the noodles and takes a bite. As he chews, Katherine picks up her fork, excited to try it as well. Ian nods his head.

"Wow, this is really good, Mom . . . it tastes sweet," he says excitedly. Even though he's tired of spaghetti, at least her cooking is actually edible this time around.

"That's the brown sugar you're tasting. The recipe calls to cook it in with the meatballs." Katherine takes a bite of her culinary masterpiece. While she chews, she thinks, *I'm one hell of a cook.* "So, this Friday we have to go and register you for school. Then I was thinking we could go to the mall this weekend and do some school shopping for you. Get school supplies, clothes, new shoes, how does that sound?" Ian doesn't look too thrilled. He looks at Katherine with doubt in his eyes. "Ian what's wrong?" she asks.

"I—maybe this is a mistake. What if I don't make friends? What if people make fun of me because of my condition and—"

Katherine cuts Ian off mid-sentence, a stern look on her face. "Sweetie, listen to me, you do not have to do anything that you are uncomfortable with, okay? No matter what you decide to do, I fully support you every step of the way."

Ian, looking directly into his mother's eyes, takes a deep breath in. "Okay . . . I think I'd rather stay homeschooled," Ian says gently.

"Ian, I can't support that decision." Confused, Ian looks at his mother, taking note of her contradiction.

"But you just said—"

"This is a great opportunity for you to gain some real-world experience and prepare you for life. I wouldn't force you to do this if I didn't think it was the right thing to do." The compassion in Katherine's voice almost convinces Ian, but his mind is still torn.

"So, I have to do this?" he says questioningly.

"Of course you do, sweetie. But just remember, do not mention to anybody about your medical condition. That is between you and Dr. Price, okay?"

"Okay," he says, blindsided.

Katherine smiles and gently places her hand on Ian's face. "My baby boy is growing up." Katherine fans her face to dry the tears that have welled up in her eyes, then continues to eat her dinner. Ian's fake smile quickly disappears as soon as his mother's face turns back to her plate.

Saturday afternoon at Lakehurst Mall, Ian looks around inside a trendy clothing store. The pop music is very loud. The atmosphere, along with the clothing options, seem to be of the stereotypical cookie-cutter, frat-boy variety, which is not Ian's style. Katherine holds up a pair of pants that detach with zippers at the knees. For those individuals who are unsure if they want to purchase pants or shorts, here's two-in-one.

"What about these? They seem to be hip and fashionable? And look, they turn into shorts!" Katherine tries enticing Ian by dangling the pants in front of him, but to no avail.

"Mom, I won't make any friends wearing that. Those pants are going through an identity crisis." Ian laughs.

"Oh, you're so dramatic. These are cool. They're *the bomb*, right? Isn't that what you kids say?"

"No, they're not."

"I'm just trying to help. Making friends is hard. You gotta fit in somehow," Katherine says as she folds the pair of pants, putting them back on the shelf.

"I thought the idea was to be yourself no matter what," Ian proclaims. As someone who has experienced public high school, Katherine isn't so sure about that statement. Instead, she remains silent. After purchasing a few sets of clothes, they both exit the store and make their way through the busy mall.

"I was thinking we could get your hair cut. You know, to make a good first impression on your first day. Oh, you're going to look so handsome . . ." Katherine continues to go on, but Ian is distracted by his surroundings. The neon lights advertising every store, the fresh smell of popcorn and Japanese style hibachi, the coin-operated kiddie rides in the food court, and of course the observation of kids his age hanging out at the mall together have Ian's head swirling. Ian's no stranger to the outside world, but he doesn't go out often, so every trip somewhere different is an immersive experience for him. He sees the comradery of friendship in full effect. He notices a group of teens hanging out near the entrance to the food court. Ian sees a girl with shiny, light red, shoulder-length hair. Samantha Harvey. She's beautiful, warm, and accented with a perfect smile. Wearing tight blue jeans and a white polo shirt, she takes a sip of her giant slushy. Ian is mesmerized by her. He notices how the sun gleams off her lips as she licks the remaining frozen treat from her mouth. She looks over and sees Ian looking at her. Startled, he quickly looks away, only to look back and see that she is still staring at him, not angrily, but in a shy and flirtatious way. Ian smiles at her and she smiles back, only to be interrupted by a tan guy sporting a white T-shirt and a leather jacket that is almost as black as his greasy combed hair. He is Alex Castillo. Half-White, half-Hispanic, full asshole. He looks as if he styles his hair with motor oil. He grabs Samantha by her waist, pulling her closer to him.

"Ian! Are you listening to me?" Katherine scolds.

"Yeah, yeah, I'm here," he responds.

Alex is conversing with his group of friends. His demeanor is cocky, pretentious, and borderline misogynistic. Leaning up against the banister to the food court lobby, he places his arms around Samantha's shoulders, looking directly into her eyes.

"Hey babe."

"Hey," she says, smiling.

"Let me get a sip." Samantha looks down at her red slushy and lifts it up to his mouth. He coquettishly puts his lips around the straw and slowly begins sucking.

"Hey Sam, are you sure you know where Alex's lips have been? It would be a shame to ruin that face with herpes sores," says another in the group. Jason Cunningham. A sluggish stoner-type, he's wearing sagging pants and a tie-dye shirt of that sixties band that's grateful for the dead. He sports a peach-fuzz mustache. He begins laughing at his own joke as the girl sitting next to him, Ashley Campbell, swings her hand, hitting him in the chest for being so rude. She's filing her black painted nails. She's a goth type with heavy black mascara, jet black hair, and a glum attitude to match. Gothic apparel aside, Ashley is just as feminine as her best friend, Samantha. These two opposites couldn't be closer. She's the darkness to Samantha's light.

"Thanks, Ash," Samantha says as she holds her middle finger up to Jason. He dismisses her *fuck you* with a hand wave and a roll of the eyes.

"Well, if I have herpes, then you must have the fucking plague. You're a walking disease, dude." Alex looks at Ashley "How do you even kiss this thing?"

"Easy—like this." Ashley leans over, shoving her tongue in Jason's mouth. The display is tasteless and vile. Both Alex and Samantha cringe a little.

"I think that's enough PDA for everyone today, don't you think?" Alex says. Samantha agrees, nodding her head.

"Absolutely," she replies modestly, a pitch above a whisper. She takes a gander at her beautiful, stainless-steel watch, a birthday gift from her parents this year. It's an expensive brand. The time reads,

5:14 p.m. "Oh shit, babe I gotta go. I've got to meet my mom in a few. We're going over college applications," Samantha says, proudly. She's ready to start the next chapter of her life after high school. She feels mature enough to move on with her independence and wants to put that to the test. It's a challenge, one that she is confident she can succeed at. She and Alex couldn't be more different. Samantha is much more mature and level-headed that her greaser boyfriend. Her future is already mapped out due to her planning and setting goals that as of now seem pretty obtainable. Graduate high school, get accepted into State, major in healthcare management, graduate with her Master's, and work her way to managing a hospital in the city. A larger city. The suburban atmosphere of Lakehurst is a fine place to raise a family and settle down, but it is beneath Samantha. She envisions living in a large city with skyscrapers, expensive coffee shops, trendy restaurants, and an even more exciting nightlife. She would love it if Alex can be a part of that journey with her, but the status of their future relationship is still hanging in the air. The primary issue in their relationship now is that Samantha is not sure exactly what Alex wants to do with his future. She brushes off the thought because she needs to focus on her own plan and make sure that she achieves her goals regardless of whether Alex is a part of her future.

"Okay, let's go," says Alex as he puts his arm around Samantha's shoulder. "Hey, we'll catch you both later." He and Samantha walk off.

"Bye Ash! Call me later!" Samantha blows a kiss to Ashley. As she receives it, she returns the same friendly gesture. Jason looks at Ashley, blank faced.

"You two are so fucking gay," he says playfully. Ashley wishes she had a rebuttal. Instead, she gets lost in Jason's eyes and gives him a nudge. They smile at one another.

"Shut up. Come on, take me home." They begin walking in the opposite direction from Alex and Samantha. Jason gives her butt a slap, followed by a firm grasp. Ashley yelps, then grabs his shirt and pulls him in close for yet another obnoxious make-out session.

Moments later, Alex and Samantha hop into Alex's navy-blue '97 Ford Mustang V6. It used to belong to his father, and in a traditional passing of the torch, now belongs to Alex—if he can keep it up. And he does. Alex has kept it in great condition since taking ownership. The floorboards of the car are always vacuumed and the black leather interior always seems to look as if it were freshly polished. The seats shimmer slightly in the summer sun. Samantha places her slushy in the cup holder, then lowers the sun visor. Alex keeps a silver rosary with white beads hanging on the rearview mirror, a sense of protection for him. He grew up in a Catholic household, but as of today, he doesn't really consider himself to be a hardcore religious type of person. But something about this rosary given to him by his grandmother seems to do the trick at keeping evil at bay. He is reminded of that every time he looks at his rosary and thinks about an incident that occurred where he narrowly avoided getting t-boned by an eighteen-wheeler while grabbing a bite at a fast-food joint. Since then he thinks the rosary is his grandmother looking out for him and his cherished Mustang.

Samantha sets her purse on the floorboard and turns to look at Alex, who has just plopped in the driver seat. He's preoccupied fixing his hair in the rearview, then places the comb in his shirt pocket. He proceeds to start the ignition but can sense Samantha staring. He slowly turns his head. She stares in a perplexing way, like she's waiting for Alex to give an answer to a question she didn't ask.

"What?" Alex says, taking his hands off the keys. Samantha shifts her body to get more comfortable.

"I'm just excited. I mean, starting college, being on our own. This is our last year of high school. Aren't you excited?"

"I guess. I haven't given it that much thought." Alex is clearly uninterested by college talk and has no desire to discuss it.

"Have you been looking at colleges like we talked about? I mean it's pretty obvious we both should go to State. That way we'll be close to home but far enough away from the parentals." Samantha reaches over and grabs Alex's hand. Her silver floral-pattern ring flickers on her middle finger in the sunlight. Alex squints his eyes and turns his head away. He really does not want to talk about this shit right now. He pulls his hand away from Samantha's.

"Babe, we talked about this. With the way my grades are, there is no way I'm getting into State. I barely passed junior year—"

"Alex, you have all senior year to improve your grades. I can help you and we can—"

Alex cuts off Samantha in pure frustration. He throws his hands up. "Sam, stop! There's no way I'm getting into State, okay? And to be perfectly honest, I might not even go to college at all."

Samantha looks confused. She sits back in her seat. The sunlight bleeds past the edge of the sun visor, illuminating half of her face.

"College isn't for me, okay. I'm just gonna stay here and—"

"What? Stay here and work at your dad's mechanic shop? You and I both know that is not going to happen. I'm just looking out for your future, okay? *Our* future to be perfectly honest."

"Sam, you're not my guidance counselor. I don't need you looking out for my fucking future. I need you to be my girlfriend. I'm not some academic project for you to excel at, alright? Go try and save someone else." Alex cranks up his car. The engine roars, vibrating the seats.

Samantha looks pissed. She slaps up her sun visor angrily. "You know something? Do what you want, okay. Piss away your life, become a crackhead, I don't give a shit. But come a year from now, I'm gone. And you can either choose to be a part of that journey with me or not." Samantha opens the car door, grabbing her slushie before her exit. "I'll catch a ride with Ash," she says, slamming the car door shut.

Alex let's out a heavy sigh. He doesn't give this little altercation much thought. He's just tired of defending his future plans, whatever they may be. He reaches into the glove compartment and pulls out a cigarette. His brand, American Spirit. He lights it up and takes a long, deep inhale, then exhales.

He looks at himself in the rearview. "What? Work at your dad's mechanic shop," he says, mimicking Samantha. "Whatever . . . bitch." He drives off.

CHAPTER 3

Clicks of a mouse and the typing of a keyboard are the only sounds present inside the messy bedroom of Brandon Scott, who is seated at his computer researching serial killers, a topic he has great interest in. With his Caesar-cut and thick-framed glasses, Brandon gives the impression of a typical teenage nerd. He hates it when kids compare him to Steve Urkel. He knows his glasses are the reason for the ridicule and teasing, but he doesn't need the approval of those who make fun of him anyway. Besides, he hates putting contacts in. His bedroom could use a bit of tidying up. Empty wrappers of various snacks cover the majority of his computer desk. A pile of clothes sits in the corner of his bedroom next to an ajar closet door. Even he isn't sure if that pile is clean or dirty. He prefers the former. His bed us unmade. A Nintendo 64 controller stretches from his bed to the floor console. As much as he'd like to clean his room, it's the weekend, and he would much rather spend his time researching macabre and dark-themed stories of true crime and serial killers than wasting energy cleaning his room.

Brandon finds the subject of serial killers and what makes them tick very fascinating. He has a passion for investigative journalism and mystery. The O.J. Simpson trial five years earlier had really impacted him. But working for the school paper for the past two years has led to an ambition to major in journalism and reporting once he makes it to college, a thought he's optimistic about. He wants to be socially accepted and build connections with others who share his interests. But right now he chooses to be more reclusive and a loner. That is where he feels more comfortable. He knows nobody wants to be bothered hanging around the nerdy kid who likes reading, serial killers, and Japanese anime. The only person who Brandon considers anything close to a friend is his cousin James, who he only gets to see when his family travels to Chicago from time to time. So investigating true crime and serial killers is a normal hobby for him at this point. Like the article he's reading now about a serial killer who killed two people and mutilated their corpses to make fashionable house décor like soup bowls and lampshades. Then, he took it a step further and practiced necrophilia, robbed graves, and developed masks out of human flesh. The striking details captivate Brandon. The article then goes on to explain that his murders were the inspiration for major Hollywood productions like *Psycho* and *The Texas Chainsaw Massacre*.

Art imitates life, he thinks. His mind wanders to the thought of necrophilia. *What would that even feel like?* He imagines the guilt, shame, and disgust that he would feel, but guesses that for serial killers, necrophilia must be a normal Tuesday routine. He thinks about the grave robbers who take the time and energy to travel to graveyards in the dead of night, find a grave, dig up the helpless corpse, and still have the energy to fuck it. And that's just time spent on the recently deceased. *What are the lengths to fucking a mummified corpse? Do you just add water?* Brandon grosses himself out at the outrageous thought.

"Brandon! Breakfast is ready!" his mother shouts from downstairs. Perfect timing. His thoughts were getting way too messed up. He hops away from his computer then heads downstairs. Stepping into the kitchen, he sees his mother, Tina, whipping up some grits on the stove. The kitchen has a classy feel to it. Black and white tile floors and black kitchen appliances are surrounded by white cabinetry. Brandon's father, Marcus, sits at the glass kitchen table, reading the paper while drinking his coffee. Three plates are set in their isolated portions of the table. The layout is gluttonous. Scrambled eggs, waffles, sausage, bacon, biscuits, fruit, orange juice, and coffee. The only thing missing are the grits, which his mother carries to the table. Brandon pulls up a chair and sits between his mom and dad. He begins piling food on his plate. Tina walks over and scoops a couple spoonful of grits onto their plates. She doesn't get any. She's never been a fan of what she calls, "bland oatmeal." She takes a seat at the other end of the table. The family begins eating. The atmosphere is calm until Tina breaks the silence.

"Ready for your last year?" she asks Brandon. His mouth full of eggs and bacon. He nods as he swallows his food.

"Yeah, ready for it to be over with," he says nonchalantly. Brandon wants this year to fly by so he can start his college journey and never look back. Brandon is a loner, even a victim of bullying from time to time. His social life is non-existent. Sometimes he thinks life would have been easier for him and a lot less lonely if his parents had given him a brother, especially if he'd had an older brother who could defend him. But since that didn't happen, he finds solace in knowing this will be his final year of high school.

"You think you're gonna make valedictorian this year?"

Brandon is getting annoyed by his mom's inquisitions. He just wants to eat his breakfast in peace. He responds, sounding snarky. "I don't know. School hasn't started yet."

"I'm sure you'll get it. I just hope it's not that one girl . . . what's her name? Whitney? Wendy?" Brandon ignores Tina. "You know her name. What is it?"

"Wendy Toreleski," he says, holding back his frustration.

Tina snaps her fingers. "That's it! You ever think about asking her out?"

"Jesus, Mom can I eat?" he shouts with a mouth full of food.

"Hey! Watch the attitude, alright?" Marcus says sternly.

"Right!" Tina says, agreeing. "You know better than to take the Lord's name in vain. You must've forgot this is a Christian household," Tina says as she reaches for the orange juice.

Brandon loves his parents, but at times they can be a bit much. For him, it seems they pick and choose when they want to be snobbish and when they want to act Black. In the household, they're unapologetically Black. In public, they're snobbish. Plus, given the location they live, which is predominately White, they feel behooved to act a certain way in public so society doesn't judge or stereotype them. Yes, it may seem easy for them to do, but Brandon hasn't grasped the concept of turning his Blackness on and off. He acts the way he acts. But if you ask his cousin James, Brandon's an Oreo—Black on the outside and White on the inside. A dynamic that he's been dealing with ever since middle school. He's too Black for the White kids, and too White for the Black kids. An oxymoron that doesn't fit in anywhere, which is why he puts his energy toward success and higher education. A necessary *fuck you* to all the people who doubted him throughout his high school years.

After finishing his breakfast, Brandon sets his plate in the sink and heads upstairs with his glass of orange juice in hand. He gets to his room and sets the orange juice on the floor and starts playing his Nintendo 64. The glass leans on the cushioned carpet. The video game is getting intense. *I just need to beat this one level and*— "YES!" he shouts as he completes the gaming task. Brandon jolts up in excitement, knocking over his glass of orange juice directly over his gaming console.

"No, no, no, shit, shit, shit!" he shouts, watching the sparks fly. The television scrambles with a billow of smoke evaporating from the 64 like a punctuation mark concluding the terrible accident. He grabs a nearby t-shirt and pats the system dry. It's fucked. The rest of his summer has literally just gone up in smoke.

CHAPTER 4

everal weeks later, it's a typical weekend morning for Ian as he sits in Dr. Price's office for yet another therapy session. The color scheme in the office is dreary, a flat and mundane color pallet of blue walls and gray furniture. Having the blinds closed doesn't help liven up the space either. Ian wonders if Dr. Price chose these color patterns in particular to influence his patients to succumb to a state of depression or melancholy. It's a smart move on Dr. Price's part if true—keeps business flowing and adds more money to his pocket. But over the years, Ian's become accustomed to therapy and embraces the release of emotions, tensions, and whatever else he may be feeling that day. Today, Ian is feeling rather confused, mostly because his therapy sessions are supposed to be between himself and Dr. Price. *Why is Mom here sitting next to me?* he wonders.

Katherine brushes off her tiny black dress. She looks like she's just come from a funeral. But she knows, if there is anything that is going to get a guy's attention, it's her favorite little black dress. A subtle hint to throw out to Dr. Price because she knows he'll be watching. She looks on his desk and sees a picture of him with a blond bombshell of a woman. His wife, Jessica. Perfect smile, perfect skin, perfect body, the perfect couple. They smile at one another on a beachfront landscape. Katherine silently acknowledges the photo, then digs in her purse for a stick of gum. She offers Ian a piece, but he turns it down.

"Why are you here? These sessions are supposed to be private."

"Oh, I know. Dr. Price knows I'm here." She doesn't give much information.

Still confused, Ian brushes it off and mumbles, "Whatever," under his breath.

The office door suddenly swings open as Dr. Price makes his entrance. "Good morning, Kathrine. Hey Ian, how's it going?" Dr. Price extends his hand and gives Ian a firm handshake. He sets his briefcase down, removes his blazer, rolls up his shirt sleeves and leans up against his office desk. "I bet you're wondering what your mom is doing here, right?" he asks.

Ian nods his head and replies, "Yeah."

"Well, your mother and I just want to make sure that you are aware of some things and to get a better sense of how you are feeling going into the public-school system." Dr. Price looks over at Katherine for reassurance as she nods her head in agreement.

"Aware of what? How school works? I've seen *She's All That*," Ian says. Dr. Price laughs. Katherine laughs with Dr. Price, but forcefully, hoping to gain his attention. Dr. Price then takes a seat in front of the two on a couch similar to the one they are sitting on.

"Yes, well, that is a movie, but you need to know that although we want you to be open and make as many friends as possible, your medical condition should remain private. In fact, the only ones who will know are the school nurse, which is where you will get your medication—if need be—and the school principal."

"Got it. I will not talk to anyone about my condition," Ian declares.

Katherine feels this meeting is just as unnecessary as Ian does, but it's the weekend and she wants to have a bit of fun flirting with the therapist. She needs to prolong this meeting just a tad, so she interjects with concern, hoping Dr. Price will back her up on the comment.

"Well . . . there are also things like bullies, drugs, and promiscuous girls to worry about." Ian looks at his mom in an offended *are you serious?* kind of way.

"Absolutely. Ian, public schools are a ground zero for STDs. Herpes, gonorrhea, genital warts. You'll hear them referred to in all sorts of ways. Clap, drip, Jesus pox, blue waffle—" Ian cuts off Dr. Price.

"Wait, what is blue waffle?" he asks, looking back and forth at his mom and Dr. Price. Katherine is lost. Dr. Price takes the reigns.

"Well, kids these days sometimes refer to vaginas as *waffles,* and when women get some of these diseases, that area can swell and ooze puss in a way that looks like a sun-dried oyster that was dipped in honey mustard and grape jelly," he says informatively. "It's not really a separate disease. And any of them can be nasty. And all can affect men, too . . . sometimes even in the anus." Ian is shocked. He looks at his mother, who looks studious, focused. She nods her head, taking in the useful information.

"Oh my God!" Ian says, disgusted. This is now confirming his suspicions on what an unnecessary meeting this is. Not to mention grotesque.

"Yes, most men won't need to worry about it, but statistically there are just as many men as women that get raped in school. Think of public school like a prison. You are coming in as fresh meat and there may be plenty of students that want to assert themselves as alpha by turning you out. Do you know what that means? Turning you out?" Ian doesn't speak. He just shakes his head. "It means they will try to make you, for lack of a better word, their bitch."

"It's true sweetie," Katherine says, chiming in. "And sometimes it may be a group of people who will try and take advantage of you. That's called a gangbang, right Doctor?" Dr. Price agrees.

"That's right," he says, going further into his explanation. "Once that happens, the entire school finds out and will tease you with nicknames like snake burglar, pogo stick, cream pie. I've seen it happen far too often. But I'm sure you'll be fine. If push comes to shoving it in, we can always go back to homeschooling." Dr. Price looks down at his watch. "Oh, will you look at the time. I'm sorry, I have another scheduled appointment coming up. But Ian, if you have any questions or concerns, feel free to contact me at any time." Ian is dumbstruck by this gathering of horrendous information.

"Oh I have a *bunch* of questions and concerns right now!" he pleads. Katherine stands up and grabs her purse.

"Ian please, Dr. Price has other engagements, there is plenty of time to address your issues. That is why we had this meeting. Thank you so much for your insight, Doctor." Katherine holds out her hand. Dr. Price gives her a soft handshake, caressing her hand with his. Katherine is not sure if that was intentional or him just being nice, but the flirtation is definitely there.

"The pleasure is all mine," he says, staring into Katherine's eyes. They're interrupted by a light knock on the office door. Jessica enters with a basket of muffins.

"Hey babe," she says excitedly. She sets the muffins on his desk and gives Dr. Price a kiss on the lips.

"Honey, this is Katherine and her son, Ian. Wonderful people."

Jessica turns to look at Katherine. With the biggest smile on her face, she says, "Nice to meet you, Katherine." She peeks over to Ian. "Hi Ian," then diverts her attention back to Katherine and continues. "I think it's so wonderful that my husband dedicates himself to helping out families in need like yours. Don't you think?" Jessica quickly grabs her basket of pastries and offers Katherine a muffin.

Katherine stares her down, then punches Jessica square in the face. Bloods gushes from Jessica's perfect nose.

Katherine snaps out of her daydream. She presents Jessica with a fake smile. "Oh, no thanks, I'm on a diet. Come on Ian, let's go," Katherine says blandly.

"Can I have a muffin?" Ian asks, walking toward Jessica. She extends the basket his way, but Katherine pulls Ian by the hand.

"No, you're on a diet too," she says as they both exit the office.

"Have a great first day of school, Ian!" Dr. Price shouts as Jessica holds a muffin up to his mouth. He takes a bite.

CHAPTER 5

On the first day of school, Ian, sitting in the passenger seat of his mom's Lexus sedan, stares out the window. His nerves are high and fueled by anxiety. Rays of sunshine periodically peak through the dark clouds, as if sending Ian a message of hope in some strange, God-like way. Or at least he imagines it that way. Katherine is talking to Ian quite loud over the radio station that plays softly in the background, though her voice sounds muffled to Ian. The radio begins to muffle as well. Ian is in his own world at this point, taking in the built-up anxiety on his first day.

The streets are empty. The overcast sky forecasts rain. The wind blows scattered leaves across the empty road of the suburban streets. *Where is everyone?* Ian thinks, anticipating seeing other forms of life in the way of kids his age laughing and being thrilled to be going back to school. Not a person in sight. *Maybe all their parents are driving them to school this morning, too.*

He then notices a lone figure standing by a stop sign at the end of the road. Katherine pulls up to the red sign. Brandon, standing by the road with his thumbs placed under the straps of his bookbag, glances over at the vehicle. This is awkward for him. Ian realizes this and tries his best not to make eye contact.

"Should we give him a ride?" Katherine says, with a motherly softness that combines kindness with pity. Ian is unsure of what to say. He begins stumbling over his words, which begin to sound jumbled and glitchy like the radio station he was barely paying attention to. But before he can answer the question with a simple yes or no, a blaring bus horn disrupts his focus. Katherine and Ian both jump at the deafening honk. Brandon casually walks back toward the bus and hops inside. Ian catches his breath for a moment after being startled. He looks over to Katherine and says, "You can go." Katherine nods, then drives away.

Ian is sweating in his seat, nervous they will be approaching school soon. Seems they have been driving forever when in reality it's only been ten minutes since leaving the house. Katherine looks slightly to her right and notices a giant sign that reads *LAKEHURST HIGH SCHOOL*. The marquee under the school's name says, *Welcome to the new school year everyone!* and *PTA meeting 9/08*.

Katherine pulls up to the front entrance of the school. Ian looks out as the clouds break and sun shines brightly over the high school landscape. Kids exiting buses, hugging each other, and walking about the campus really gives Ian the high school feeling that he was hoping for all along. This is exactly how he pictured it. He looks over to see a couple of students playing Hacky Sack. He sees another student a few feet away sitting on the low brick fencing to the front of the school writing in a notepad, a brooding look on his face. That's when it hits Ian. Although this is very new and different for him, he knows he needs to stay focused. With this being his first, and hopefully last school year, his academics are priority. But the excitement is within him as well.

"Want me to walk you to the office?" Katherine says as she begins to unbuckle her seatbelt.

"No!" Ian says, with a quick turn toward Katherine, his hands outstretched like a referee making a call on the play. He then cracks a smirk and points both index fingers toward his mother. "I think I can handle it from here, Mom. Thanks for the ride." Ian grabs his plain black bookbag off the floor of the car and slings one strap over the side of his left shoulder.

"Are you sure honey? I know this is a lot to take in." Katherine reaches for the keys to turn off the ignition.

"Mom, no. Please. I can handle it from here. Plus, it's kind of embarrassing," he says in a low and soft tone, hoping he doesn't offend his mother or hurt her feelings in any way.

She responds with a smirk. "I know you'll be fine, sweetie. Since you don't want me to embarrass you, promise you won't embarrass *me* by getting in trouble while you're here," she says in a defiant manner.

Ian agrees with a slight nod. "Of course, Mom. You know me," he affirms with a returning smile.

"And most importantly, do not discuss your business with anyone at this school except the—" Ian interjects into Katherine's sentence and they both say simultaneously, "School nurse and the principal."

"I got it, Mom. Okay?"

"Okay. I'm just making sure." Katherine gives Ian's hand an affectionate squeeze. "Alright . . . I love you, sweetie."

"I love you too, Mom." Ian opens the car door and steps out into the brightly chaotic setting.

"Have a wonderful first day bab—" Ian unknowingly slams the door shut on his mom. He takes in a deep breath, grabs hold of the straps on his bookbag, and begins walking into the juvenile abyss. He already feels like an outsider. Walking alone in the swirling atmosphere of friendships and relationships only enhances the experience, which ranges from nervousness to excitement to fear.

He tries his best to seem as normal as he can, blending in with his peers as if to become one with the shared reunion of old faces. But every face is new to Ian. As he walks through the crowd, he smiles at everyone and greets them with a friendly "hello." Most of the students ignore him. The others look at him in a strange way, their faces reading, *who the hell is this kid?* He looks over, noticing a nearby sign, *PRINCIPAL'S OFFICE/MAIN OFFICE* pointing to the left. A long brick corridor leads to a separate building sitting in front of a side parking lot.

Ian enters the main office and quickly picks up on the smell of popcorn. To his right is a beautiful red-haired woman sitting at her desk, freckles subtly sprinkled on her cheeks, arms, and chest. Ian visualizes the many constellations he can connect the freckles into that run across the top of her perfect C-cup breasts. She notices Ian and removes her headset. The golden name tag on her shirt reads *Heather*. She smiles at Ian.

"Good morning. How can I help you?" Heather adjusts herself more professionally in the rolling chair, not that she was slouching before, but she feels the need to really assert herself.

"Hi. I'm here to pick up my schedule." Ian walks toward Heather with a slightly timid posture, but at his best, he's being cool. No limited amount of human interaction is going to stop him from making his presence known to Heather. "Are you making popcorn?" Ian places his hand gently on her desk. Heather grabs a stack of folders to her right and sets them in front of her. She looks up at Ian, smiling.

"I did. Would you like some?"

Ian ponders her question for a moment. He doesn't want to turn down her friendly offer, but he feels it's way too early for popcorn. "No thanks, I'm fine," he says.

Heather shrugs her shoulders. She places her hands over the stack of folders and takes a good look at Ian. Ian gives off a look of intrigue but confusion.

Heather smiles and lets off a laugh. "I know it's too early for popcorn, but I just love the smell. You must think I'm weird," she says, laughing.

To Ian, she has the perfect smile. "Not at all. And if that's considered weird, I guess I'm weird too," Ian says nervously. *Is this what flirting feels like?*

"What is your name again?" she asks curiously.

"It's Ian. Ian Moss." He leans over her desk to get a peek of the alphabetically labeled folders of names. She pauses for a moment and looks up at Ian. He slightly moves back, hoping he didn't offend her by getting too close.

"Are you new here?" Heather asks with a puzzled look on her face.

"Yeah. This is my first year . . . ever," he says with a crack in his smile.

"Right! You were homeschooled. Oh my God." Heather pushes her chair back a bit and stands up from her desk. She pulls her dress down a bit and clears her throat. She extends her arms like a magician's assistant to showcase the bronze lettering of the school's name above her desk window and lets out a greeting.

"Welcome to Lakehurst High! Home of the Tigers! Rawr!" Heather curls her fingers into tiger claws, laughing. Ian starts to clap. Not only was this a cute gesture, but also welcoming. Not to mention that he now has a better view of Heather's body.

"Thank you. That was so nice." Ian grins from ear to ear. He grabs the straps of his bookbag and walks a bit closer to Heather's desk.

"I just want you to know that if you need anything, you can always come to me," Heather says, looking directly into Ian's eyes. Before he can respond, the loud voice of a jolly middle-aged man cuts Ian off unknowingly.

"Either I'm crazy, Heather, or I just heard you welcoming another student to our wonderful school." A tall, stocky individual, Principal Owens, with a salt-and-pepper military buzzcut and a racoon-sized mustache walks from around the corner. He places his left thumb underneath one of his suspenders, extends it out, and releases it, lightly slapping himself across the chest. He's holding a marbled coffee mug that reads, *CEO of Lakehurst High School* in golden letters. His presence is intimidating, but only because of his size. He sets his coffee mug down on Heather's desk.

"Good morning! And what's your name young man?" Principal Owens says in a whimsical, larger-than-life type of way.

"I'm Ian Moss . . . sir," he says, pointing to himself for assurance of his identity, even though he's the only one in the office besides Heather. Principal Owens realizes *who* this kid is. His eyes grow wider than saucers.

"Right! Ian Moss," he says excitingly, walking over to welcome Ian with a firm handshake. Ian catches a glimpse of Principal Owens' gold wedding band that's slightly more visible than the gray hairs on his knuckles. "It is so nice to meet you, Ian. Come on back to my office with me so we can get to know each other." Principal Owens puts his arm around Ian like they are long lost friends and begins pulling him in the direction of his office.

"Oh, I have to get my schedule and get to class," Ian says, trying to evade the invitation.

"Oh it's fine. I'll give you a pass that excuses your tardiness." Principal Owens gives Ian a quick buddy slap on his back as he grabs his coffee mug and walks to his office. Ian follows him as he gives one look back at Heather who is wiggling her fingers goodbye to him.

Once inside the office, Ian takes a seat right in front of the principal's desk. He looks down and sees a shiny gold placard mounted to a cherrywood base. *PRINCIPAL OWENS.* The gold really shines off of the plaque as it seems to sit in the right direction to the window where the sun illuminates the lettering. As Principal Owens takes a seat, quick cloud coverage turns this bright welcoming office into a disciplinary chamber. But Ian realizes Principal Owens doesn't give off that persona. He scans the desk, which is neatly organized with office supplies, an American flag sticking out of a pen slot mounted to a lamp, and a photo of Principal Owens standing in front of a tent dressed in military attire. His hands are placed behind his back as he looks into the camera with a stern facial expression. Ian can barely make out the desert landscape on the edges of the photo that branch out to a golden frame. Behind Principal Owens' desk are a series of graduation photos that have been labeled with their corresponding years. From 1995 to 1999. The photos show Principal Owens standing in the middle of an enormous gymnasium with the graduating class behind him on the bleachers. Rows and rows of diverse high school youth are either smiling, looking bored, looking away, or demonstrating gestures of peace, bunny ears, or the ever-popular flipping of the bird.

Principal Owens is smiling the same stiff smile in every photo. But none compares to the lovely family photos that line the top portion of the bookshelf behind him. His wife, two kids, and a German Shepherd appear in several photos. Principal Owens couldn't look happier in the ones he is in.

"So how are you, Ian?" Principal Owens says, seated calmly in his chair with his fingers interlocked on his desk. The sun begins peeking through the clouds again, affecting the lighting in the room.

"I'm good," Ian says. His nerves are beginning to calm.

"I know this is all very new to you but let me start by saying if you need anything at all, please do not hesitate to let me know. I have been in charge of this school for five years and for someone who is just starting their high school journey, I want to make sure you have the best experience here and succeed in walking across that stage with a diploma in your hands from Lakehurst High, signed by me." Principal Owens expresses in the most sincere and cheerful way. He gives Ian optimism. This is the type of motivation and excitement that he needed to hear. Principal Owens breathes new confidence in Ian.

"Yes sir! Absolutely," Ian replies.

"Now, I know of your condition, as well as Nurse Murphy, so we want to make sure that you have everything you need to make you feel as comfortable as possible here without any hiccups. Last thing we need is for you to go crazy on us." Principal Owens says, laughing in a deconstructed pattern, realizing his joke may have come off offensive. His demeanor invites Ian to laugh with him to eliminate the awkwardness of his off-color joke. But Ian is not offended. He actually finds the joke to be quite refreshing, an introduction to life outside of his household. He sees now that it is possible for him to be treated like any other student instead of receiving special attention because of his mental illness. The school bell rings. Ian grabs his bookbag.

"Hang on one second. Let me get you that late pass." Principal Owen grabs an excused tardiness slip from the top right drawer of his desk and signs it. He hands it over to Ian. "And don't forget to grab your schedule from Heather, okay?"

"Yes sir. Thank you," Ian says, as he stands up and slings his bookbag over his shoulder.

"Oh, and Ian." Ian stops and turns back. "Welcome to Lakehurst, *pardner*," Principal Owens says. He points at Ian using a cheesy handgun gesture, following it with a wink and a clicking sound as he pulls the invisible trigger. Ian smiles, then exits the office.

Walking through the empty school halls, Ian admires the waxed, light-gray vinyl flooring, accented with royal-blue squares throughout. The matching royal-blue lockers extend down the hall on both sides, some covered in graffiti. A few have some dents, while others look to be in pristine condition. His footsteps echo through the halls in a way that seems as though someone might be walking behind him. He turns around, finding no one. Posters dot the walls of the hall, which all have a different inspirational and welcoming slogan such as, *Welcome back students!* and *Tiger Pride*. There are a few D.A.R.E. campaign ads. Another poster stands out. It reads, *Don't do it, you are loved* and is accompanied by a sticky note pad attached with a phone number on it to a suicide hotline. Ian thinks how many students must have killed themselves for there to be an entire poster dedicated to preventing teen suicide.

He looks down at his schedule. His first class is homeroom, located in room 237. Ian walks pass classroom 109 and sighs. He then looks over to a sign on the wall which has an arrow pointing upstairs to rooms 200-300. *How big is this fucking school?* He obviously knows the exterior of the school is a bit intimidating, but that pales in comparison to once you actually get inside. And he knows he has only scratched the surface of the school's interior as he then starts to think about the gymnasium, cafeteria, football field, and all of the roofed outdoor corridors that lead to those places and many more. His nerves reappear. He gets more and more nervous with each step closer to room 237. He approaches a polyurethane-coated wooden door and looks at the plaque. *Room 237.* He takes a quick peek through the rectangular window on the door and sees a woman standing in front of the class giving some sort of lecture. Ian takes a deep breath and opens the door.

The classroom is bright, not only from the fluorescent lighting, but from the sunlight piercing through the windows. An outside glare shines on Ian as he walks through the door, a natural spotlight so the entire class can get a good look at him. And they are. All eyes are on Ian as he notices some students whispering to each other, some laughing, and some looking completely unimpressed.

"Which brings me to my point class, show up on time." The teacher says, looking over to Ian. She looks too young to be a teacher with her short brown pixie cut hair and slight body structure. Ian nervously walks toward her and hands her his signed slip from the principal. He looks over at the blackboard and sees her name written in chalk. Mrs. Ashford. She glances at the excused tardy slip Ian hands to her and responds with a stern question for Ian.

"Are you sure you're supposed to be here?" Ian hands over his schedule. She looks and sees that he is right where he is supposed to be. She nods her head then hands Ian his schedule.

"Okay. Welcome to homeroom. Please introduce yourself to the class," she says, gesturing her hand toward the class like an auctioneer. He looks at Mrs. Ashford trying to silently communicate that it would really help if he didn't have to introduce himself. He then notices the entire class staring at him in silence. His anxiety is beginning to boil over. He takes in a deep breath and begins counting backward from five. *Okay, you're good.*

"Hello, everyone . . ." Ian says as his voice begins to crack a little from the nerves. He clears his throat and tries his best to exude confidence. "My name is Ian Moss and I'm new to this school." Ashley is seated in the back of the class and notices Ian. She begins staring at him in a very peculiar way as if she either recognizes him or that they may have known each other in a past life. There's something about him she finds familiar, but she can't quite put her finger on it.

"Where are you from, Ian?" Mrs. Ashford says, aware of his nervousness.

"I'm from here," he says quickly. The two begin staring at each other awkwardly. Mrs. Ashford ushers Ian to further expand on where he is from and more about himself, but to no avail. Ian stands nervously in front of the class hoping she will just stop probing and let him blend in with the rest of the class by taking a seat somewhere. More awkward silence passes as she doesn't seem to be budging. Finally, she gives in.

"Okay. Class, please make sure you make Ian feel welcome. You can take that empty seat right over there." Ian makes his way to the empty desk placed next to a window on the last row to the right side of the classroom and takes his seat, relieved that part is over.

Ian is able to find his next few classes without too much problem. As the bell rings for lunch, Ian navigates his way down the crowded hall of students. He seems a bit lost, but the general crowd seem to be going the same direction, and since it's lunch time, Ian can only assume they are on their way to the cafeteria. He gets shoved a few times by a couple of rude students who call him "loser," "fuck-face," and "dick cheese." Ian has heard them all before, except dick cheese. He has no idea what that is. *Is it an STD? Maybe that's in the Blue Waffle family.* Regardless, he tries erasing the terms from his mind when he begins to smell the food from the cafeteria. Because who can eat when you're pondering dick cheese? For a split second, he wonders what that would even taste like. He cringes at the thought, nauseating himself. But all of those insignificant thoughts fall by the wayside as he enters through the rusted blue metal doors leading to the cafeteria. All he can hear is the jumbled mumbling of students, shrieking laughter, and the occasional teacher yelling at a student to watch their mouth or to stop tormenting others. He observes all of the cliques and groups of friends and realizes that high school movies aren't all that cliché after all. Just beyond the numerous rows of lunch tables is a gigantic wall of windows and a door leading to a courtyard where several students are enjoying their lunch break outside playing hacky sack, skateboarding, strumming the guitar, tossing around a football, or sneaking a couple tokes off of a joint.

Ian stands in line waiting on his food as he contemplates where he should sit. He feels he needs to assert himself and approach whatever group is willing to accept him, so he won't feel so alone. He steps up to a lunch lady with a mustache as thick as that actor from that 80s television show *Magnum, P.I.* whose name he can't recall at the moment. She looks at Ian with a uniform scowl over her face as if she hates her job and all the people she comes into contact with.

"Salisbury steak or orange chicken?" she asks with attitude. Frazzled, he makes an impulsive choice.

"Uh, Salisbury steak, please ma'am," he says timidly, extending his tray. She slaps the wet piece of meat onto the lunch tray, followed by an ice cream scoop of mashed potatoes. Next, she piles corn and a roll onto his tray and nudges it back to Ian.

"Thank you," he says politely, delivering a friendly smile.

"Next!" the lunch lady yells. Ian stands at the head of the lunchroom trying to decipher where he fits in and where he could sit. He nervously begins to sweat in the midst of this fearful choice. *I'll avoid the jocks,* he thinks as he does not have much knowledge or interest in sports at all. *The nerds may seem more welcoming.* But how is this going to help his social status in school? Although he believes in treating everyone fairly, he knows that sitting with the nerds is not going to better his first high school experience. He then sees a table of four individuals who seem pretty friendly. He makes his way over and sets his tray down. The four guys stare at Ian then look at each other in confusion. Ian takes a seat and sits down next to them.

"Hi, my name is Ian. Nice to meet you." Ian holds out his hand to the one who seems to be the leader of the group, a grungy, greasy haired guy wearing a denim jacket covered in button pins of several rock bands, and ideological sayings encouraging anarchism and to fuck the system.

"Hi, my name is I don't give a fuck!" The rest of the group begins laughing as they hop up and walk away from the table. Ian tries his best to put on a tough face, but he is deeply hurt. If this is how the rest of the school year is going to go, he might as well go back to the comfort of his home-schooled routine than deal with this level of rudeness. He begins eating his unsavory lunch in isolation as if he's in some obscure high school version of solitary confinement.

The boy's restroom is moldy, grungy, and is already littered with toilet paper, cigarette butts, and crumpled up school papers on the tile floor. The first day of school and this bathroom looks like it hasn't been cleaned all year. Nothing about this bathroom seems sanitary. Urine drips from the toilet seats and onto the floor in most of the stalls. One urinal in the far back corner next to a rather widely large window up above looks like the cleanest in the space, which is only because someone deliberately pissed on the wall instead of in the urinal. Some chattering and snorting sounds can be heard in the last stall. The rusted blue stall door rattles a bit. Alex and Jason have set up a makeshift platform for snorting Percocet. A thick Algebra II book is set on top of the toilet. Alex shakes a couple more Percocet pills from his medicine bottle and places them on top of the book. Jason has his metal spoon in hand, carefully placing it on top of the pills, gradually presses down to crush the medication. He was successful with the first two. His attempt on the next two sends one of the pills flying across the stall, ricocheting off the wall, and dropping into the toilet directly in the provided gap between the toilet bowl itself and the powder covered Algebra book.

"Dude, stop wasting my shit!" Alex shakes out another pill and hands it to Jason. Jason is crouched down, an apologetic expression on his face.

"Fuck man, my bad."

"My dad is getting low on this shit, so we can't be wasteful," Alex proclaims.

"I don't understand why we're here instead of where we usually go."

"Cause Coach Matthews is cleaning the storage room out today, for some odd fucking reason. Just hurry up, alright. I'm coming down," Alex demands. Jason crushes the new pill with expertise and begins separating the powdered drugs with his school ID card. Alex crouches over and snorts a line. He squints then tilts his head back and holds his nostrils together. This line hit him harder than he expected. Jason was never much of a pill-type of guy. He likes to stick to weed and shrooms, but he follows suit and snorts a line as well. His eyes bulge after the hit. Alex laughs. Jason snorts the rest of the white lines. He and Alex exit the stall as Alex lights up a cigarette. Jason slings his bookbag over his shoulder and checks his nostrils in the grimy and rusted mirror.

"Have you seen Emma yet?"

Alex coughs a bit after he takes a drag. He shakes his head to Jason's question, thinking about the last time he and Emma saw each other. "She's probably pissed at me anyway," he says, taking another drag. "Like, how do you get mad at me for telling Greg you give amazing head, and then go and give Greg amazing head?" Alex says, cocking his head to one side.

"He *told* you?" Jason asks.

"Yeah, like the next day he said 'Alex, dude, you were right. Emma, hands down, has the best tongue in town, man,'" Alex says, doing his best impression of Greg's dimwitted jock voice. They both laugh.

"Hey, aren't the cheerleaders practicing now?" Jason asks. Alex has a light bulb moment.

"Yeah. I need to talk to her anyway. Shit, let's go."

The two exit the bathroom with haste. Alex is startled as he bumps into Brandon, who drops his books and papers on the ground. "What the fuck man! Yo, watch where the fuck you're going!" Alex shouts.

Brandon bends down to pick up his books. He glances up at Alex, who looks strung out and sweaty. His eyes are bloodshot.

Alex recognizes Brandon—a soft-spoken nerd he'd enjoyed bullying all throughout last year. Alex chuckles. "Not this fucking kid again," he tells Jason. "Watch where the fuck you're going, dipshit."

Brandon whispers to himself. "Whatever, junkie."

Alex tilts his ear closer, hearing what Brandon said. Alex yanks Brandon up by the shirt and slams him against a locker. The impact echoes down the hall. Not another soul is in sight.

"What the fuck did you say, faggot?" Alex asks. Specs of spit land on Brandon's face and glasses. He is frightened but tries his best not to show it. Jason gawks at the interaction. "I can't hear you. Say what you just fucking said!" Alex stares directly into Brandon's soul. He is waiting for him to utter just one syllable, so he'll have a good reason to knock his fucking lights out. The built-up tension has them both sweating.

"Alex, man, come on. Fuck this nerd," Jason says. The animosity between the two is sharp, drugs fueling Alex's rage. He's intense but knows it's not worth it to kick Brandon's ass right now.

"That's what I thought, you fucking pussy." Alex pushes Brandon against the locker once more. He brushes himself off and begins walking away. He yells back, "Stay the fuck outta my way next time!"

Brandon is frozen. His lips quiver in fear and anger. He takes off his glasses and wipes the lenses with his shirt. He bends down to pick up his books, papers, and dignity, then heads down the hall in the opposite direction of his tormentors.

Clouds roll over the sky in a rather fast motion. The sun flickers between extreme brightness and a hazy glow. A group of cheerleaders sit in the grass of the enormous football field. The field grass is kept up to precise and immaculate standards, even height throughout the entire field, a glorious olive shade of green that could be misinterpreted as faux. Freshly laid chalk line the edges of the field as the school maintenance man rolls the line marker across the turf while slyly gazing at the girls in the middle. A tall and busty blond, Amber, stands in front of her squad addressing the girls with excitement. It would be safe to assume she is always like this. Emma Parsons, beautiful and tan, leans back on her arms, her long blond hair dangling down her back. Unenthused, she rolls her eyes at Amber and smacks her bubblegum. Amber talks about the upcoming football season and all the routines and changes that will be happening to the cheer squad over the course of the school year.

Noticing Emma's annoyance, Amber politely addresses Emma with a little bit of a snide tone in her voice. "Emma, could you please act like you want to be here?" Amber's right-hand girl, Amy, agrees. Emma stares down her cheer captain with a menacing glare but dials it back, not wanting to cause any unnecessary problems on the first day back, even though she thinks she deserves the spot of cheer captain over this prissy, wannabe Barbie cunt. She sits up and spits the gum out of her mouth like a cowboy aiming for a spittoon, then gracefully positions herself cross-legged with a fake grin on her face.

"Is this better?" she says sarcastically.

"Much better, thank you. Anyway, girls . . ." Emma drops the fake smile and rolls her eyes. She looks over and sees Alex standing by the bleachers smoking a cigarette. Alex notices and sends her a two-finger salute, then takes the same two fingers and spreads them over his mouth sticking his tongue between them.

"Oh my God," Emma mumbles to herself. She thinks, *what are the odds of multiple people annoying me on the first day back in school? God, I hate it here.*

Amber checks her watch. "Okay. Well, classes are about to start soon, so we'll catch up with some routine layouts on Wednesday. I'd love to hear some pitches, so brainstorm girls! Amy and I will narrow down some of the routines, so see you all Wednesday!"

Emma is the first one to get up. She casually walks toward Alex thinking, *what the fuck does he want?* She barely acknowledges him as she opens the gate to exit the field. She walks right past him. Alex steps in front of her. She stops and sighs. Alex takes one last drag of his cigarette and flicks it toward the bleachers. Emma fans her face as he exhales the smoke.

"You know those things cause cancer, right?" she says, squinting her eyes from the bright sun. Alex reminisces about their summer fling. He is not done with Emma yet. If he had it his way, he and Emma will continue to fuck on the side—just as long as she keeps her mouth shut to Samantha.

"So I've heard." Alex holds up his pack of smokes and points out the bold lettering of the surgeon general's warning on the back. "As if people who smoke don't know the fucking consequences."

Emma is starting to lose her patience. "What do you want?" she asks. Alex doesn't want to piss her off. He decides to play it smooth, kind, and flirtatious.

"Obviously to talk to you. Look, things got a little out of hand and I wanted to make up for it."

"Making up for it would be to keep your fucking mouth shut. Now everyone thinks I'm some kind of slut who just goes around blowing everyone," Emma says, starting to get mad. She's questioning herself why she's even talking to this bozo right now. "You know what . . . bye."

"Wait!" Alex says, grabbing her arm. "I know that sucked, okay, and I'm sorry. Most people don't even remember that shit, honestly. Everyone has more important things to worry about other than your amazing head-giving skills," Alex says with a smirk.

Emma is not amused. She steps to the side in an effort to walk away but is once again stopped by Alex.

"Seriously, Alex, what do you want?" Her voice gets loud, catching the attention of a few cheerleaders.

"I told you I wanted to make it up to you. Just come by my house this weekend. My dad's leaving for some car auction thing, and I thought, *You know, this would be the perfect opportunity to get back on*

Emma's good side. So, whaddaya say?" Alex tilts his head and frowns in an attempt to give her a puppy-dog look.

A couple of cheerleaders are walking by whispering to one another. Emma notices and brushes them off. She looks back at Alex. She cannot stand him, but the attraction still lingers. The puppy dog look is working for him while simultaneously his attraction to her starts to boil over again.

The wind blows Emma's hair in her face. She brushes her hair back with an inquisitive look. "Wait a minute. Are you still with Samantha Harvey?" she asks. Alex looks like a deer in headlights. He doesn't quite know how to answer, so he just decides to tell the truth.

"Well, yeah. I mean, she's my girlfriend," he says, with an obvious tone.

"Okay, well either you break it off with her, or leave me the fuck alone. It's that simple." Emma brushes her hair back once more. She blows a kiss to Alex, turns around, and walks off.

Alex is now more determined than ever to accomplish the mission of hooking up with Emma again. Or at the very least, secure another blowjob. He watches her seductively walk away and yells, "This isn't over!" She continues to walk away, ignoring him. The school bell rings.

Later that afternoon, Ian walks from the bus to his house and notices his mom's car is in the driveway. He checks the mailbox and pulls out a few envelopes. Stepping to the doorway, he opens the door and is met with utter silence. Nothing seems out of place. The house is in tip-top cleanliness as usual. Ian then walks toward his mom's bedroom and opens the door. Katherine turns around, startled, as she's buttoning up her shirt.

"Jesus, Ian, you scared me." Katherine catches her breath. "How was your first day of school?"

The depressed expression on Ian's face tells it all. He looks completely devoid of happiness. "I don't want to talk about it," he says, as he turns around and walks off.

Now fully dressed, Katherine quickly follows Ian into the living room. She knows something is bothering him. "Honey, wait. What happened?"

Ian slings his bookbag on the recliner seat to his left and plops down on the couch. He grabs the television remote and turns on the TV. "I want to be home schooled again," he says.

Katherine sits down next to Ian, her motherly instincts kicking in. She needs to get to the bottom of whatever has her baby boy in a funk.

"What happened?" she asks, brushing his hair back with her hand before placing it on his shoulder.

"I don't like it there. The food is gross, the people are mean and repulsive. I saw a guy take a dump under the bleachers today. A *dump*! Was he trying to be funny? I wasn't laughing. Why not use the bathroom? Which are disgusting, by the way. That school is a petri dish of germs."

Katherine understands where Ian is coming from, but she does think he's overreacting a bit, which is totally expected given that this is his first public school experience. She can only console him with a little bit of optimism. She tries to approach it in a light-hearted way that gives Ian hope for returning.

"Ian, sweetie, I know this is a little tough for you, but just give it some time. No one said this was going to be an easy transition, but it is a necessary one." Katherine puts her hand over Ian's and looks him in the eyes. "Trust me, sweetie, it gets better."

Ian sighs.

"I just hope you know how proud I am of you for doing this." Katherine pulls his head toward her, kissing Ian on the temple. As she stands up, Katherine begins to question Ian about what she should make for dinner while making her way to the kitchen. Ian has a perplexed look on his face. The same look he shared when he walked up to the driveway and noticed her car. He stands up and follows her into the kitchen. Katherine starts pulling out pots and pans from the lower cabinet by the stove. "I was thinking lasagna. Is that okay?"

"What are you doing home so early, anyway? I thought you'd be at work?"

Katherine stops, a bit surprised by Ian's questioning. She doesn't quite know what to make of it, but she nonchalantly explains herself. She knows how Ian can be when he gets a little worked up and starts feeling out of the loop.

"I had an appointment today," she says, continuing to grab cookware, utensils, and food from the fridge. "Which reminds me— they have me coming in thirty minutes early for work from now on, which means you'll have to take the bus to and from school every day."

Why would Ian be surprised by this news? Life seems to be doing what it wants at this point. "Perfect," he says sarcastically while walking away, mumbling under his breath, "This day just keeps getting better."

CHAPTER 6

A late-summer dawn approaches the cookie-cutter suburb the following day. Cars, mailboxes, and perfectly manicured front lawns are covered in dew, an indication of how hot the day is going to get. The sun barely peaks over the horizon as the landscape of neighborhood house roofs begin to steam from the heat. Ian walks out his front door, trying his best to embrace a new attitude for the day. So much so, that he figures he could appeal to his peers more if he updated his wardrobe a bit. Straight-legged Levi jeans, a white Henley shirt, a red and blue flannel shirt tied around his waist and a pair of white canvas Chuck Taylors complete his modern grunge look. On the contrary, he seems to have a way with style, but Ian is not comfortable wearing these clothes. He would have been more comfortable in what he wore yesterday—a polo shirt, jeans, and his favorite Adidas sneakers. He makes his way to the bus stop, second guessing himself. He thinks these assholes at school probably won't even notice his wardrobe change anyway. But what else was he to do? It's not as if he can back out now. Well, he can, but that idea makes him feel worse than facing the public-school system head on. He figures he might as well give it another shot, no matter how bad he wants to crawl back inside the house and finish out the rest of the school year from home. The streets are dead. Not a bird chirp, not a squirrel to be seen. It makes him feel like he's the last person on Earth. He gets to the bus stop, which is just a yellow bus sign attached to a rusted metal pole. He is the only one there.

As he waits for the bus, he begins contemplating a means to an end. If he's going to continue to torture himself with the "all-American high-school experience," then it shouldn't be in vain. Ian has never really been passionate about anything except taking care of himself and making sure he presents himself as an upright citizen to the world. He has thought about having a career that supports awareness for his mental condition or one that researches more treatments and cures for it, but he doesn't know what that is, or even what that could be. *A therapist maybe?* But he knows he wants to go to college, so if that means getting over this hump that is high school, he's willing to sacrifice his feelings for it.

The loud roar of a car engine startles Ian. It sounds thunderous. He figures the person driving is deliberately being loud and causing a disturbance for the sole purpose of being a dick. Or just maybe this person is in a rush and needs to get where they need to be fast. He turns and sees a pretty sleek muscle type of vehicle heading in his direction. Alex is behind the wheel revving the engine intentionally to disturb the peaceful neighborhood. He doesn't live here, so why should he give a shit? It's like breathing anarchy into the normalized law and order of neighborly settings.

Samantha is in the passenger seat doing some last-minute cramming for her human biology class. She finds the human body fascinating, but the way her teacher teaches the course drives Samantha to the brink of wanting the drop the class and study the materials on her own. Better yet, she thinks she is more capable of teaching the class herself since her teacher seems inexperienced and lackadaisical about the subject as a whole. Even though Samantha herself is a virgin, she has had a few sexual experiences in her past, mainly with Alex, but she tends to think she is an expert when it comes to the human body. She knows how her body works and seems to have insight on everyone else's body as well. Like a nutritionist shaman.

Jason is in the back seat rolling up a joint. He portrays himself as the group's modern-day hippie. A true stoner to the trade. He comes from wealth, but his appearance would say otherwise. Usually sporting a band T-shirt, jeans with rips in the knees, and flip-flops, Jason is the complete opposite of his older brother Mark. Mark would fashion a tucked polo, trouser pants, and a pair of fancy loafers and complete the ensemble by dousing himself in Drakkar Noir. Something Will Smith's cousin in *The Fresh Prince of Belair* would sport. Jason's Drakkar Noir is weed. As he rolls, he's ranting about his kiss-ass of a brother, who just started college at MIT. Samantha and Alex ignore him. Ashley, sitting next to him in the back, stares out the window.

Glancing out the window, Samantha notices Ian standing alone at the bus stop. He looks familiar to her, but she can't quite figure out where she's seen him before. One thing is for sure, Ian looks very timid and nervous in his stance.

"I think that kid is in my homeroom class. He looks so familiar . . ." says Ashley, staring out the back passenger window. Samantha acknowledges her comment but makes no effort to try and make conversation. She slightly tilts her head back so Ashley can hear her.

"Yeah, he does." Samantha again catches Ian making eye contact with her as the Mustang drives past. *I think I've seen her before.*

"He looks like a fucking dweeb," Jason says, as he lights his joint and takes a drag. Alex slightly turns his head from the road, getting a good look at Ian. He looks back to the road blank faced. *Who the hell are you to judge?* He thinks, glancing at Jason in the rearview mirror. *You're a fucking dweeb, too.*

Samantha turns around in her seat toward Jason. She's annoyed, but her facial expression reads more of confusion than anything. "You don't even know him," she says with an attitude.

"Please. I know a psycho when I see one." Jason blows smoke in Samantha's face. She coughs once, fans the smoke and turns back around in her seat. Jason holds the joint up to Ashley. She's tempted but is not the type of person who like to wake n' bake. She's the more, late-afternoon-sitting-in-the-darkness-of-her-bedroom-burning-incense-and-candles-while-listening-to-Death-Metal-type of stoner.

But she shrugs her shoulders and accepts the joint, taking a drag and immediately starting to cough. A realization hits her.

"He's in my homeroom. I think his name is . . . Ian."

Samantha is intrigued. She turns to Ashley in her seat to question her about him. "Really? Where is he from?" Alex side-eyes Samantha. He doesn't make his jealousy seen, but he questions the excitement in her voice.

"He said he's from here," Ashley replies. Samantha finds that interesting since she's lived in Lakehurst most of her life but has never seen Ian before.

"So, what's he like?" Samantha questions. Alex grips the steering wheel tighter in an effort to control his emotions.

"I don't know. He seems like a fucking dweeb to me," Ashley says. Jason bursts out in laughter. Ashley joins him. They high-five each other before Ashley takes one more hit of the joint. Samantha shakes her head and turns back around. She looks over to Alex, who has been silent the entire ride. She places her hand on his leg.

"Hey, you okay?" she asks. Alex glances over, stone-faced.

"Yeah, I'm fine." He turns the radio up louder, concentrating back on the road.

Ian is starting to wonder if the bus is ever going to come. He thinks if his mom drove him to school, he could have already eaten breakfast and have made his way to the library and pretend to surf the internet to cover up the embarrassment of not having any friends or people to talk to. *Are public school buses always this late?* The bus was supposed to arrive by 7:30, and it is now 7:42. Maybe he can just go back home and skip school. His mom wouldn't know. He'd much rather be in the comfort of his small room, lying in his bed with a bowl of cereal in his hands. Just as those thoughts were about to become a daring reality, Ian feels the pavement vibrating under his shoes. He then hears the rumbling of the oversized yellow limousine making its way up the road. The breaks squeal an unbearably loud screech as the bus comes to a stop. Ian cringes at the piercing sound that echoes in the streets. The doors open to a sound as equally unpleasant as the breaks. He takes a deep breath and enters the bus. The bus driver, a large and welcoming Black woman, nods to Ian as he nervously grips the straps of his bookbag tighter and steps on the bus. Looking down the aisle, he can feel all eyes are on him. He gingerly makes his way through row after row, hoping to find an empty seat because he is too nervous to ask anyone to sit next to them. An array of odors from musk to perfume to Pop-Tarts shift as he makes his way deeper and deeper into the bus. *Good thing the windows are open.* He spots a mildly attractive blond girl sitting in a seat by herself. He approaches to ask for a seat until she beats him to the punch by moving her bookbag in the empty spot. Ian takes the hint. Almost toward the back of the bus, Brandon sits in a seat by himself reading a book. Ian cautiously approaches because there are no other seats left.

"Could I sit here?" he says with a slight tremble in his voice. Brandon looks up. He's never seen this kid before, so he assumes he's new. Brandon can sense Ian's nerves. He feels sympathy for him because if anyone knows how nerve-racking high school can be, it's Brandon.

"Yeah, sure," Brandon says as he moves his bookbag out of the way. A weight has been lifted off of Ian's shoulders. He feels as though he can breathe again. Ian thanks Brandon and takes a seat next to him. The bus ride is awkwardly silent for a while. Bus chatter and a roaring engine are the only sounds filling the dead noise between the two. Ian looks over and sees the book Brandon is reading. *Hunter's Moon.* He figures this is his moment to break the ice and start a friendly conversation.

"Is it good?" he asks. Brandon stops and looks over at Ian, distracted.

"Is what good?" Ian points to the book. "Oh, yeah. It's pretty good so far. I heard it's supposed to be a true story, but I don't believe it."

"I'm Ian by the way," Ian offers a handshake, a bold move on his part since he seems to be getting rejected with every friendly gesture he makes. Brandon smiles and shakes Ian's hand. A solid grip, but neither are asserting dominance. It just feels right.

"I'm Brandon." The exuberance of this exchange seems like the beginning of something great. Maybe it is intuition or just the stars aligning, but Brandon and Ian both feel good about this chance encounter. For the remainder of the bus ride they continue to chat about mutual interests like film, music, current events, and parts of their background. Brandon lays out his plan of going to State in hopes of pursuing a career in journalism. He explains to Ian how he works on the school paper and plans to one day have a thriving career working for a top newspaper organization such as the *New York Times* or the *Washington Post*. He questions Ian about his future plans and what he wants to do after high school.

"I'm honestly not sure. I guess I need to see some options."

"Well, what do you like to do?" Brandon asks.

"I like watching TV, eating food . . ."

Brandon laughs. "I mean like hobbies, interests. I have a passion for journalism, so I want that as a career. Are you passionate about anything?"

Ian doesn't know. He's never been asked this question before. Not even by Dr. Price. He takes a moment and realizes his interests mostly vary depending on his medical condition, but he is not going to screw up this surprisingly friendly interaction by mentioning that.

Brandon picks up on how lost Ian looks. "Hey, the school year just started. You have plenty of time to figure it out before graduation," Brandon says, endearingly.

Ian agrees. He now realizes that he has been hard on himself about this high school experience as a whole. He's glad he met Brandon. He gives Ian the boost of optimism and companionship that he needed. Brandon feels the same. Plus, it's not like he has a rolodex of friends to choose from.

As the bus arrives at school, Brandon tucks his book into his bookbag. They continue their conversation as they exit the bus together.

"What class do you have first?" Brandon asks.

"I can't remember." Ian pulls out his class schedule and looks it over. His roster of classes hasn't quite stuck with him just yet. "Hmm, oh right, human biology."

Brandon grabs Ian's schedule and looks over his classes to see if they have any together.

"That sucks, we have no classes together." He hands the schedule back over to Ian, disappointed.

"Yeah, that does suck," Ian says, folding up his schedule and placing it back in his pocket.

"Guess I'll see you at lunch then?" Brandon asks, putting himself out there in hopes that Ian is on the same page as he is. Brandon is not usually one to offer friendship, but he has a good feeling about Ian. He believes this to be a promising friendship that has potential to be long-term. And luckily for Brandon, Ian feels the same way.

"Absolutely!" Ian says with excitement.

"Cool. Guess I'll see you then. It was great meeting you Ian."

"Same! I'll see you at lunch." Brandon gives Ian a head nod, bouncing away as if the hottest girl in school had just accepted his relationship proposal. He disappears into the chaos of the student body. Ian cannot contain the smile on his face. Maybe he was wrong about public school. Maybe this is where things turn around for him. Regardless, it feels so good for him to know that he's finally found a friend.

Alex pulls into the student parking lot and parks his Mustang. The sun slowly creeps above the school building, blinding his vision. He pulls the sun visor down. Ashley applies a layer of lips gloss to her full-sized lips. She emphasizes that asset of her body as best as she can, only to highlight the tiny mole on the upper left side of her lip, a timeless and unique quality about her that she thinks is alluring. She taps Samantha on her shoulder.

"Oh, I need to get that English book out of your locker."

"Yeah sure," Samantha replies. She glances over at Alex. "Hey, can you guys give me and Alex a minute?" Ashley and Jason both look at Samantha and Alex with concern but shrug their shoulders. Ashley knows she'll just get the gossip from Samantha later.

"Yeah, of course," Ashley says, while Jason gives Alex a comforting pat on the shoulder. He has a hunch as to what this could be about, but he sure as hell isn't saying anything about it. Especially to Ashley. They both exit the car. Alex turns the ignition key, shutting off the rumbling engine. He turns to look at Samantha, a bit nervous, but still keeping his guard up. Anything she asks that he doesn't like, he'll deny. *This cannot be about Emma. Sam knows nothing about that. Jesus, I hope this isn't more college talk.*

"I wanted to talk to you for a moment about college," Samantha says, in a fragile voice, almost like a baby bird. She knows she's beating a dead horse at this point, but she needs to say this.

Fuck! Here we go again. Alex would much rather confront the fact that he cheated on her over the summer than to regurgitate the same bullshit again. He takes a deep breath and braces himself.

"Sam, look I—"

Samantha quickly interjects. "Alex I just wanted to apologize for jumping on you about college that other day. Regardless of what you decide to do after high school, it is your decision and I should not guilt-trip you into doing anything you don't want to do." This is a surprise for Alex, if it isn't already evident from the expression on his face, which reads like a proctologist has just slipped him the finger. Samantha continues, "I just want you to be happy. I want us to be happy." Alex giggles. Samantha looks offended. He grabs a hold of her hand and gently squeezes.

"Sam, I *am* happy. Nothing is going to change. Whether I go to college or not, we will still be together, and nothing is going to change that. We'll just be together at different schools, that's all. Besides, I can't let you go to college a virgin. That cherry needs to be popped, by me." Alex gets a laugh out of her and responds with a kiss to her hand.

Samantha smiles. "Very romantic," she says. They share an affectionate giggle.

"I bet it smells like a fruit basket down there. Let me get a whiff." Alex leans forward in an attempt to smell her crotch. She playfully pushes him back. "Come on, just let me stick a finger in." Alex sucks the tip of his index finger.

"Oh my God, you perv," she says, friskily. Alex knows he's won Samantha over. "I just want to thank you for being so patient with me and waiting until prom for us to have sex. I know it must be hard for you."

"In more ways than one. And yes, my dick is trying his best to rip open my jeans as we speak." Samantha looks down and notices the bulge in Alex's jeans.

He has a devilish expression on his face as he tries to entice Samantha for a quickie. *What better way than to show me how sorry you really are?* "Morning glory?" he asks.

Samantha mischievously looks around the student parking lot for any prying eyes hoping to get a quick peep show and assess her head-giving skills. The parking lot is surprisingly less crowded than usual. Samantha looks down at her watch, checking to see how much time she has before the bell rings. She's got time. Plenty of time to satisfy his urge, give her English book to Ashley, and review the last chapter of her human biology book before the bell even rings because she knows how quick Alex can be. He unbuckles and unzips his pants. Samantha helps him pull his pants and underwear down to a halfway point just above his knees and smiles up at him as she lowers her head.

Ashley and Jason make their way through the crowded hallway of the school, passing students chitchatting and preparing themselves for the school day ahead. Jason looks over to see a huge sign on the wall reading, *I want you*, in big bold red lettering. An Uncle Sam caricature, Uncle Pete, is pointing out with a look of disdain and discipline. With Jason's loopy and euphoric state of mind, this poster is not sitting well with his buzz. Uncle Pete is staring into his soul, and he is not happy. Jason wonders if that poster has always been there or is just another tacky addition to the other cringeworthy posters on the wall that say stuff like *Hang in there*, and *You've got this, champ!*

"Has that poster always been there?" he asks Ashley. Holding a small makeup mirror in front of her, she briefly pauses her touch-up and glances at the poster.

"I don't know. Who gives a shit?"

A fellow student passing by Jason and Ashley, greets Jason as they high five each other. Jason addresses the individual as Calvin. He is what one might consider the "Pig-pen" of the school—a hygiene-optional type of guy. Calvin's only concern in life is getting high, and his appearance and attitude back that up. He spends countless hours of the day stoned out of his mind, without any regard to cleanliness or a decent wardrobe. Ashley tries to mask the disgusted look on her face as they pass. Calvin asks Jason if he is going to meet him at the "spot" before lunch ends. It's a regularly deserted section of the boy's locker room, a storage room more accurately, that Jason and Alex use as their personal hotbox location. It is perfect because no one occupies that area during the morning and lunch hours, and it sits just beyond the showers of the boy's locker room, leading to a dead end. The storage has an eight-foot wall that is lined with four windows up above. Those windows usually remain open, unless it has been raining, which helps the stoners air out the space. There is even a rusted floor drain to slip evidence in just in case faculty or Coach Matthews pops by.

"You know I'll be there. Yo, do you have papers?" Jason asks.

"Of course, dude. I'm always ready," Calvin replies.

"Sweet, I'll catch you later."

Ashley is at her locker fumbling with the combination lock. Jason leans against the other locker beside hers, seductively looking her up and down. He wants to ask her something but is not quite sure if the timing is right. Plus, she looks a bit frazzled and agitated. He figures he'll butter her up, sweet-talk her first.

"What's wrong?" Jason says.

"Nothing. Calvin is just gross, that's all." Ashley opens her locker and sets her purse inside. The inside of her locker is littered with stickers of bands she likes. She also has glittery skull stickers and a photo cut-out of Brad Pitt from that vampire movie—a bold red heart drawn around his face—and a mirror she consistently uses every time she opens her locker door. She grabs her mascara out of her purse just to touch up on her lashes a bit. Jason is talking her head off about how good of a person Calvin is and that she should not judge someone based off of their hygiene.

"And what world do you live in where that shit is acceptable?" Ashley asks. She turns her attention back to the mirror. "We wouldn't be an anything if you were that gross." She glances at the reflection of her middle fingernail on her right hand. *That doesn't look even.* She closes her mascara, then grabs a nail file.

Jason blows off her comment. "Yeah, whatever," he says. His character quickly changes back to seduction. "So, my parents are leaving town for the night. And I was thinking," he says, sliding his finger down the side of her waist, "you could stop by, and we finish that thing we started the other day." He gives her a wink and a smile.

Ashley just about has her nail where she wants it. She stops and looks at Jason.

"No," she says bitterly. Jason's disappointed. She continues, "First of all, I had to sneak and steal my dad's Preparation H, okay? And secondly, you didn't even know what you were doing."

"Of course I know what I'm doing babe, we just need to try again. And as far as the Preparation H, I can't help how big I am," he says, with a slick grin on his face.

"No. I'm not a fan."

"Of my dick?" he asks concerningly.

"No, idiot. Of anal. It hurts."

"That's why we should try it again, so it can start to feel better, ya know?"

"Is that so? Then tell me, how many times have you been fucked in the ass?"

Jason nearly answers the question without even thinking. He pauses. Before his rebuttal, the school intercom squeals before Principal Owens makes an announcement.

"Attention students. Due to the recent incidents involving school and mass shootings happening in the country, the Indiana School Boards Association is requiring a random monthly bookbag and locker search of all students, effective immediately, and lasting until the end of the school year. Students in possession of any contraband including drugs, alcohol, and weapons of any sort, are subject to immediate expulsion. That is all." The school bell rings immediately afterward, a chorus of boos following the news.

"That's so fucking gay! Just because a couple of retards decided to shoot up their school, the rest of us have to suffer the consequences?" Jason shakes his head. Ashley feels the exact opposite.

"I think it's good. This is the last fucking place I want to die . . . well, second to last," she says, thinking about the summer she had to spend with her Aunt Patrice and the disgusting chicken pot pies she'd had to eat that tasted like dog food. And the morning and late-night prayers every day. And the constant smell of moth balls in the air. It was hell for her. The only silver lining had been a gray cat Aunt Patrice owned named Charlie. Ashley loved Charlie and Charlie loved her, demonstrating his affection by sleeping on her bed every night and waking her up with face licks or cuddles. Ashley wanted to take Charlie away from her aunt and home with her, but she never got the chance. One day after running a grocery shopping errand for Aunt Patrice, she came home to find her crying at the kitchen table, a mug of tea next to her and her face buried in both hands. Ashley had asked her aunt why she was crying, to which she had replied, "It's Charlie!" She used the word *accident* multiple times as she apologized over and over. Ashley had hurried down the hall to the bathroom. Standing in the doorway, she had seen the bathtub overflowing with water, Charlie's lifeless body floating at the top. To this day, Ashley still believes Aunt Patrice murdered Charlie. Maybe she was jealous. Maybe it was some bizarre pet classification of Munchausen syndrome by proxy. But either way, she'd rather die a thousand times at school than take one step back inside that cat-murdering dungeon Aunt Patrice calls a home. Still, she supports the school's decision.

"I fully support it," she says. The hall monitor, Tim, steps up to Jason and Ashley. He's the epitome of a nerd in his brown and white plaid shirt, khakis—which rest above his naval and are accentuated with a brown J. Crew belt—and white tube socks, which are visible on account of his highwaters. His hall-monitor badge shines over his left breast. He snatches Ashley's nail file.

"This is a controlled level two weapon, and I must confiscate it," he says, waving it in front of Ashley before placing it in his fanny pack and zipping it up.

"That's just a nail file!"

"Today it's considered a shank. You easily could have used it as a weapon and stabbed this gentleman." Tim walks away, head held high knowing he may have prevented a future catastrophe. He has done his good deed for the morning. Ashley on the other hand is pissed. She scowls at Tim as he walks off. "I wish I could stab *you*," she mutters. Tim may or may not have heard her, but he continues walking either way. Ashley looks at Jason, who's laughing at her. She hits him on the arm and tells him to shut up, then storms off. Jason continues to snicker, trying to be apologetic. It doesn't work.

Ian looks down at his schedule of classes just to make sure that he is in the right place. This keeping up with different rooms and buildings is troublesome for him. Especially considering how homeroom class was an introductory course that took over first and second period on the first day. He looks up at the plastic placard hanging on the wall adjacent from the propped open wooden door with the small rectangular window and sees the numbers, 217. This should be his human biology class. He walks in and notices not very many students are in this classroom. Ian spots a frail, brown-haired girl with glasses as big as magnifying glasses sitting in the front row of the classroom on the far right near the windows. Her pale face is buried in her textbook. She looks up at Ian, then puts her face back into the book. Arms crossed, she cradles her body as if she's cold, but that's just a nervous tick. Another student is seated on the opposite side of the classroom to the far left. Yet another nerdy looking individual has set up his desk in such an organized manner that you would think he is the teacher. The only thing missing is a shiny red apple. His human biology book sits at the corner of his desk. His notebook is open to a blank page. His freshly sharpened pencil sits on the open notebook next to a couple of black ball-point pens and a yellow highlighter. Ian figures since there are only two students here and twenty other desks to choose from, he has third round pick at some great choices. He begins ruling out his options. *Not the first row. I don't want that kind of attention.* His timid nature would insist he take a seat all the way in the back, but those seats are only reserved for the wannabe unknowns and the class clowns. Then he spots it, the perfect seat. Just diagonal from the girl who looks like she might have telekinetic powers. It's tucked into the second row, which is perfect. Not the first row, and not all the way in the back, but exactly right where he needs to be. He walks over and takes his seat. The bell rings. Not a split second later, the teacher walks in. A six-foot White guy with an obvious toupee, glasses, and an outfit that resembles a bible salesman. His demeanor comes across as no bullshit as he throws his business bag on his desk and begins writing the lesson plan on the chalkboard. More and more students begin piling into the classroom.

"Please just find a seat anywhere that's available," the teacher says in a nasally voice. He writes his name on the chalkboard. Mr. Sadler. As Ian watches Mr. Sadler write his name in perfect penmanship, he notices Samantha walking into the classroom with two other girls by her side. They each engage in conversation. Samantha stops for a split second and notices Ian as well. Ian quickly puts his head downward, rummaging through his bookbag. The two other girls with her are attractive in their own right. One has skin the color of caramel with a short, stylish cut and perfect teeth. The other looks as though she spends most of her evenings with a face full of tears and a mouth full of Ben & Jerry's. But Ian is sure she has a wonderful personality. They each find a seat next to one other, opposite from where Ian is seated. He notices Samantha stand up, walking in his direction. Ian tries his best to play it cool by opening up his textbook and casually flipping pages, but his nerves are rattled. She walks right past him and delivers an "excuse me" before heading to the nearby pencil sharpener. Ian fantasizes Samantha turning the lever of the pencil sharpener in a sexual nature. She pulls the pencil out of the perfectly sized hole, then puts it back in, continuing to sharpen. Ian gulps. She pulls the pencil out once more, admiring its beautifully symmetrical point. She blows the shavings off the tip. The whole scene is in slow motion. When Ian comes to, Samantha is walking toward his desk. She stops.

"Do I know you?" she says, coming off a bit flirtatious. She is slightly intrigued by Ian. She remembers seeing him at the bus stop, but she cannot shake this feeling that the two have already met in different circumstances. Ian looks up, anxious.

"I don't think so," he says, eyes nervously scanning the room.

"You were at the bus stop this morning, right?"

Wow, she remembers me, Ian thinks. "I was. I remember you driving by . . .well, passing by."

Samantha giggles. She can sense how nervous Ian feels. But she wants him to know he has no reason to be nervous or anxious. She wants Ian to feel welcomed as she offers a friendly introduction.

"Yeah, that was me. I'm Samantha by the way. Or Sam for short."
She holds her hand out. Ian glances at her hand. It's smooth in texture.
He follows up her wrist, admiring her arm as a whole. Her complexion
radiates. The little blond hairs on her arm glow in the sunlight. Ian
does not hesitate to grab hold of her hand, greeting Samantha with a
jolting handshake, but one not too forceful. It's mostly just awkward.
Samantha tries not to laugh.

"I'm Ian," he says, still shaking her hand.

"Are you new here?"

"Yes—I mean no. I mean, I'm from here, just new to this school,"
he says timidly. Samantha nods in acknowledgment.

"Well, welcome to Lakehurst. The lunch food sucks and the school
itself sucks even more. But luckily you have me to make it not suck as
much," she says, coming across upbeat and bubbly.

Ian smiles. "That's good to know," he says.

Samantha looks over, noticing the confused look on the faces of
her friends. "Well, it was very nice to meet you, Ian, and if you need
any tricks to help you survive this place, just let me know," she declares,
ending her sentence with a metaphorical period in the form of a smile.

"I will, thanks."

Samantha walks back to her desk, chatting it up with friends. Ian's
beginning to crush on Samantha. He's mesmerized by her beauty, her
polite, bubbly personality, and her scent, which smells like a hybrid of
roses and vanilla, with a hint of sunscreen.

Soon, lunch is in session, the best part of the day for students to
socialize and replenish their stomachs with subpar and barely edible
cafeteria food. Samantha, Alex, Jason, and Ashley are sitting at their
regular table, which is positioned on the far-right side of the cafeteria in
between rows of lunch tables. They spend their lunch period gossiping

about several unsavory students and how this will be their best year of high school since it's their last. Samantha picks at her food like a finicky bird, only there to eat out of necessity. Alex's right arm rests over Samantha's shoulders as he and Jason obnoxiously debate over what they would consider to be the best movie of the year. Jason passionately defends his choice, explaining to Alex why that shark movie starring Samuel L. Jackson is the best movie of the year. Alex pays no mind to Jason's defense of a film that he believes to be, a cheesy, second-rate *Jaws*, while going on to praise his love of that action-packed film where the main character dodges an array of slow-motion bullets.

Ian sits off in the middle row of lunch tables near the front of the lunchroom close by the entrance about twenty feet from Samantha's table. Admiring from afar, Ian picks over his less-than-appetizing lunch food as well. The food is a non-issue. Not even on his radar. He takes several glances toward Samantha, admiring her prissy mannerisms as she picks at her food. They definitely have that in common. Maybe they are alike in other ways, too. He wonders if her birthday is in December, as well.

Brandon walks over to Ian's table with the biggest smile on his face. He has a friend now, and now that he has a friend, he doesn't have to inhale his food as quickly as possible and rush to the school's red room to lessen the embarrassment of eating alone. He notices Ian grinning as he sits at the table. "Isn't this the most disgusting food you've ever seen?" Brandon says. He looks up to see Ian is not even paying attention to him or anything he said.

Just as Brandon's curiosity pries on what has caught Ian's attention, he snaps out of his day fantasy, apologizing to Brandon. "Huh? I'm sorry, I didn't hear you," Ian says.

Brandon points down at Ian's tray. Ian looks down at his tray of beef stroganoff. He hears Brandon rant on about how disgusting the food looks and tastes. Ian agrees. The more he picks at the stroganoff, the angrier it seems, bubbling and oozing aggressively with each flick of the spork.

Ian decides he's just going to eat the garlic bread. "Oh yeah, this food smells like it looks . . . gross," Ian says, dropping his spork down on his tray. He glances over at Samantha once more but tries to be a bit sly about it. Brandon notices. He turns his head around and sees who has Ian's attention.

"Ah, someone has a crush on Samantha Harvey, I see."

"What? No. She's just a nice girl who's in my first period class. But who's that guy with his arm around her?"

"You mean the druggie in the leather jacket? Yeah, that primate's her boyfriend, Alex. And as a friend I think it's only right to let you know that if you do have a crush on Samantha, let it go. I'm telling you that guy is a grade A jerk."

"In that case, I'll steer clear," Ian says sharply.

"So how do you like this school so far?" Brandon changes the subject.

"It's okay, I guess. Better than yesterday, now that I have someone to talk to. It's ironic that it took a school full of people to remind me what being alone felt like."

"You are not alone there, no pun intended. I'm reminded of that every time I look at myself in the mirror."

"Where are your friends?" Ian asks inquisitively.

"There are a couple of students I associate with on the school paper. But I wouldn't call any of them *friends*. I've just kept my head in the books and put all my focus on graduating. Plus, going this long without friends, what's one more year?" Brandon says with a smirk.

"Well, this year is different because you have a friend now. And neither one of us are going through this school year alone . . . deal?" Ian asks.

Brandon looks down at Ian's hand. He grabs hold as the two engage in a firm handshake, a non-verbal promise to have each other's backs the rest of the school year.

"Deal," Brandon says, right before he takes a bite of his garlic bread.

Sipping her Coke through a straw, Ashley seems very uninterested in Jason and Alex's movie talk. She rolls her eyes at the heated debate until she notices the geeky hall monitor, Tim, walking down the aisle of the lunchroom with his tray of food. Ashley is vindictive, and this nerd rubbed her the wrong way by having the audacity to take her fucking nail file away on the grounds of paranoia because nationwide schools are on an anti-violence, anything-can-be-a-weapon, authoritative police state of a fuck-train at the moment. She wants payback. She nudges Jason and notions him to look forward. He sees Tim, looking even more pathetic than before, proudly showcasing his nutritionally balanced lunch like the fucking holy grail of midafternoon meals. If the food pyramid was a person, it would approve Tim's lunch. Jason looks back toward Ashley and without a word, shares a devious smile with her. Jason waits for the perfect opportunity and just as Tim passes by, he sticks his leg out in front of him, causing a catastrophically hard fall to the vinyl flooring. The crash echoes throughout the lunchroom as the entire tray of food explodes in Tim's face before smearing across the floor. The full cafeteria is in hysterical laughter, but no one is more satisfied than Ashley. Samantha wants to help him, but the poor kid hops up and instinctively begins picking up spilt pieces before he even registers what happened. Ian and Brandon are not laughing as they helplessly watch from afar. Brandon turns his head back to Ian.

"You see what I mean. I guarantee you, if I weren't already sitting here, that would've been me."

"I don't get it. Sam seems so nice. Why are her friends so mean? Is it a high-school thing?"

"High-school thing, violent video games and tv shows, who the hell knows," Brandon says plainly. Ian seems intrigued by the idea of this group's behavior. He wants to psychoanalyze them. He's also intrigued by how Samantha feels about her friends' behavior as well since she seems to be on an opposite agenda from the group. Nonetheless, he's glad he's not in Tim's shoes right now.

The remainder of the school day is not as exciting or eventful as the cafeteria incident. Brandon and his team of somewhat enthusiastic members of the school paper generate a generic list of current events with things that are happening during the next couple of weeks of school—a blood drive, the football game, the lunch menu for the next week, all of which sound pretty boring.

Ian is trying his best to concentrate in trigonometry class. Although he is quite good at math, he does not enjoy it at all. He understands the importance, which is why he is enrolled in a trig course. But he figures his trajectory in life will more than likely leave the problems and solutions of letters interacting with numbers interacting with triangles far behind.

Ashley files her nail and sporadically pays attention to her English teacher. She looks down at the *English Literature Before the Twentieth Century* textbook in front of her. *Fuck, this is boring. Someone please shoot me now!* She sighs, pausing from her manicure, then continues filing.

Jason is fast asleep in his class. Luckily, the student in front of him is always at attention and focused on the lesson plan, which gives Jason the perfect human shield for catching some necessary z's.

Alex is counting the minutes on his watch until the bell rings. He is unfocused on class. Tuning out into a daydream. His teacher is starting to sound like a Charlie Brown character, words mumbling together like underwater gibberish. He gains a moment of clarity and turns his attention to Emma, who is seated in the same row, two desks down. Both desks separating them are empty. He provides her with a delicately flirtatious wink followed by a devious smile. Emma is on the brink of blushing. But by no means does she want Alex to think that she is interested or that his advances are even working. So, she decides to roll her eyes at him and sigh in disgust. She's playing hard to get, and even though she would rather jump off a cliff than hook up with Alex again, she figures a little harmless flirting won't hurt. It beats trying to stay engaged with this boring lecture.

Samantha is presenting a science project she and a fellow classmate worked on together to demonstrate the affects of global warming and the melting ice caps. As they both take turns explaining the science behind the overheating Earth, and that we as humans are speeding up the process of global warming by our careless and selfish actions of vanity and greed, the classroom seems to be split on believing what they are explaining is evidence to be true or not. One student closest to the back of the classroom coughs the word "bullshit," loud enough for everyone to hear. Samantha and her presentation partner are not at all amused by the outburst as the class begins laughing. Their teacher, sitting behind his desk, urges the class to settle down and pay attention. The two awkwardly get back in the groove. After completing their presentation, the bell rings.

The school bus arrives at Ian's bus stop. He hops off and journeys his way home. He glances at Brandon, sitting by the window. They both wave goodbye to each other. Ian grips the straps on his bookbag and heads down the asphalt to his sanctuary of peace. With a gleeful smile and a pep in his step, Ian seems to have embodied an entirely different attitude when it comes to school and friends. He'd had a really good day. Besides the always horrible lunch food, he made a friend in Brandon, learned a few interesting things in class, and to top it off, he gets to see Samantha's beautiful face every day, first thing in the morning.

As he approaches his house, he sees Katherine's car is in the driveway. *I thought she would be at work still;* he thinks to himself as he checks the mailbox. No mail. Walking through the front door he's immediately hit by the smell of food. *Jesus, spaghetti again!* He walks into the kitchen to see Katherine, cheerful, as she sports her favorite cooking apron, the epitome of the suburban housewife. She greets Ian with an overly enthusiastic smile and a kiss on the cheek.

"Hi Mom."

"Hi sweetie. How was your day?" she says, stirring the pot. Ian takes off his bookbag, holding it by the top strap.

"It was good, surprisingly. Really good," he says with a smile. "I thought you'd still be at work?"

"Oh, today was a short day for everyone, so I decided to come home a little early and cook your favorite—meatball subs." *Nice change of pace,* he thinks. Especially after the terrible lunch he'd had, Ian's thrilled about dinner. "So did you make any friends at school yet?"

"I did. I met several nice people today. Some of the kids were pretty mean, though. But as far as I know, I don't think I've met anyone that has blue waffle."

"Oh, that is wonderful, sweetie. I'm so happy for you." The telephone rings. Katherine takes a step forward to answer but Ian is closest to the landline. She almost shouts to Ian that she'll answer it, but she stops herself once Ian picks up.

"Hello?" Silence. Ian repeats it. He hears a quick hang up and a dial tone. He hangs up the phone. "They hung up," he says, confused. "Well, I've got a little bit of homework to do, so I'll be in my room."

"Okay, dinner should be ready soon." Ian heads upstairs. Deep in thought, Katherine stops stirring the pot. She walks over to the telephone and attempts to dial star sixty-nine. She stops herself, hangs up the phone, and walks back to the stove to resume cooking.

CHAPTER 9

A picturesque Saturday afternoon could not be more perfect for a stroll in the park, a day at the lake, or even a nice backyard barbecue. Instead, Ian sits in Dr. Price's office for a follow up since his last therapy session a couple weeks ago. And things look very different since he was last here. A major upgrade. Before, the windows and blinds were closed, as if Dr. Price assumed his patients would seize the opportunity to jump out of an open window or burst into flames from the sun. Now, the windows are open, letting in a nice breeze. The silk khaki office curtains gently flap against the beige colored walls. The glaring sun illuminates a sepia tone that complements his office and makes Ian feel more comfortable, almost in a state of Zen.

His office is pristine. Not a spec of dust is seen anywhere, from his professionally manufactured mahogany desk to the combination lock on his briefcase. His desk is littered with a rolodex, a mini globe, a pen and pencil holder, as well as a coffee mug with a design on it of a prescription pad with *#1 Shrink* written on it. The drug: caffeine. Instructions: one to two cups daily—three when life gives you shit. The only thing that has remained the same is his stainless-steel picture frame with the photo of him and his wife. The frame is also dust free. Not until now, has Ian noticed his book collection, which is impressive with a wide arrange of literature from famous authors, poetry books, biographies of public figures, and of course the DSM series. Ian sits on a couch that bears a similar color to the curtains and really gives this office a touch of anal precision in appearance and professionalism. *I see he changed the couches, too.* Dr. Price sits across from Ian on a couch that is identical in style, color, and comfortability. A small coffee table separates the space between the two as Dr. Price writes on his notepad. He then crosses his legs and turns his attention to Ian. But before he can speak, Ian chimes in.

"I see this office has had quite the upgrade." Dr. Price laughs.

"Compliments of the wife. She said my office needed to look *less depressive*," Dr. Price says, using air quotes and shaking his head.

I couldn't agree more, Ian thinks.

"But you seem to be in good spirits. That's good. How have you been adjusting to the new changes in your life? How has school been going?"

"Things have never been better. School is going great. I made some friends . . . life is good," Ian says in the most relieved of ways.

Dr. Price smiles. He writes down in his notepad, *overly optimistic.* "I'm glad to hear it, Ian. It's not every day that one can transition from such a crippling disorder to embracing the unknown changes in one's life. That shows signs of great maturity on your part."

"I've also been thinking about college and what I want to do with my life after high school."

"Well, that's great! So, what have you decided to focus on?"

"I want to do what you do. I want to be a therapist. Or a psychologist, whichever works better for me in the long run."

Ian is excited to be sharing this news with Dr. Price, who is a bit taken aback by Ian's career decision. He does not want to crush Ian's spirits, but he also does not want him following in his footsteps. Dr. Price sees it as a slap in the face to him and everything he has worked hard for. The nerve that a patient thinks he can do a better job at counseling than Dr. Price himself is not only an insult, but also ironic as fuck. But he must remain encouraging and supportive.

"That is wonderful, Ian! I am so proud of you!" The overt sarcasm is hard to read on Ian's part. Dr. Price awkwardly smiles as he jots down in his notepad *DELUSIONAL!* "So, what made you want to pursue this career field? Did I have anything to do with this sudden revelation in career choices?" Hoping Ian praises him for everything he has done up to this point, Dr. Price is surprised when he is hit with a nonchalantly dismissive no.

"I became interested just by the drive to help people. I obviously understand what it's like to live with a mental disability so I want to help those just like me overcome their illness and be a productive member of society because I know it can be done. I also want to research possible cures and maybe find a link between my own illness and my dad's."

"Is that the reason why? You don't want to end up like your daddy?" Dr. Price questions, very condescendingly. "I do find your tenacity to be very brave, Ian, but you have to be careful. Going down the rabbit hole of mental illness can trigger suppressed emotions within yourself. Next thing you know . . ." Dr. Price puts his fingers to his head like a gun and demonstrates a figurative suicide. The gunshot is a fart noise coming from his mouth.

"I know I won't end up like my dad. I can't tell you why, but I just have a gut feeling of optimism I guess."

"Do you resent your father for what he did? Because that would mess up any kid, I'm sure," Dr. Price says with a chuckle. Catching himself, he reasserts his therapist character, repositioning himself and clearing his throat to come across more professional.

"I don't resent him at all. I miss him. I just wish he would have stuck around to see all the progress I've made." Ian shrugs.

"Well, technically if he had stuck around, we wouldn't need to be having this conversation right now. But I understand exactly what you mean. Tell me a fond memory you have about your dad, if you can. I know you were pretty young when he ate it, so just try really hard to focus on a good memory you have of him." Dr. Price clicks his pen, crosses one leg over the other and focuses all his attention to Ian's story.

Ian reminisces about a day much like today. It was hot, the sun was blazing, and cotton candy clouds floated in the sky. Ian tells Dr. Price a memory of him, age five at the time, and his father washing his car on a late Sunday afternoon. Young Ian had been in the living room catching up on old cartoons when Ray walked by holding a bucket with sponges, rags, soap, car wax, and tire shine. Dressed in flip flops, a wife beater, and Richard Simmons-style shorts, Ray had stopped at the front door and called to Ian, asking if he would assist him in washing his prized '84 Cutlass Supreme. Ray loved that car almost as much as he loved Ian. He treated it like it was his own son. In comparison to Ian, the attention was borderline even, until that day. That day, the love was shared by all. In fact, Ian cannot even recall the last time he had seen the car dirty. He remembered the shiny red body, the light almond-colored leather seats, and the inside that always had this fresh smell of cherry pie. Ian was excited to share this moment with his father.

The two went out into the eighty-degree weather and began washing the car. Ray sprayed the inside of the bucket full of water to get the suds foaming, then guided Ian's hands as they both sprayed the car. Ray tossed Ian a sponge. It bounced off his forehead and landed directly into the bucket. The two laughed instantaneously. Ray scrubbed the topside of the car, while Ian worked the bottom half. During the course of the wash, Ray sprayed Ian with the garden hose a couple of times. Ian giggled as he ran from the stream. He threw the sponge at Ray, who caught it like a soggy football then tossed it into the bucket. Ray then sprayed tire shine on his tires and showed Ian how to buff out the scuff marks and scratches on the rims.

Ian remembers this being a very teachable moment. Even though he did not understand the concept of how to drive a car, he knew he wanted no one but his dad to teach him how to drive when he got to be old enough. After the chore was complete, Ray and Ian high fived each other. Ray told Ian to have a seat on the front steps of the porch while he walked into the house for a moment. Ian stared at the beautifully shiny car looking as if it had just been driven off the lot. Ray returned and sat next to Ian, handing him a popsicle. Cherry flavored, Ian's favorite. Ray explained how he was proud of Ian and thanked him for his help. He said what a good job Ian had done and that one day, Stella would belong to him. *Stella?* Yes, Stella was the name of that gorgeously shiny red boat sitting in the driveway. Ray then made Ian promise him that he would take care of Stella once it was passed down to him so that when he has a kid, he can pass Stella down to his son. Ian promised. Ray kissed Ian on the forehead and told him he loves him. Ian responded with, "I love you too, Dad."

Dr. Price clicks his pen a couple of times, then jots something down. He seems to be moved by Ian's recollection of his father. Dr. Price can sense that Ian holds his father in high regard, despite his suicide. He can tell that above all, Ray was a great father.

"That was very touching Ian. But I'm curious, what happened to Stella?"

"After my dad passed, my mom sold it and put the money in an account for me when I turn eighteen."

"I'm sorry to hear that," Dr. Price says, in a genuinely concerning way this time.

"So am I. That was one thing of my dad's that I wanted to hold onto for as long as I could. I wanted to keep his promise. But I know my mom's intentions were in the right place. A part of me feels that having Stella around would be more upsetting to her than it would be beneficial to me."

"That's a very selfless way of looking at it." Dr. Price looks at his watch and notices their session is ending. He closes his notepad and sets it down with his pen on the coffee table. "Well, it looks as if our session is over today. I gotta say, Ian, you have shown me tremendous progress and I know for a fact that your father is very proud of you."

Ian silently agrees.

"Now, if you will excuse me, I have to get ready for my next session. This woman is over forty and is just now struggling with bulimia, blah," Dr. Price says, holding up her file to Ian as he motions gagging himself with his finger. He laughs hysterically at his own joke.

Ian finds it a bit amusing but thinks Dr. Price's laughter is excessive. They both make their way to the office door. Katherine sits in a cushioned single chair just outside the office. She stands as they exit. Katherine places her hand on Ian's shoulder to comfort him.

"How was it, sweetie?"

"Fine. I'm gonna go get something from the vending machine." Ian walks away. Katherine turns to Dr. Price, hoping to get a little bit more of an insight as to what was discussed and how he feels about Ian's progress.

"I hope I can get a little more out of you than just *fine*," she says with a slight giggle at the end. Dr. Price stands with his feet sternly planted at the doorway; arms crossed like a bouncer blocking the entrance to a nightclub. It does not come off as rude, more so authoritative, and marginally appealing. He sighs, which concerns Katherine.

"Ian has shown me a level of maturity today that makes me question whether he should continue with these therapy sessions. I recommend he does, but with his remarkable growth and demeanor, Ian has proven that he is more than capable of being a productive member of society." Katherine's facial expression sparks, like discovering Disneyland for the first time.

"Oh, Doctor! You have no idea how great that makes me feel." Katherine sighs in relief as she places her hand on Dr. Price's shoulder. She unintentionally slides it down to his chest where she can tell he must have an amazing body underneath his white-collar attire. Her reaction is embarrassed as she notices where her hand is placed. She quickly pulls it back while Dr. Price looks down with the notion that Katherine is possibly flirting with him again.

There's no "possibly." She's definitely flirting with me.

"Oh my God. I'm so sorry," she says, rubbing her promiscuous hand as if she just touched a hot stove.

Dr. Price smirks. He's flattered and figures he could fuck Katherine if he wanted to—a risk he's not willing to take. Best to just keep leading her on.

"It's fine. Don't worry yourself," he says. Katherine's childish glow slowly morphs to the expression of a scolded orphan. "But when you get the time, I think it's best that you and Ian have a conversation sometime about his father. Whether that's reminiscing on past memories or answering unanswered questions about him, I think it's time you two normalize the relationship you shared with your late husband. Ian truly misses him and getting him familiar with his father's condition as it may relate to him, I feel, is the final step in Ian's evolution as an adult."

Katherine hears everything he is saying but is a bit distracted by his handsomely chiseled face. She is normally not this horny for someone, other than the time she went to a bar downtown and ended up fucking a twenty-one-year-old bartender that night because she wanted it and he was there. Katherine owns a vibrator, but has not used it in over a month, so the idea of fucking Dr. Price is just enough to get her wet.

"That sounds like a great idea, Doc. I will definitely discuss that with him." She sees Ian down the hall with a grape soda in hand. "Well, again, thank you for everything."

"Absolutely. And if you need anything, or have any questions, you have my number. Feel free to use it anytime," Dr. Price says with a dash of flirtation. He knows it's cruel to lead her on, but he is having too much fun.

Katherine wants to jump his bones and fuck on his office desk right this second. She wonders how erotic it would be to push him against his desk, strip his pants off and suck his dick until he comes in her mouth. She would then spit the cum on the picture of him and his wife out of spite because, well, his wife's a bitch. Instead, she gives Dr. Price an assuring head nod and walks away. Dr. Price yells goodbye to Ian, waving from his end of the hall. Ian raises his hand to acknowledge his departure. He sees Katherine is a bit flustered as she approaches.

"Why are you so red?" he asks.

"I'm just a bit lightheaded. Come on, let's go." She rushes out of the lobby, quickly pressing the elevator button as she fans her face. Ian just assumes she must be having a hot flash or some kind of menopause episode.

CHAPTER 8

As the school bell rings, students are settling into class and getting ready for the day. Nothing is out of the ordinary this morning, as it seems to be a boring, typical school day. Ian, who's grown accustomed to the mundane, and the rest of the class await instructions from Mr. Sadler, who always gets flustered in the morning. Ian's a step ahead of Mr. Sadler in what the lesson plan for the day is. He confidently opens his human biology book to see that today's assignment is going to be getting an in-depth look at the human reproductive system.

Ian is mature enough (as most seniors should be) to handle the illustrations of the male and female anatomy in the textbook, or so he thought. He repositions himself at his desk to avoid the pain of his boner pressing up against his ruggedly stitched Levi jeans. His pencil drops by the side of his desk. As he leans over to pick it up, he's startled by a striking set of yellow painted toenails standing right beside him. He looks up and notices Samantha, looking fuckable as ever. She's wearing yellow flip flops that match her toenails and Daisy Duke shorts with a small fringe that goes all the way around to her perfect apple-shaped derriere. Her top with its semi-transparent spaghetti-strap covered in sunflower designs just barely reaches her belly button, exposing her stomach and a red cherry tattoo located on the top of her left hip. He stares as she sucks on a big red lollipop. If Ian could not contain his boner before, it's definitely now on the brink of busting through his jeans. He quivers at the suction sound as Samantha pulls the lollipop from her mouth. She bends over and picks up Ian's pencil.

"I believe this is yours," she says with the seductive tone of a seventies porn star. Ian is at a loss for words. He holds his hand out to grab the pencil, but his fingers don't bend. Samantha places the pencil in his hand, but again, it drops to the floor. "Listen, I need a partner for this human reproductive assignment and was wondering if you would like to do it together?"

Ian points to himself and exclaims a questionable "me?"

"Of course. I think you are so cute." She giggles a bit. "In fact, ever since we first met, I've been fantasizing about what you might taste like." Ian's mouth nearly drops to the floor. He can barely comprehend what to think at this moment while simultaneously in disbelief that this is actually happening.

"You know what . . . fuck it." Samantha drops to her knees, crawls under Ian's desk, then proceeds to give him head. Ian grabs ahold of his desk and yells out a pleasantly surprising, "Oh shit!" The entire class is witnessing the actions taking place and cheers on the dirty duo with whistles and applause and slap their hands on the top of their desks. Mr. Sadler is trying his best to get the class under control.

"You two stop that!" he yells, while witnessing the sex-capade from the view of his desk.

"Hey buddy," a voice says. Ian looks to his left and sees his dad leaning up against the window next to him.

"*Dad?*" Ian asks.

Ray pulls a toothpick out of his mouth. "Oh, don't mind me, but I think it's time for you to cum, wouldn't you say?" Ray says as he checks his watch.

Ian braces himself as he gains a tighter grip of his desk. He yells out a primal "Oh my God!" before abruptly waking up to the sound of his alarm clock. He hits the alarm and immediately feels the wet and sticky situation going on in his underwear. He lifts up his comforter just to be sure.

"Shit." Yeah, he definitely came in his PJ's. He hops out of bed and looks out his window to see that his mother's car is gone. *Guess she left already,* he thinks as he walks to the bathroom and turns on the shower. He takes off his sticky garments, throws them into the dirty clothes hamper, and steps into the shower, the beginning of his morning routine. He then brushes his teeth, gets dressed, combs his hair, and admires himself in the mirror for a moment. He doesn't consider himself to have model or movie star looks, but he does know he is not the ugliest thing to walk the earth. If he just added a boost of confidence to his demeanor, maybe that would be enough to get Samantha's attention.

What a crazy dream. Even though Ian is obviously crushing on Samantha, she has a boyfriend. A boyfriend who, according to Brandon, is a crack-headed neanderthal or whatever, so it's best not get on his bad side. Regardless, he just has to keep reminding himself that there are plenty of fish in the sea, if only he could stop thinking about his insanely erotic wet dream.

He goes to the kitchen and grabs a box of Cookie Crisps from the top of the fridge. He sees a note written by Katherine:

"Good morning, sweetie, I will be late coming home today. There are leftover meatballs in the fridge. If you want to order something, there is $20 by the phone stand. Have a wonderful day. Love, Mom

Ian picks up the twenty-dollar bill sticking out from underneath the phone and proceeds to make his breakfast. *Today has been wonderful so far. Let's hope it stays that way.*

During first period, the day starts off normally. The teacher is preparing for a presentation while students chatter and talk amongst themselves before class actually starts. Ian pulls out his book and sets it on his desk. His pencil falls to the floor beside him. As he reaches over to pick it up, he sees a set of feet standing there. He looks up to see Samantha. *Oh shit, just like in my dream. This is weird. Control your boner, Ian. Control your boner.* Samantha bends over and picks up the pencil.

"I believe this is yours," she says with a smile. Ian gently grabs the pencil from her.

"Thank you," he utters nervously.

"You're welcome," she says cheerfully. She then makes her way to the pencil sharpener. Ian looks down and tries to realign his pants. *It's leaning to the left, good. Not showing, not hurting.* All he needs to do now is think about something non-sexual related. *Baseball? The solar system? School work? Yeah, that is perfect. Just focus on the lesson plan for the day.* Mr. Sadler then sets two model diagrams of male and female genitalia on top of his desk

"Alright class. Today we will be exploring the human reproductive system. So, let's be mature when discussing things like penises and vaginas okay? Now, who wants to hold the penis first?" Mr. Sadler takes the model penis off his desk and hands it over to an eager student in the front row. Ian sighs. *Fuck me.*

As first period ends, the school hallways have now become a traffic jam of students who are all making their way to their next class. Ian is beginning to feel a bit nauseous. Things become overwhelming for him. Tiny beads of sweat trickle down his forehead. He wipes the sweat into his hair. *Something's not right.* He hears his name called from a distance.

"Ian! Ian!" His nauseousness begins manifesting into paranoia and confusion. He's not quite sure if someone is actually calling his name or if it's an auditory hallucination. The scene is chaotic. People seem to be giving Ian weird looks as he navigates through the crowd. The structure of the hallway bounces off of itself. The walls are made of rubber. Things are becoming disorienting for Ian.

"Hey, Ian!" *That voice is not real.* The grip on reality is slipping away. He figures he just needs to calm himself down. Maybe water is what he needs. He locates a water fountain near the end of the hall. Ian stops and takes a few sips. His nerves are a bit more relaxed, but his body temperature seems high. His head feels hot and he's still slightly disoriented.

"Ian!" the voice calls out. Ian turns around furiously and screams, "WHAT?" He notices Brandon standing behind him, startled.

"Yo. I was calling your name back there. You didn't hear me?"

"Shit, dude. I'm so sorry."

"Are you okay?"

"No, I—I'm just not feeling so good right now."

"You're not going crazy on me, are you? And if so, I don't blame you. I sometimes question my own sanity whenever I get . . ." Ian tunes out Brandon as it finally dawns on him that he forgot to take his medication this morning. *How could I be so careless? How could I forget the most important part of my morning routine?* After all these years of maturing and solidifying his independence. After all the praise given to him by Dr. Price. For the first time ever, Ian feels like he really fucked up.

"Oh shit!" he says, terrified. Ian does not want to experience the effects of skipping his medication. A steel cage door that has always been deadbolted and welded shut has now been left ajar.

"What? What's going on?" Brandon says, lost and out of the loop. He can see something is obviously bothering Ian.

"Uh, where is the nurse's office?" Ian says frantically.

"Oh, down this hall, down the stairs, it will be on the left side." And just like that the Flash, Ian dashes down the hall with a quickness. Brandon, still left confused, shrugs his shoulders, and walks in the opposite direction. Ian narrowly evades student after student as he rushes down the hall, sounding like a broken record in repeating, "excuse me," and "sorry," every few seconds. He gets to the end of the hall and looks to his right to see the staircase. He sprints forward, skipping several steps as he makes his way down. He finally gets to the first floor of the building and sees an office with the blinds closed. The wooden door is labeled with a plaque that reads, *Nurse Murphy*. Ian gets to the door and turns the knob. It's locked.

"No, no, no! This can't be happening!" He starts banging on the door, ignoring the office hours on the placard. Mon–Fri. 10 a.m. – 4 p.m. His banging intensifies. It's becoming aggressive. Passing students gawk.

"Hello! Is anyone in there!" Ian looks down at his watch. 9:58 a.m. *You gotta be fucking kidding me!* He continues banging on the door. His efforts become useless, as he realizes no one is going to answer. *This can't be happening. What the fuck am I gonna do now?* Ian begins hyperventilating. A seemingly perfect and ordinary day for him has now become consumed by a dark cloud of doubt, paranoia, and panic. He begins second-guessing this journey and wonders if he can keep up this charade of pretending to be like everyone else, pretending that he's not stained with the curse of schizophrenia and that his actions right now are completely justified.

"Oh my God! Are you okay?" a voice says. Ian is crouched on the floor, leaned up against the door with his hands covering his face and his elbows on his knees. He looks up at a young, beautiful blond. Nurse Murphy. Ian knows his mind is playing tricks on him, but Nurse Murphy comes to him in the form of an angel. He sees a bright light behind her. He hears the gentle and beautiful sound of a soft harp. He wants to speak, but his words are fragmented.

"I—medication—stop—" Trying to understand, Nurse Murphy quickly reacts by unlocking the office door. They both enter into the dark space, which mimics a morgue until Nurse Murphy turns on the bright florescent lights. Now it's a brightly lit morgue. She helps Ian sit on the brown leather loveseat just to the right of the office entrance.

"Can I get your name?" she says as she sets her purse and coffee mug down onto her desk.

"Ian—Ian Moss." Nurse Murphy knows exactly who Ian is. Principal Owens has brought her up to speed. She assumes Ian forgot to take his medication and is now suffering from a panic attack. And she is right.

She removes her light jacket and tosses it across her desk chair.

"Right, Ian. Nice to meet you. I'm Nurse Murphy. Everything is going to be fine; you're just having a panic attack okay. Just focus on your breathing for me." She grabs her keys off the desk and unlocks the medicine locker near the back of the office. All of the medication is labeled alphabetically by last name. She immediately finds the section for M and sees a bottle. *Moss, Ian.* She quickly grabs the medication, then heads to the water cooler dispenser and fills a cone paper cup. She walks over to Ian and hands him the water and shakes a pill out from the bottle into his hand. Ian pops the pill and takes a swig of water. His breathing starts to get back to a normal rhythm. He looks at Nurse Murphy with a little more clarity now. Like he had noticed before, she's beautiful, blond, and possibly a recent college grad given her young looks. There's a sparkle in his eyes. He delivers a gratifying "Thank you."

Nurse Murphy acknowledges and walks over to her desk, scribbling on a piece of paper. "Do you often forget to take your medication?"

"No, not at all. This is the first time it has ever slipped my mind."

"It happens. I'm sure this is a lot for you to get used to," she says in a supportive and comforting manner.

"It is. Thank you again."

"Absolutely. And I'm here to help, so you have nothing to worry about. Are you okay to go back to class or should we call someone?"

"No, no. I'm fine. Thank you."

Nurse Murphy hands him a slip of paper. He takes it and notices it is a signed excused tardy slip. A bit confused, he looks at Nurse Murphy. She points her finger in the air. The school bell rings.

"Have a great rest of your day, Ian."

Brandon is hurrying through the now less-crowded halls, bookbag sliding off his shoulder as he carries a stack of papers almost up to his chin. *The Lakehurst Journal*, a semi-popular school newsletter that he prides himself on contributing to. The school bell continues to ring for another five seconds. He knows he will be late for class. Most teachers give Brandon a pass when he's late because he is normally very punctual. And his grades are top tier. Either way, he knows he gets a pass, but doesn't want to take advantage of their generosity and aims to be on time every day. Luckily, the drop-off point for the school newspaper is just a few doors down from his next class. Looking down the hallway, he sees none other than Alex and Jason walking in his direction. *Shit!* He figures maybe if he keeps his head down, passing them quickly, they won't really notice him. As their paths reach closer to one another, Alex swiftly slaps the stack of papers out of Brandon's hand, scattering the sheets over the vinyl flooring. Alex and Jason both laugh hysterically.

"Looks like you've got quite a mess to clean there, darkie," Alex says, patting Brandon on the back then proceeding down the hall. Bent down to gather his newsletters, Brandon shouts at Alex.

"Fuck you!" he says angrily, turning back to collect the newsletters. Alex and Jason look at each other in shocking amusement. They turn back, then step directly in front of Brandon.

"Fuck me?" Alex says. He then kicks the stack of newspapers Brandon has reassembled, laughing at the humiliation on his face. Brandon is tempted to retaliate but is fearful of the consequences a fight would do to his reputation and education. He's almost at his breaking point, but he also sees the finish line to graduation. Why risk everything now? He sighs, then proceeds to once again, stack the dismantled pile of papers. Alex waits until he gets a decent number of papers stacked. Brandon hears him say, "watch this." He kicks over the stack once more, high-fiving Jason after.

"And what the fuck are you gonna do about it, pussy?" Alex says, leaning into Brandon's face. Brandon takes one final look at Alex. His face is demented. He reaches into his bookbag and pulls out a handgun. He stands, pointing the weapon at Alex's chest. A silent beat before Brandon pulls the trigger. The bullet punctures Alex's chest, quickly soaking his gray shirt red. He falls to the floor.

"HOLY SHIT!" Jason screams, as he runs down the hallway in a clumsy yet rapid speed. He sneakers squeak with each step. Brandon stands over Alex who is whimpering in pain while holding his leaking gunshot wound. He slowly begins crawling back from Brandon, using his feet for propulsion. Pleading and apologizing, Alex knows he's not getting far. He's too fearful to think. Brandon stands over Alex. He points the gun and fires off six more rounds. The feeling is borderline pleasurable for him. Dead silence fills the hall as Brandon remains impassive, staring at Alex's lifeless body, blood leaking from the bullet wounds.

Brandon snaps out of his manic daydream and continues to stack his newspapers. He turns back and sees Alex and Jason walking away in a playfully nonchalant manner. He was just an inconvenient speed bump on their journey. Brandon picks up the five-pound stack of newspapers and continues his destination feeling frustrated and defeated.

Ian, who's now got a hold on his mental and emotional state, gets to his next class—keyboarding. Upon entering the classroom, he walks over and hands the teacher his tardy slip. His teacher, a slightly obese gentleman, takes his slip and points for Ian to find somewhere to sit.

"As I was saying, we will be having a timed quiz tomorrow to test your home key skills. If I have to warn you again not to go on the internet without my instruction, there's going to be a problem. And do not let me catch you typing with one finger at a time. Again, if I catch you fingering your keyboards, I will fail you on said quiz immediately." Several students can be heard giggling at the instructor's keyboard innuendo. Ian quickly finds an empty seat next to Emma. They both smile at each other as he sits down. Ian notices Emma slightly bobbing her head in his peripheral. She leans over and whispers in his ear.

"If you don't wanna die of boredom, I suggest you invest in a CD player." Her hair is covering her headphones. The silver band from the headphones is disguised as a headband for her hair.

"I'll keep that in mind . . . who are you listening to?" Emma takes the headphones off and presses it against Ian's ear. The infectious beat and raunchy lyrics reverberate through Ian's ear canal. He has never heard this song. It's vulgar and unapologetic but full of energy. Ian likes it. "Wow," he says as he looks ahead for a moment to make sure the teacher does not see him distracted. Emma pulls the headphone away. "Who is that?" Ian asks.

"It's old-school 2 Live Crew. Good shit, right? Makes me miss home," Emma says, as she stuffs her CD player back into her bookbag.

"Where is home?"

"Orlando. My mom got a good paying job here last year and I've been hating it ever since. Glad this is my final year so I can get the fuck outta here and go back to Florida." Ian giggles. He finds her honesty and bold personality refreshing.

"I understand," Ian replies. "I've been here my whole life and I have to say, I'm not a fan either." The two share a laugh. Emma looks at Ian with a smile.

Keyboard clatter, mouse clicking, and the occasional cough are the only sounds present through most of the class until Emma leans over and whispers to Ian. "No fingering the keyboard, okay?"

Ian covers his mouth to muffle his laughter. "Is it okay to play with my hard drive?" he responds.

She smiles bashfully at his joke, stifling a giggle. *Finally, this class has gotten more interesting.*

As night falls on Saturday, the wind sweeps the dead brown leaves across the metropolitan landscape. The city glows from illuminated fast food signs, beaming headlights, and the dazzling marquee from the city's local movie theater. A freshly washed gray Dodge Caravan pulls up to the front entrance of Lakehurst Regal Cinemas. Sitting in the middle row, Ian is excited to finally have a chance to go out on the town with someone other than his mom. Brandon sits next to Tina in the passenger seat. He unbuckles his seatbelt, ready to hop out. Tina is trying to get a good look at the marquee from the driver's seat. Maybe there is something of interest she would like to see.

"What movie are y'all going to see?" Neither of the boys answer. Brandon is not sure, and neither is Ian. Brandon typically knows what movie he's excited to see before he gets to the theater, but things are different this time around. He figures he will leave it to Ian to decide what movie they see—it's only polite. Ian usually knows the movie he wants to see, also. He figures Brandon likes to be spontaneous about his movie choices and hopes they can agree on something.

Tina's been waiting on an answer. Her voice gets more direct. "Hello? What movie are you two seeing?"

"Mom, we don't know," Brandon says, somewhat annoyed.

"Well you need to figure it out if you want me to come pick you up afterward." Ian hops out of the vehicle. Brandon follows. Staring at the marquee, they both see the title of a movie that appeals to the both of them. They look at each other and nod. Brandon closes the car door behind him. He turns to Tina speaking through the window.

"We're gonna go see *Fight Club*," he says, excitedly.

"What time does it start?"

"Eight thirty."

Brandon looks at his watch. 8:16 p.m.

"Okay, I'll be back in two hours. Y'all behave yourselves."

Ian nods and delivers an assuring, "Yes ma'am."

"I love you," Tina says, in a demanding way, expecting Brandon to return the favor.

"I love you too, Mom," he says embarrassingly. She rolls the window up and drives off. Brandon and Ian hop in line. It doesn't seem that long, but they just hope they have plenty of time to get their tickets, their snacks, and be in their theater seats in time to catch the previews.

"Man, I can't even tell you the last time I had someone to go to the movies with besides my mom," Brandon says.

Ian feels the exact same way. "I understand completely. My Saturday nights usually end with my mom passed out on the couch from the Blockbuster movie we rented and me cleaning all the popcorn off the floor that she spilled while falling asleep," Ian says, mundanely.

Brandon laughs. "Well hey, let this be the start to better Saturdays for the both of us. Deal?" Brandon holds out his hand.

"Deal." Ian shakes his hand enthusiastically. They each purchase their own ticket to the film and express how excited they are as they enter the theater building. The theater lobby is decked out in a Halloween phantasmagoria of spider webs, jack-o-lanterns, rubber bats, strings of orange pumpkin lights hanging around and of course life-like mannequins of a few iconic horror movie villains: the Wolfman, Dracula, and the popular Ghostface killer from that teen slasher flick. The dazzling Hollywood lights from the concession stand and upcoming film posters around the lobby add to the allure. The theater scene is a horror geek's wet dream. Standing in the concession line, they both debate on the best theater candies and contemplate what they'll get to munch on during the well-reviewed film. Finally approaching the counter, Brandon has his eyes fixated on the popcorn bursting from the kettle in the machine. The smell is heavenly. A frail kid with jet black hair and a ring tattoo around his middle finger steps from behind the counter and offers his assistance. Ian is overwhelmed by the choices. Brandon immediately requests a large popcorn, M&Ms, and a medium Sprite.

Brandon turns to Ian and assures him in a considerate way. "We can just share my popcorn if you want."

Ian was not expecting that from him. His social skills aren't too noticeably awkward when it comes to human interaction, but when confronted with seemingly easy dilemmas, his decision making is foggy. He truly doesn't know what is the best option. He awkwardly looks at the blank-faced cashier waiting on an answer. He looks back at Brandon, who he thinks would feel offended if he didn't take him up on his offer.

"Okay, sure. Then, just a large Coke, please," Ian says, confidently. Walking to their designated auditorium, Brandon points out a couple of arcade games along the left side of the corridor. Specifically pointing out *Space Invaders* as a classic and recommending they play a couple of rounds after the movie. Continuing down the hall they approach the auditorium.

The lighting is dim, with red carpet illuminated by tracking lights on both sides. Upon entering, they smell dried soda, popcorn, and a flowery scent of perfume presumably from a woman who entered the auditorium moments before. They find a pair of perfectly placed empty seats in the very center of the theater. They plop down and begin enjoying handfuls of popcorn. Brandon looks down at his hands and can see a glaze of butter glistening from the dim theater lights. He wipes his hands on his pants and grabs another handful. The previews start, which seem to be a hit with the audience. Moments later, the movie starts. Ian and Brandon are both glued to the screen in fascination. As the movie progresses, Ian starts to feel a bit uneasy with the relatable concept of the film. Sure, this seems to be an exaggerated take on something that is very real to him, but watching it play out in front of him in graphic and surreal detail is putting him on edge. He periodically looks over at Brandon to see if there may be any signs of judgment as he reacts to the movie. None. Just laughs and shock and awe.

After the film and a few rounds of *Space Invaders*, Brandon and Ian wait outside of the theater for Tina. Ian seems to be left in a bit of a daze from the film. Brandon is going on and on about all of the action sequences and how great the acting was. He then brings up the plot twist of the film which catches Ian's attention.

"I mean, I did not see that coming at all," Brandon says, as he pops a couple more M&Ms into his mouth. Ian agrees. He explains that the film and the characters seemed real and authentic. Brandon again attributes that to the acting in the film. There clearly seems to be something on Ian's mind other than the film. He looks over at Brandon with concern. Brandon keeps an eye out for his mom's hard-to-miss minivan. Ian takes a deep breath. Katherine's voice pops into his head, warning him about telling others about his mental state. Ian ignores it. He exhales deeply.

"There's something I want to tell you," he says, abruptly. Brandon is at full attention. He stops chewing his M&Ms and lowers the bag from his mouth. Ian continues. "Watching that movie has got me thinking about my own life. Taking chances you know?" Brandon is confused. He is unsure what is happening right now, but he is definitely intrigued to hear more. "I want to be honest with you because you're my friend. My only friend really."

"Be honest about what?" Brandon asks.

Ian takes another deep breath in and just comes out with it. "I have schizophrenia," he says, slightly cowering as he expects judgment and criticism from Brandon. He has completely disregarded Katherine's wishes. But for what it's worth, Ian feels he can trust Brandon. At least he hopes he can. He nervously anticipates Brandon freaking out on him, but the reaction is actually opposite from expectations.

"Schizophrenia? Like Tyler Durden?" Brandon says, pointing back to the theater. "Is that why you've been homeschooled this whole time?" Ian nods his head. Brandon is in amazement at this point. He now has so many questions for Ian about his past, how he grew up, his condition, his favorite breakfast meat, etcetera. But Brandon can sense that this is taking a lot of courage for Ian to say. He's also flattered Ian chose him to open up to. So instead of interrogating him, Brandon feels he should show sympathy and be supportive. "Man I don't care about that. You're my friend and I'm here for you. You can come to me about anything. I swear."

"Really?" Ian says in an upbeat manner.

Brandon is surprised he has to sell his sincerity this much. He figures Ian's lack of social skills is just masking over his trust issues with society. But then again, he just admitted to having a mental illness. And Brandon knows his social skills are not top tier either. Again, he figures sympathy and support is the way to go. Brandon places his arm around Ian's shoulder.

"Of course dude . . . I got you." Brandon holds his fist out for a bump.

"Thanks dude." They fist bump then share an embrace. The hug gets a bit embarrassing when Tina pulls up beside them. They quickly let go of one another and pretend as though they were just rough housing. Ian clears his throat as they both hop inside the van.

The two boys continue enjoying each other's company during a sleepover at Brandon's. Potato chip bags, cookies, soda cans, and a pizza box are scattered on the floor as the two unwind over small talk and late-night television, a low-budget horror movie on screen. Ian sits on the floor with his back against the foot of Brandon's bed. Brandon is lying on his bed down by the foot. He reaches and grabs a couple of chips from the Lay's bag sitting on the floor next to Ian. Ian looks over and notices Brandon's gaming system tucked in the corner under some clothes.

"Dude, you have a Nintendo 64? I haven't even played one yet," Ian says.

"And you won't because I broke mine over the summer, unfortunately."

"Oh," Ian says, disappointed.

"So what will happen if you don't take your medication?" Brandon says with a mouth full of chips.

"Not sure. The last time I had an episode I was really young, so I don't really remember it, but . . . I guess it's like a more intense me.

I forgot to take my medication the other day and nearly had a panic attack."

"So you have another personality?"

"I don't think so. It's still me, just me with a shorter fuse, I guess. Regardless, I do everything I can to keep that part of me hidden away," Ian declares.

"Makes sense. So are you still crushing on Sam or what?" Ian looks back at Brandon nervously.

"What? No. I just think she is attractive. But there is this other girl in my keyboarding class . . . uh . . . Emma Parsons—"

"Whoa, you do *not* want to get involved with her."

"Why not?" Ian says, confused.

"She's a very promiscuous girl."

Ian is not sure he quite follows. He gives Brandon a befuddled look.

"She's a slut, dude."

Ian gets it now. He's wondering if her borderline abrasive introduction was actually her flirting with him. "Wow. I guess that makes sense, now that I think about it. She's so nice though, and funny."

"Duh, that's what sluts do; they flirt."

"I guess you're right. Is Sam a slut?"

"I don't think so. She's got pretty big tits though."

"No doubt. But like you said, she's with Alex, so I'm just gonna step aside."

"Good. See, where would you be if I wasn't here to show you the ropes?" Brandon asks.

Ian laughs and shrugs his shoulders. Brandon grabs a few more chips.

"Speaking of sluts, do you know anyone at school who has blue waffle?" Ian asks.

Brandon looks confused. "What the hell is that?"

"My therapist said it's some kind of STD that looks like blueberry cobbler or something."

"Blueberry cobbler?"

"Something like that. I wasn't really paying attention too much." Brandon ponders for a moment.

"Why don't we ask Jeeves?" Brandon says.

Ian agrees. "That's a good idea!" Brandon hops in his computer chair and gets on the internet search engine, talking as he types.

"What is blue waffle . . . search!" Brandon says, with the click of the mouse. Several websites pull up a warning for graphic content. "This website has photos." Brandon clicks the highlighted webpage and reads through. "This says that it is an STD that . . . wait what?"

"There's a link to the photos!" Ian says, pointing at the screen. Brandon clicks the link. As the photos load, the two simultaneously begin to gag over the graphic depiction. Ian turns his head and urges Brandon to exit the webpage. Brandon is repulsed but is too curious to turn away. He scrolls further to a photo of a violent STD attacking a person's anus. Brandon instantly gags and turns his head away.

"Dude, turn that shit off please! It's disgusting!" Ian shouts.

Brandon quickly hits the *x* at the top right of the screen. He hops up from his chair and turns to Ian.

"Man, what the fuck is wrong with your therapist?" Brandon asks. Shocked, Ian shrugs his shoulders. "I'm gonna go get some bleach for my computer," Brandon says, shaking off the grotesque image from his mind as he walks out the room.

"Good thinking," Ian responds, giving a thumbs up.

CHAPTER 9

The October morning is brisk but not too cold. Tacky Halloween decorations can be seen lined along several houses. Dawn is just starting to approach over the silent suburban community. Ian stands at the bus stop waiting for his chariot to arrive. As he stands in the mild wind, he realizes that he is the only person in this neighborhood who waits for the bus. Is he the only high-school-aged kid in this neighborhood or is every other student privileged enough to own a car? He begins pondering that now would be a good time to learn how to drive. After all, kids his age should already have their license. *Maybe I'll ask Mom if she can teach me sometime this weekend.* As he begins to envision himself driving down a smooth interstate, he hears the rumbling of Alex's Mustang approaching. He knows the distinct sound of his car, as he's become accustomed to the engine's disturbance since the school year started. Usually the car just drives by. Lately, Ian's been treated with a slight wave from Samantha from time to time. But today is different. As the muscle car approaches, it comes to a stop directly in front of Ian. Ian watches as Samantha rolls down her window. The rumbling engine vibrates the asphalt under Ian's feet.

"Hey!" she says, waiting for Ian to respond. It takes him a minute to build up the nerve to even speak. At this moment, Ian has realized that his social anxiety comes in the form of being the center of attention. But he figures others must go through the same thing and the only way to conquer this uncomfortable feeling is to dive headfirst into social interaction. *That's why I chose to do this in the first place, right?*

"Hey!" Ian shouts awkwardly. He hopes Samantha can't hear the slight pitch change in his voice.

"Do you want a ride?"

Ian is unsure how to respond. On one hand, if he accepts, he'll have the awkward pleasure of riding with complete strangers in the midst of boiling anxiety. On the other hand, he can calmly ride the musty smelling and unsanitary school bus next to his friend Brandon. He prefers that hand.

"Oh, that's okay. I'll just wait for the bus," he says politely.

"I'm not taking no for an answer. Get in!" Samantha opens the passenger side door. She turns to Jason behind her and tells him to make room. She hops out of the two-door car which looks like it has had a fresh wax job. The sun glimmers off the body. No smudges, fingerprints—not even a smear from the applied wax. If anything, Alex is a master at detailing vehicles. She gestures like a game-show hostess while Jason pushes the passenger seat forward and gets out, allowing Ian access to the middle of the back seat. Ian takes a deep breath and says to himself quietly, "Ah what the hell." He hops in and settles between Ashley and Jason.

Samantha closes the door as Alex speeds off. For the first few minutes of the ride, everyone is in complete silence. This is what Ian was afraid of. Sitting uncomfortably in between two strangers, he just knows he's making things awkward for everyone. Music is blasting from the speakers. It's a band that Ian is unfamiliar with, but the song is quite catchy.

"Thanks for the ride. I really appreciate it," he says, timidly. No one responds. Samantha thinks she might have heard something, so she turns back to Ian.

"Did you say something?" With the music blasting and both windows down, it's a miracle Ian is able to make out everything she said. He knows he'll have to enunciate himself this time with a little more volume.

"I SAID THANKS FOR . . ." Samantha turns the music down mid-sentence "THE RIDE I . . ." Ian adjusts his voice. "Uh, really appreciate it."

Ashley looks at Ian, annoyed. Ian cringes in his seat and awkwardly smiles at Ashley and sheepishly says "Sorry." She rolls her eyes.

"It is no problem at all, right Alex?"

Alex, who has been slyly peeking at Ian from the rearview mirror responds. "Right. So Ian, where are you from?"

"I'm from here. Born and raised."

Jason jumps in on the inquisition. "How come we've never seen you at school, then?" Ian looks over at Jason, who looks stoned beyond belief. His eyes red and watery, Jason's question and response time moves at a sloth's pace.

"Well, I was homeschooled."

The car goes silent as the song ends.

"Really? That's interesting. So this is your first time ever going to a public school?" Samantha asks.

Ian nods his head. "Well, technically it would be my second. I stopped going to elementary school when I was around five or six."

Alex chimes in. He has a ton of questions for Ian but plays it cool. "So why start public school now?"

"My mom thought I needed the experience to prepare me for college next year."

"Well you picked a great school to graduate from," Samantha says, smiling brighter than the sun.

Ian returns the smile. "I hope so."

"Yeah right. This school fucking blows donkey dick," Jason says while squirting drops in his eyes.

"Don't mind him. He was dropped on his head as a child," Samantha says in an attempt to curb the vulgar comment made by Jason. Ian realizes it's a joke and awkwardly laughs. He turns to Jason, who stares at Ian for a moment just before letting out a deep and abnormally long burp. Again, Ian awkwardly laughs at Jason's vulgar and repulsive sense of humor. Alex is going above the speed limit at this point. Ian checks the middle seat but can't seem to find the seatbelt anywhere.

"Do you have seatbelts?" he asks, rather concerned. He looks over at Ashley, who is not wearing a seatbelt. He looks at Jason, who isn't wearing one either.

Looking through the rearview, Alex responds. "Don't worry Ian. I am a very safe driver. See, I don't have on a seatbelt." Ian then looks over at Samantha, who is the only one being a safe passenger.

"Oh, I see someone's being safe at least," he points out.

"Yeah, unlike these daredevils, I don't put much faith in his driving," Samantha says, pointing at Alex. Alex presses down a little more on the gas pedal. The engine revs as the speed increases. The road goes through a residential area with a maximum speed limit of thirty-five miles per hour. Alex is now traveling at fifty.

"Alex, slow down," Samantha says, sitting back into her seat in a more braced position. Ian notices the speedometer increasing to fifty-five, sixty, seventy. His heart nearly pounds out of his chest. He wants to scream for Alex to slow down but he also knows he'll come off as a pussy in front of everyone if he does. He places one hand on the back on Alex's seat and the other against Samantha's for support. Seventy-five, eighty. Houses, mailboxes, and landscaped shrubbery all begin to blend together as Ian looks out the window. His eyes nearly pop out of his head when he sees an approaching stoplight.

"There—there's a stoplight coming up," he pleads.

Samantha also chimes in. "Alex, slow down! I said slow down now!"

Alex gives a quick glance over to Samantha. "You don't want to be late for class now do you?" he increases the speed to eighty-five miles per hour. The threat becomes too real as they approach the stoplight. They see merging cars and lane changing on the horizon. God forbid they end up a teen-driving statistic.

"Alex, please slow down," Ian says, faintly.

"Oh shit!" Alex screams out but keeps up the momentum. The stoplight is fast approaching. Now everyone in the car is beginning to panic. Samantha, Ian, and Ashley are all yelling and screaming for Alex to slow the car down before they wreck. He suddenly slams on the breaks as the car skids forward several feet before stopping directly in front of the white line just below the red stoplight. Alex shouts out a celebratory "Woo!" as he feels the rush from his adrenaline-fueled brush with death. "Now that was fucking awesome!" Alex says, as he and Jason share a mutual laugh together.

"You're an asshole! That was so irresponsible, Alex!" Samantha screams as she hits him on the arm.

"Relax. I know what I'm doing," he responds. Samantha turns her attention to Ian, who looks as if he just seen his life flash before his eyes.

"Ian are you okay?" she asks. Ian's face is frozen. He is in too much shock to even speak. So instead he looks at Samantha, smiling creepily and nodding his head as he answers with a "Mmmhmm."

"Are you sure? Cause you look like you're about to cry," Samantha says.

Ian starts rapidly blinking, trying to dry up what visible tears Samantha may see in his eyes.

"What? No way uh . . . that—that's uh, lame as f—fuck—to cry," Ian says, laughing nervously. "Not me. Maybe . . ." Ian throws the blame to Ashley by nodding his head in her direction. Ashley blankly stares back. Samantha's not buying it.

The crew finally arrives in the school parking lot. Alex parks in his usual spot as they all exit, still complaining about Alex's little Nascar stunt. Ian's just glad to get out of that death trap of a vehicle and plant his feet firmly on reliable ground. Samantha and Ashley walk ahead. Alex yells for her to give him his morning kiss before she heads off to class. Samantha flips him the bird and walks off, disappearing into the crowd of students. Ian then spots Brandon in the crowd and tries walking ahead of Alex and Jason to catch up to him. Just as he's about to call out Brandon's name, a hand is placed on his shoulder.

"Where do you think you're going?" Alex asks, as they stop in the school courtyard.

"Uh, to class?" Ian asks.

Alex shakes his head. "Nope. You're coming with us," Alex says, menacingly.

"Where?" Ian asks.

Alex puts his arm around Ian's shoulders as the three begin walking in the direction of the gymnasium, which is attached to a far-left building of the school where most elective classes and after school activities are held. "Well, first I just want to apologize for that stupid car stunt earlier. I tend to show off a bit in front of new people. So to make up for my . . . childishness, I have a surprise for you. Well, me and Jason have a surprise for you."

Ian is hesitant. He wants to break free and do the responsible thing, which is to go to class, but Alex's grip is pretty tight around his shoulders and he's honestly worried about what would happen if he tried to run away. "But won't I get into trouble for skipping class?"

"Ian, we are not going to get you into trouble. Come on it'll be fun I promise." The trio walks toward a side entrance to the gymnasium. Ian's expression resembles a cartoonish gulp.

They make their way inside of the vacant gymnasium. Only the squeaks from their sneakers can be heard echoing throughout the vacant building. Even though this gymnasium has been unoccupied for at least a good twelve hours, the smell of sweat and plastic and a thick humidity still linger in the air. Walking past the left side of the bleachers, Alex turns the corner to an entrance labeled *OFFICE*. He looks down the proceeding corridor to see a vacant office with the lights out. He motions for the other two to follow him quickly to pass the office toward the locker room and showers at the long end of the L-shaped corridor. They pass the showers to the open storage area. Ian notices the shift in smell to mildew and a hint of body soap. He looks around the storage space and sees they are just in front of a storage cage filled with sports and activity equipment, including a basketball goal, cornhole boards, several stacked blue mats, and some folded chairs. Mold leaks from two high up windows, the streaks stopping midway down the wall.

"What is this place?" Ian asks, while looking around in confusion. Jason pulls a joint out from his shirt pocket.

"This is *the spot*. Jason and I come here to smoke." Ian looks at Jason, who sparks up a joint. His eyes bulge.

"Oh, uh, guys I'm sorry but I don't smoke." Jason and Alex look at each other and start laughing. Ian is not in on the joke. Alex places his hand on Ian's shoulder and looks at him intently as Jason hands him the joint.

"Ian, have you even tried weed before?"

"No, but I hear it's a gateway drug."

Again, Alex and Jason start laughing. Ian has caught on to the joke at this point. He knows they are laughing at his exceptional lameness. Alex takes a slow hit and blows the smoke in the air. He steps closer to Ian and holds the joint up to Ian's mouth. Ian nervously looks down at the burning joint then to Alex, then to Jason, then back to Alex. He seductively whispers to Ian, "Just do it."

Ian sighs. He could think of a million other things he would rather do. Ultimately, he gives in. He leans his head forward putting his lips around the joint then taking a small drag. Immediately he begins coughing while smoke projects from his mouth and nose. His eyes begin to water from the coughing. Alex and Jason are in stitches. They pass the joint back and forth to one another.

"See Ian, you're still alive, you're not in trouble, and you haven't got hooked on heroin yet . . . Dare I say it, DARE is full of shit, right?"

Ian smirks. "I guess," he says with a now euphoric expression on his face. Jason passes the joint to Ian, who now handles the joint himself to prove he can take a hit on his own. He takes a longer drag. This time, Alex tells him to hold it in as long as he can. Ian tries but he doesn't last long. At this point, Ian is for sure feeling the effects now. His body starts to feel weightless. His reaction time has drastically slowed. His mind is clouded with haze and a false reality. *This seriously is not happening right now.* Ian is now in his own world. Giggling at the shenanigans he's now a part of. Alex and Jason join in on the laughter.

They jokingly tease Ian about how high he is and telling him that his weed cherry has just been popped. Ian now realizes that weed is not that bad. In fact, he kind of likes it. The three continue toking until they hear a door close. They immediately stop moving. Footsteps can be heard from a distance.

"Oh shit!" Alex whispers. Jason puts out the joint as the three retrace their steps from the storage area. Ian is feeling paranoid. He knows what he did was wrong and is instantly regretting this idiotic venture of stoner activity. He wants to escape unnoticed but his confidence in not getting caught isn't too high. Definitely not higher than he currently is. *Maybe I deserve to get caught.*

They sneak back to the L-shaped corridor and see Coach Matthews walking back to the gymnasium from his office. Alex and Jason then rush past his office and run out of the exit from the short end of the hallway. Coach Matthews hears the door close behind them and immediately turns around and heads back to the hall. Ian knows he's going to get caught. Alex and Jason had left him to manage his own escape. Stoned and confused, Ian looks around then heads back toward the locker room. He finds a small space between two large lockers and hides. Just feet away, Coach Matthews walks into the locker room and takes a moment to look around. He then heads to the shower area. Ian peeks to see the coach walking opposite his escape. He sneaks by and runs down the corridor and exits out of the hallway. He feels pavement under his feet and the sun on his face. He sighs in relief but comes to realize he is way too high for this. *Fuck!* Walking about the perimeter he sees the courtyard to the school and knows immediately where he is. Now he just has to get to class and provide a good enough excuse as to why he is late.

He gets to his prospective building, still thinking of excuses to use. He hopes he would have bumped into Alex or Jason along the way, but to no avail. The hallway is empty and dead quiet. The sound of Ian's footsteps ricochet through the vacant hall. As he turns the corner, he sees Principal Owens casually strolling down the hall.

"Oh shit." Ian turns around and tries finding a way to disappear. He sees a water fountain. As he makes his way toward the fountain, he hears his name called.

"Ian Moss!" Principal Owens shouts. *This isn't good.* Ian's late to class and higher than a giraffe's pussy at the moment. He knew he was going to get caught sooner or later, and here it's happening. Ian turns around as he's approached by the principal.

"Good morning, Ian. How are you?" Principal Owens asks in a very upbeat manner. Ian is unsure if he even remembers how to talk. His body is basically levitating off the ground and everything seems like a bizarre dream. He looks over and sees he is near the nurse's office. His only thought is to point to the nurse's door. "Oh okay. Well let me escort you to class. I'll be your hall pass so you don't get any crap from your teacher. Where you headed?" Ian doesn't speak. He's afraid if he says anything the principal will know he's stoned. He instead pulls his schedule from his pocket and hands it to Principal Owens. "Oh human biology, that's right down this way. Come on."

They both walk to class, but for Ian, it's more so floating alongside the principal as he goes on and on about the school year, upcoming school events, and how unappreciative his wife was to receive a treadmill for her birthday. *This is taking forever.* Principal Owens' ranting starts jumbling. His words are now sounds reverberating off of each other. It's hard for Ian to follow. He justifies by periodically making eye contact and smiling at the principal, not knowing anything that's being said. They finally reach the classroom as Principal Owens escorts Ian inside. Ian walks straight to his desk and takes a seat. Samantha makes note of Ian's slightly odd behavior. His clandestine mannerisms make it seem like he's keeping a secret.

"Don't mind Ian. I'm just escorting him from the nurse's office," Principal Owens explains to Mr. Sadler, who nods his head. As he continues teaching his class, Principal Owens again interrupts. "Just know kids, that if you apply yourself, you can do anything you want in this world. Some of you have the potential to become the president of the United States. Some of you will probably go on to a more humbling job like a mechanic—"

A student then shouts out, "Or a school principal."

The class bursts into laughter. The offhand comment stung Principal Owens' feelings a bit, but he's not going to show it. He scans the classroom trying to figure out who made the outburst. No luck. "Ri—right! And that is the best . . . the best. You kids have an exceptional day," Principal Owens says before exiting the classroom. By this point, Ian and his desk are floating to the ceiling. With a child-like grin on his face, Ian swings his feet enjoying the view from up top.

Later that day in the lunchroom, typical high jinks ensue as kids unwind with their peers over the luxury of below average school food. Brandon walks over to a vending machine to his right. He sets his tray of food down and tosses in a couple of quarters. After pushing a couple buttons he grabs his dispensed soda and starts walking to his favorite lunch table. He is surprised to see Ian already sitting down eating. Brandon sits down at the table. Without saying a word, he watches Ian with intrigue and confusion as he devours his tray of food. So much so, his tunnel vision hasn't even noticed that Brandon is sitting in front of him.

"Yo, where were you this morning?" Brandon asks. Ian stops his frantic eating for a moment to glance at Brandon.

"I don't know what it is about the food today but oh my gosh . . . it's incredible! I mean this casserole alone is fantastic!" Ian says with a mouth full of food. He continues to gorge.

"Yeah, I think it's only one-week-old casserole instead of the usual two," Brandon criticizes, as he picks over his semi-burnt school version of shepherd's pie. Ian laughs hysterically at the joke.

"I don't know if enough people know this about you, but you are *hilarious.*"

"Thanks. So where were you this morning? I didn't see you on the bus."

"I got a ride," Ian says, not breaking rhythm of his aggressive eating.

"From your mom? You could've picked me up, then." Brandon cracks open his soda and takes a swig. Alex and Jason walk up to the table and greet Ian with a pat on his back.

"My main man, Ian! Are you feeling okay? Just wanted to come over and check on you," Alex says, with a sly grin. He and Jason share a laugh. Brandon can't believe what he is witnessing. He slowly sets his soda on the table and continues to watch this interaction. Jason glances at Ian's face.

"I think someone's got the munchies," he says, as he and Alex laugh.

Ian let's out a half-assed chuckle. "I'm doing well, guys. Thanks for asking," he says. Alex turns his head slightly and sees Brandon sitting across the table. He is taken aback. Brandon looks at Alex and braces himself for whatever is coming next. Alex laughs then places his hand on Ian's shoulder.

"Ian my man, you really gotta start keeping better company," he says, continuing his laughter as he pats Ian's shoulder. He walks off, but not before shouting out a "Catch you later, buddy." Jason follows.

Ian looks at Brandon like a timid puppy. Brandon's eyes are nearly as big as saucers. They read of shock and deceit.

"Are you serious? You know I don't like that dude, so why the hell are you hanging out with him?"

"Relax, he gave me a ride this morning to school. They pass me every day and he—Sam, offered a ride."

"So you hang out with dickhead for one day and you're already smoking weed? Man, are you crazy?"

How the hell does he know that? "How do you know that?" Ian asks.

"Ian, I'm no idiot. Your eyes look like tomatoes, and you are literally the first person in Lakehurst history to describe anything that came out of that kitchen as 'incredible.' Just be cautious, man. That's all I ask."

"Oh, you don't have to tell me. I almost got caught twice skipping class. And the person who caught me was the principal, of all people."

"Wow, skipping class, smoking weed, hanging out with Beavis and Butthead over there, what's next? Gangbanging?"

"Gross dude. I'm straight," Ian says.

CHAPTER 10

Moments later, Alex and Jason make their exit from the cafeteria. Jason senses the school bell is going to ring as soon as the cafeteria clears, and the skeletal halls of the school begin to crowd with students. He looks up at a hanging clock. 12:26 p.m. He looks worried and slightly confused.

"Yo. You okay, man?" Alex asks, not in a concerning way, but in a more sarcastic fashion that gives way to having some much-needed ammo for his artillery of Jason-insult jokes. Jason snaps out of his daydreaming episode and looks at Alex with worry.

"No, I'm not okay," Jason says.

Alex now feels guilty about downplaying Jason's emotional state and genuinely wants to know what is bothering his friend.

Jason continues. "I'm just trying to figure out how I can get Ashley to have butt sex with me again."

Alex is now regretful that he even asked. "What? That's what's been bothering you? Jesus, dude. Just do what you did last time."

"I can't. Last time we did it, I just shoved it in. There was no discussion or foreplay involved. Just some lube I snuck out of my pocket and then—" Jason shoves his right index finger into the closed hole of his left fist.

Alex is repulsed. "That's fucking disgusting."

"Hey, don't knock it until you try it."

"I'm knocking it. You know shit comes from there, right?"

"Now you're just judging. Look, forget I said anything." Jason is about to walk away from the conversation until Alex grabs him by the shoulder.

"Look dude, just do something nice. Be romantic and shit, and I'm sure she'll come around . . . or turn around or bend over or however you two sickos do what you do."

Jason ponders this proposal. The thought of being romantic hasn't crossed his mind. He's more of a go-straight-for-the-kill kind of guy. "That's actually good advice."

The school bell rings. Alex looks down at his watch. "Listen I gotta get to class. See you after school." Alex and Jason fist pump and Alex walks off as Jason takes a deep breath and heads in the opposite direction.

Later that day, Jason exits from Alex's car. He throws Alex the peace sign as Alex honks his horn and drives off. Jason makes his way up the driveway of his upper middle-class residence. The lawn is perfect, the driveway is spotless. Not an oil stain, cement crack, or random pebble is visible. He opens the brick-layered mailbox and takes out a couple of envelopes. He walks onto the porch of his three-story home and puts the key inside the lock of the mahogany door with a mid-frame glass design. He opens the door and is greeted with the beeping sound of the alarm. Jason walks over and enters the code, stopping the beeps, then places the mail on the kitchen island. As he makes his way to the stairs, the phone rings. He looks at the caller ID and recognizes the number immediately.

"Hello? What's up Stu . . . sure, I can come by. Give me like fifteen minutes. And I only have twenty bucks. Okay . . . see you soon." Jason hangs up and heads upstairs to his room. He throws his bookbag on his lavish queen-sized bed. The comforter is a pretentious royal-blue color accented with equally pretentious royal-blue sheets. Jason's room is a mess, but given the size, it's hard to tell what is in place and what is carelessly thrown about. Posters of musical artists like Cypress Hill and Soundgarden, clutter his walls. A double panel window sits just after a nook where Jason has a massive pile of unfolded clothes. A computer sits on a cluttered desk that is littered with papers, crumpled tissues, sketches, and a lava lamp. A state-of-the-art boombox sits on a dresser that Jason is rummaging through. He opens the top right drawer and digs through socks until he grabs hold of a wad of cash. A thick roll of cash at that, tied together with a rubber band that's about to give way. Jason unrolls the cash and pulls out a twenty-dollar bill. He rolls the cash back up and stuffs it in the back of his drawer.

He hears the garage door opening. Jason looks out the window and sees his mom pulling up in the driveway. He doesn't want to talk to her—or even hear her voice—at this moment. Jason rushes downstairs and grabs a set of car keys hanging on a key ring in the kitchen. He opens the side door and sees his mother pulling into the garage. Jason unlocks the '95 off-white BMW parked on the other side of the garage and hops inside. His mom, Elizabeth, hops out of her vehicle, trying to get Jason's attention by telling him to roll down the window. She's a sweet, woman with bushy red hair and way too much makeup on her face. Jason sees her but turns the music up to almost full blast. He rolls the window down and motions that he cannot hear what his mom is saying. She yells for him to turn down the music. Jason turns it up more.

"WHERE ARE YOU GOING?" Elizabeth screams.

"I'M GOING TO ASH'S TO STUDY! I'LL BE HOME FOR DINNER!" Jason yells back. He then speeds out of the garage and into the neighboring streets. Elizabeth watches in concern. She knows that's not all Jason is going to do. She hates to view Jason as the black sheep of the family, but that is the role he chooses to play. Suddenly, she feels something crawling onto her toes. She looks down to see a spider tickling her petite red-painted toenails. She screams and kicks the spider off, stomping it until she is comfortable it's dead. She shivers at the thought of the creepy arachnid and smoothes her hair back a couple of times before closing the garage and entering the house.

Jason pulls up on the side of the road next to a rusty and discolored trailer home. The lawn is patchy and unkempt. Several useless items are scattered throughout the yard, including a bicycle with a missing wheel, four stacked cinderblocks, various toys that look to belong to a pet or small animal, and four bags of trash that are piled just beside the front porch. Jason walks up the steps and knocks on the door. He hears a voice yell, "WHO IS IT?"

"It's Jason. Open up." Several seconds pass before the front door swings open. A tall, skinny dude answers the door. His appearance is also unkempt and he looks perpetually strung out, with terrible skin, matted White-boy dreadlocks, stubbly facial hair, a dingy white T-shirt, and a pair of wrinkled blue jeans that looks like they've been worn for almost a week straight at this point. They greet each other with a handshake as Jason makes his way inside. He immediately takes note of the trailer's soaking wet carpet. He feels the soggy indentions, hearing the squishes with every step. "Why is your carpet wet?" Jason asks. Stu turns around, a bit confused at first. He's licking the inside flap of a joint paper.

"Huh? Oh, we had a pipe burst or a flooded sink or some shit in the kitchen." Stu plops down on the couch. Jason sits in the adjacent single recliner looking at Stu's pit bull lying in her crate.

"Hey Lady," Jason says, while enticing the dog to come to him with a slight clap and sounds of smooches. Lady the pit bull is either depressed or too lazy to get up and greet any guests. She is more than comfortable lying in her crate only occasionally checking into the conversation between the two with a watch dog's eye.

"Yeah, she's been really fucking lazy lately. I think she's pregnant," Stu says.

"Really?" Jason glances once more at Lady. "I think she might be depressed."

Stu laughs. "Depressed? That's the stupidest shit I ever heard. Dogs don't get depressed man. She's just high or lazy or um . . . pregnant." Stu continues to roll up the joint. "You're graduating this year, right?"

"I am . . . I mean I think I am. Class of two thousand." Jason thinks about his less-than-stellar academic record. He gets worried thinking about school and his grades.

"Well, whatever you do, man, don't go to college. That shit is a scam, dude. Paying for education that's going to put you in debt only to be a slave to a job you're eventually going to hate but have to stick with so you can pay off all the debt you collected in college? Yeah, fuck that."

"I see," Jason says, not knowing if this information is beneficial to him or not.

"Yeah dude. Why do you think I never went to college? It's a fucking joke."

"So what did you do after graduation?" Jason asks, as Stu grabs a lighter off a cluttered coffee table and lights up his joint.

"I started selling weed, dude!" He says, followed by laughter. Jason also laughs, but in a more subdued manner. "Seriously man, I make my own hours, I get paid every day, and I get to smoke every day. I'm living the motherfuckin' dream!" Stu passes the joint to Jason.

"That does sound like a pretty sweet life," Jason says, as he takes a couple of drags and hands the joint back to Stu.

"So what do you plan on doing?" Stu takes a big drag and starts coughing a bit.

Jason looks to be deep in thought. Or it could just be the weed kicking in, but he responds with a somber, "I don't know."

"Just don't end up like your sell-out of an older brother. You know we made plans to go to Cali after graduation." Jason was fully aware of this plan. Mark has mentioned it to him plenty of times. "Guess he decided to shove a stick up his ass, buy every J. Crew sweater he could find, and ditch us for the East Coast."

Stu has no idea, but Jason knows all too well that his father is the reason for Mark's sudden change of heart. He can remember the constant arguments the two would have over Mark's future, until their father finally guilt tripped him into doing what he wanted him to do. Even to this day, Mark still has regrets about not standing up for himself and planning out his own future. Since then, Jason has vowed to himself to be in control of his own life and not appease his father's demands, whatever they may be.

On the drive back home, Jason is pondering his conversation with Stu. He doesn't want to admit it, but graduation and his future is now starting to burden him a bit more because he has no clue what he wants to do, and the clock to graduation is ticking. Jason pulls up and parks his car on the side of the road in front of his house. A gloomy yet grungy rock song is playing over the radio. He looks at the clock on the car radio. 7:38 p.m. *Just in time for dinner.* He pulls a joint from his jacket pocket and sparks it up. The dusk sky ignites a pinkish-orange tint as the sun slowly sets. The music is starting to intensify Jason's emotions with every drag. His worrying and paranoia about his uncertain future is starting to take a toll on his high. He begins to imagine a life with no worries and no responsibilities.

He envisions coming home from a beach somewhere far from Indiana. Maybe California. Tan lines on his arms and legs as he walks from the roaring shore holding a beer. He chugs the remaining beverage and tosses the bottle out into the sand. He walks into a beautifully crafted beach house to find Ashley in the kitchen cooking dinner—his favorite, steak and lobster. Ashley gently stirs the hollandaise sauce heating over the stove. He grabs another beer from the fridge and pops it open. He tosses the bottle cap into the trash. A perfect shot. Jason walks over to Ashley and plants a kiss on her cheek. He sits down at the island of the kitchen and starts rolling up a joint. They both begin discussing their day and how wonderful life is. Jason lights the joint and takes a couple of drags before passing it to Ashley. He admires her taking a toke as he thinks, *this is the perfect life.* A loud thud is heard coming from upstairs. Jason ignores it. Ashley passes the joint back. Jason takes a few more tokes but is startled at the sound of two loud thuds.

"What the hell is that noise?" he asks.

"Those rugrats upstairs," Ashley says, as she begins prepping the salad.

"Rugrats? We have kids?" The loud thuds continue to increase in volume. More rapid by the second. The sounds are getting closer. Suddenly, three kids pop into the kitchen, as they all yell simultaneously, "DADDY!" A boy and two girls. Startled, Jason coughs up the weed smoke and fans it through the kitchen. He puts out the joint in an ashtray sitting on the kitchen counter. "Hey kids!" They all rush over and give Jason a group hug. "We have kids!" he says to Ashley.

"Duh. Remember, this is your dream not mine," Ashley replies.

"I guess you're right." Jason picks up his youngest daughter, a bright, blue-eyed blonde sporting pink all over. Jason plants a comforting kiss on her rosy cheek.

As he snaps out of his fantasy, he remembers the advice Alex gave him to just be romantic and shit. *Ash's birthday is coming up . . . perfect!* Jason fantasizes about the possible gift options. He imagines himself knocking on her door dressed in a black and white tuxedo. She opens the door in a cream-colored and beaded dress with enough cleavage to shove your face in. The scenario plays like a film noir of sorts. Thunder and lightning disrupt the otherwise peaceful suburb. The rain begins to pour. Everything is black and white. Ashley is seductively leaning up against the open door.

"To what do I owe the *pleasure* of such late company?" she says. Jason doesn't say a word. He pulls a bouquet of black roses from behind his back. Ashley is mesmerized.

"Happy birthday, doll face," he says with a wink. Ashley eagerly accepts the roses. She walks over to a polished wooden credenza against the wall in the foyer. A perfectly placed crystal vase filled with water sits on top.

"Oh these roses are beautiful Jason, just beautiful." She places them in the vase. Jason steps inside, closing the door behind him.

"Stick with me, baby, and there's more where that came from." The excitement in Ashley's expression is unmistakable.

"Really?"

"Absolutely. Doll face, I'll give you the moon if you want it."
Ashley rushes over and gives Jason a tight hug.

"Oh, I love you, Jason," she says, as Jason grabs her body and tilts
her back to plant a wet kiss on her lips. "Oh Jason, I want you to fuck
me. Fuck me right in the ass."

"You got it, toots." They continue passionately kissing for a brief
moment. They soon begin ripping each other's clothes off as they rush
upstairs to the bedroom.

Jason nods his head, smiling at the thought of his erotic fantasy.
He looks down at the clock on the car radio once more. 7:52 p.m. He
flicks his joint out the window and cranks up his car then pulls it into
the driveway of his home.

Walking inside the house, he sees his mom and dad sitting at the
kitchen table eating dinner. The home is dimly lit aside from the dining
area. The television in the living room is tuned to the news as the
coverage explains how department stores are now going to be taking
extra precaution this year on Black Friday amid the growing crisis
and fear of violent shootings happening around the country. Jason's
father, John, does not take his eyes off his plate. His bulky arms are
highlighted by a white polo muscle shirt. His grayish buzzcut gives the
impression that he must have served in the military, but it's quite the
opposite. His newfound disciplinary attitude is only attributed to his
father whose untimely passing a few years ago really hit him hard. His
father was a successful owner of a car dealership and since taking over
the business, John owes it to his own father to do everything in his
power to make sure his family is on the right track to success.

Elizabeth hears Jason going up the stairs. She calls out, "Dinner's
ready!"

"I'm gonna take a shower first!" Jason yells. His parents continue
their meal, attentive to the news broadcast.

Getting out of the shower, Jason dries himself off. He wipes the
fogginess off the mirror and takes a good look at himself. He is very

aware of the fact that he still looks completely stoned, but at least he doesn't smell like weed. He exits the bathroom, throws on some lounging clothes and heads back downstairs. He walks into the rustic and minimalist style dining room, as his parents are seated at opposite ends of the table, still eating dinner. Like usual, Jason's empty plate sits in the middle between them as the spread of food litters the remaining space on the table. Dinner rolls, green beans, a mixed salad, and a pork roast feels like a king's meal to Jason. He is way beyond the point of munchies. Now, it's more like starvation. He sits down and starts piling his plate. Elizabeth looks as if she wants to say something but is too timid to speak. She continues to eat instead. John takes his time eating his meal. His way of eating comes off a bit aggressive. He stabs his food with his fork. He quickly pulls the fork from his mouth as it grates against his teeth. His chewing is slow. He looks as if something's bothering him.

"So when does your Christmas break start?" John asks. Jason looks over with a slightly paranoid reaction time. He spoons another helping of salad onto his plate.

"The twenty-second. And we go back on the sixth," he says in a drab tone.

"Perfect. We're planning a trip to Boston to go see your brother for New Year's Eve."

"I'm not going," Jason replies. Everything stops. You could hear a pin drop in the dining room. Even the living room television seems momentarily muted. John sets his silverware down onto his plate and interlocks his hands with his elbows resting on the table. He wants a thorough explanation.

"What?" Elizabeth says, almost choking on her glass of water.

"You're not going? And why the hell not?" John demands.

"I promised Ashley I was gonna spend time with her and her family for New Year's." John and Elizabeth look at one another.

"Oh honey. It almost seems as though you like *her* family more than your own," Elizabeth says, in a tongue and cheek fashion.

"I do. Besides I don't want to be around you guys kissing Mark's ass the entire trip." John snaps. He slams his fist on the table. The bang startles both Elizabeth and Jason.

"Hey! Watch your fucking mouth, okay? And maybe, just maybe, we would kiss your ass a little more if you had a sense of what the fuck you're going to do with your life after high school!"

Elizabeth tries her best to calm John down. She thinks he might say something regrettable if he continues his rant. She's unsuccessful. "You can sit here and be jealous of your brother and get so fucking high that your lungs fall off. But let me tell you something—once you turn eighteen, your ass is out that door. Period!"

"John!" Elizabeth shouts.

"Beth, save it. It's no secret all Jason wants to do is get high and fuck around. I'm sure he's high right now! And at this point, I'm tired of reiterating the same shit! Whether you graduate next year or repeat the same grade or go to college or decide to work at fucking McDonald's, your ass is out of this house as soon as you turn eighteen. I can fucking promise you that! Your mother and I have worked our asses off to be able to provide a good life for you and your brother, and if you can't even appreciate that or have some sense of a fucking clue about your future, you can leave!" John stands up from the table and grabs his beer. "I'll be in the living room watching the game."

Elizabeth stands up from the table. "You know, your father is right. We only want what's best for you and your future, sweetie." She grabs her husband's plate and stacks it on top of hers, then heads to the kitchen. Without so much as missing a beat, Jason continues eating his food in silence with a blank I-don't-give-a-fuck expression on his face.

Weeks later, it's just another day in the halls of Lakehurst High. Ashley is setting some books and miscellaneous items in her locker.

Something is on her mind. With a sigh, she gazes into the mirror hanging in her locker to apply some eye shadow. The halls are chatty, but abnormally low in volume and excitement. Maybe there is something bothering everyone else as well. Some hive-mind depression sweeping the halls of Lakehurst. Ashley closes her locker and is startled by Jason's presence. He's standing there leaning against the other lockers with a devilish grin on his face. She screams.

Jason puts his hand on Ashley's shoulder to comfort her. "Oh my God, baby! I'm so sorry I scared you. Are you okay?" Jason leans in and kisses Ashley's cheek. He notices something is bothering her, more so than just being startled. He again begins questioning. "Ash what's wrong?"

"Well, besides starting my period today of all days, I'm stressing over this goddamn midterm, and I haven't even started studying for it yet. I wanna cry so bad but I know I'll mess up the makeup I just put on." Jason feels for her. As much shit as they give each other from time to time, neither one wants to see the other upset.

"Aww baby. I'm so sorry." He gives her another peck on the cheek. "Maybe this will cheer you up a little." Jason pulls a half-dozen roses from behind his back and presents them. "Happy birthday, baby." Ashley is in utter disbelief. She begins to cry.

"You don't like them?" he asks.

"No, I love them. These are tears of *joy* . . . and now I'm ruining my makeup." Ashley pats her eyes dry with her shirt sleeve. She grabs the roses, looks at Jason, and smiles. "Thank you, baby. I love them." They give each other a few kisses on the lips. Ashley opens her locker and gently places the roses inside for the time being.

"That's not all I got you," Jason says, in a slick approach.

"You got me something else?"

"Yeah. I'm sure you're gonna love it."

Ashley's intrigued. "My parents are working late tonight, so why don't you come by around eight and bring it then," she says, closing her locker door.

"It's a date." The two admire each other in silence until the bell rings.

"Thank you. For the flowers, for putting me in a better mood—for being my ace." The two share another kiss.

"Anytime, babe. So I'll see you tonight, then?"

"You better," Ashley demands. Jason smiles, ending their conversation with a wink then heading down the hall.

Later that evening, Jason pulls up to Ashley's house. It's a decent-sized brick house with beige shutters to match the trim of the roof and the front door. The home is decked in Christmas lights. Ashley's folks are the type to throw up decorations as soon as November hits. The yard is kept up rather nicely but could use a mow. From outside, the only visible lights are in the foyer of the house and Ashley's bedroom. Her window is not seen from the front of the house, but off to the side, which reminds Jason that he should park his car a little farther down the road just in case her parents decide to come home a little earlier. He drives about twenty feet down the road almost to the neighbor's driveway. From his side mirror he can see Ashley's bedroom window. A faint meow catches Jason's attention. He looks over at part two of Ashley's birthday gift—an all-black kitten with amber eyes that pierces through one's soul. Jason picks up the kitten, leering with a smile. The kitten stares back, and again meows. Jason seems to have already gotten slightly attached. He's not really a pet kind of guy, but this kitten is just too damn cute.

"Ashley is going to love you, I promise." Jason gives the kitten a kiss on the cheek. He starts heading toward the house. Silent lightning flickers the sky. The air is brisk and slightly windy. Dead leaves skip the neighborhood streets. The night feels desolate, borderline creepy. Jason opens his navy-blue workman's jacket and places the kitten in a spacious pocket on the inside. He gets to the front porch and rings the doorbell. A cheesy chime blares throughout the house. *Ding-dong-ding-dong-dong-dong-ding-dong.*

Jason rolls his eyes at the over-the-top chime. "So stupid," he mutters to himself. A faint meow is heard from inside his jacket. "Hey, hey, shush. It's a surprise, okay."

Ashley opens the front door, looking absolutely stunning. She favors a sexy 1930s burlesque model. Her allure is classic and erotic with just a hint of danger. Jason is taken aback. *Oh I'm definitely getting laid tonight!* "Hey babe," he says, astonished. "You look incredible!"

"Thank you. Come in," Ashley says with a smile. She grabs hold of Jason's hand and pulls him inside a neat and clean entryway and into her slice of suburban Americana. Being the only child, you can say she is a bit spoiled, but the love is on full display with the house décor. Family photos line different portions of the walls, a Thanksgiving photo here, a soccer photo there. A section of diplomas on the wall highlights her parents' accomplishments.

Christmas decorations give the atmosphere a warm and welcoming feeling. Lights are strung about, garland weaves around the staircase railing, and a choo-choo train circles the ceiling trim from the foyer to the living room to the kitchen and all the way back to the foyer. The house feels like a true Christmas wonderland. Jason closes the door behind him then leans over and gives Ashley a kiss. She cannot stop smiling. Her excitement and happiness are a total one-eighty from how she was feeling earlier today. "So . . . what is it?" she says, eagerly.

"Whoa, slow down. Give me time to really show off my romantic side. I gotta get the people to like me somehow, you know?" Ashley rolls her eyes.

Jason smiles and grabs hold of both her hands. They lock stares. "Baby, you are the most important thing to me, and I feel so lucky to have you in my life . . . especially considering the family I've been dealt. And I just wanna show my appreciation and to thank you for putting up with all my shit. Happy birthday." Jason reaches into his jacket pocket and pulls out the tiny black kitten. Ashley's eyes light up brighter than the Christmas lights in her home. The kitten sounds off a tiny "meow," wiggles a bit, then looks directly at Ashley.

"Oh my God! It's so cute!" Ashley carefully grabs the kitten from Jason and cradles the feline like a baby.

"It's a *he*, and his name is Salem."

"Like on *Sabrina the Teenage Witch*! Oh that's perfect!" Ashley says, giving Salem kisses to the face. Jason is a bit confused as to who Sabrina is, but he goes along with it.

"Uh, yeah, absolutely. I know how you like animals and wanna be a vet and stuff, so I figured you should have your own pet to look out for."

"Jason, he's perfect. You're perfect. Thank you so much." Ashley gives Jason a peck on the lips. She then walks over to the kitchen, holding Salem as gently as a newborn. Jason follows. The outdated kitchen is spacious, complete with an island, off-white paint for the walls, wooden cabinetry that looks straight out of the seventies, and a matching off-white fridge and stove. A separate dining area sits further into the kitchen with a side door leading to the backyard. A dimly lit dining room light adds a warm and soft glow to the otherwise harsh fluorescent kitchen lighting. Ashley grabs a bowl from the cabinet and sets it on the island, along with Salem. She grabs a carton of milk from the fridge and pours a little for Salem. Jason, looking through the fridge, spots exactly what he wants sitting on the bottom shelf to the right. He grabs a beer and cracks open the tab.

"Your dad doesn't count his beers, right?" Ashley gives him a sly look. Ashley grabs Jason's hand and they make their way up the stairs while Salem enjoys his fresh bowl of milk.

The staircase wall features more family portraits ascending to the top. A corridor off from the main hall is where Ashley's parents' bedroom is located. Straight ahead and to the right is Ashley's bedroom and her bathroom is to the left. They get to Ashley's bedroom. Jason removes his jacket and throws it on the floor. The bedroom has various posters of musical artists on the walls. A rustic-style vanity table sits near the far end of the bedroom. A small television sits on top of a tall wooden dresser, which is positioned to his right, against the wall and facing her centered queen-sized bed that's accented with red silk drapery. Twinkling lights hang from the ceiling, adding a whimsical charm. Jason feels a slight draft. He sees her bedroom window is cracked open. Her silk curtains gently flow with the breeze. He takes a good swig of his beer and plops on Ashley's firm bed.

"Do you always like your room to be this cold?"

"I like to make sure it's aired out."

"Why?"

Ashley closes her bedroom door. She takes her panties off and flings them at Jason. They land on his crotch. "Because you're gonna fuck me, that's why." Ashley walks over to Jason and sits between his legs. "You've been so good to me and have made this a very special birthday. So I just want to show my appreciation and return the favor," she says, seductively. Ashley begins kissing Jason's neck. He is liking every part of this, but still has one question on his mind.

"But babe, you said you're on your period, right?"

"I am. But I have other holes," she says. *Jackpot!* Jason's ecstatic. His pants get tighter. He reaches into his pocket and pulls out a small tube.

"Good thing I keep this little bottle of lube on me. It's cherry flavored." They share a laugh then begin their second exploration at back-door fucking. After some much-needed foreplay and oral pleasures, Ashley turns around, bending over in front of Jason. Jason mounts her from behind. He squeezes some lube onto his hand and masturbates with it. Ashley hears the wet suction sounds and turns to look with curiosity.

Jason smiles. "Just revving up the engine."

"Well, be gentle this time, okay? You're not drilling for oil back there." The start is a bit awkward for Jason and a bit painful for Ashley. But soon, they find their rhythm. Even though it only lasted a little over five minutes, to their surprise it is a success. After the deed is done, they cuddle next to each other on the bed.

Jason cannot stop smiling. He takes a swig of his beer. "Oh my God. That was incredible," he says.

"Much better than last time."

Jason laughs, finishing the rest of his beer. He hops off the bed.

"I'm gonna grab another beer. You want anything from the kitchen?" Ashley ponders for a moment.

"No, I'm fine. Hurry back so we can do it again."

"Yes ma'am!" Jason rushes out of the bedroom and heads downstairs to the kitchen. He looks and sees Salem still drinking his bowl of milk from earlier. "Man, you're still drinking that? I'm on my second beer, dude." Jason opens the fridge and grabs another cold one. As he closes the door, he notices car headlights shining through the blinds of the living room. He gets to the window and peeks through one of the blinds and sees Ashley's parents have just pulled up in the driveway. "Oh shit." He rushes upstairs, sneakily in a jogging tip-toe motion, trying to avoid making noise. He gets to the bedroom and starts to panic.

"Your parents are here! They're right in the fucking driveway!"

Now Ashley starts to panic a little. But she has a plan. "Shit! Okay, out the window."

"What? You're on the second floor!"

"Out the window!" she says, pushing him. Jason hops out of her window onto the sloped side of the roof. "Just move over to the side a little." Jason moves out of sight from the window, nervous about the steepness of the roof. He also realizes he may be up here a while, and the temperature outside is not getting any warmer. Ashley closes the window to a crack. She turns on the television and lays back in bed. She spots the condom wrapper on her bed glistening from the glare of the television. Quickly, she grabs it and throws it under her bed.

"Hey, sweetie," her dad, Derrick says. A clean-cut and heavy-set man, he pokes his head through Ashley's door frame.

"Dad! You scared me."

"I'm sorry. Just checking on the birthday girl," he says, stepping into her bedroom.

"I'm fine, Dad."

"Okay, okay. Just making sure." He sets a bouquet of an assortment of flowers on her nightstand, roses, lilies, and tulips. "These are for you." He takes a seat on Ashley's bed.

"Dad, they're beautiful."

Derrick places his hand on Ashley's. "I know we made other plans on your birthday, but tomorrow I'll make it up to you. Starting with your favorite—chocolate chip pancakes."

Ashley smiles. "Thanks, Dad."

"I'm so proud of you. Happy birthday." Derrick leans in and kisses Ashley on her forehead. He sniffs a few times, catching wind of an odor. "What's that smell?" he says, puzzled.

"What smell?" Ashley asks. He sniffs a couple more times. It smells like sex and candy.

"It smells like—" Before Derrick can answer, he is interrupted by a shrieking scream coming from downstairs.

"Pam!"

"Mom!"

They both rush out of the bedroom to investigate the sudden disruption. Pam is standing just outside of the kitchen staring. She's trying to catch her breath. She fans herself and flips back her let-me-speak-to-the-manager haircut.

"Honey, are you okay?" Derrick says, consoling his wife.

"I'm fine. Just wondering why there is a cat sitting on my kitchen counter," she says in a condescending way. Ashley rushes over and picks up Salem.

"His name is Salem. Jason gave him to me as a birthday gift." Cradling him, Ashley tickles his stomach and kisses him.

"And where is Salem supposed to stay when your away for college?" Pam asks.

"Well, he's going to stay here, so I can see him when I visit, and you guys will have something to remember me by when I'm gone."

Pam does not look happy.

"Mom, he's a gift!"

"I think having a pet around the house could be a good thing,"

Derrick says. He walks over and brushes Salem's furry face with his finger. He purrs. "He's definitely cute."

"Thank you, *Dad*," Ashley says.

Pam sighs. She knows Ashley always gets her way when it comes to her dad.

"Fine, whatever. Just keep that thing off my kitchen counters. It probably hasn't even had its shots yet," Pam says scornfully. "I'm going to bed." She walks off.

"I think he's adorable," Derrick adds. Ashley smiles. He gives her one last kiss on the forehead.

"Good night, sweetie."

"Good night." Ashley sets Salem back on the counter and pours him another bowl of milk. She takes the bowl and her new feline friend and heads up the stairs to her room. In a small corner of the bedroom, Ashley takes two folded blankets and stacks them beside each other and places the bowl of milk in front. She grabs Salem and places him on the blankets.

"This will be where you sleep for right now, okay? At least until we get you potty trained." Ashley then hears a light tapping outside her window. She gasps, turning around to see Jason waving from outside. She opens the window halfway.

"Oh my God! What are you still doing here?"

"You never told me to leave."

"Well I'm telling you now. Go home," she says, checking behind her to make sure her parents don't sneak up.

"Fine." Jason watches his balance, timidly eases his way down to the edge, and squats down. He rolls on his belly and scoots down, grabbing the gutter and dangling for a second before dropping down to the lawn below. "Ooof."

"Thank you for the cat," she says, smiling.

"Uh-huh."

Ashley closes her window shut.

The next morning, Ashley wakes up to the wonderful smell of pancakes. It's the day after her birthday and she feels a new sense of empowerment and maturity on her end, and not just the rear one. At this point, she is confident in the fact that she has mastered the art of anal sex. Sure, Jason could use a few tips, but practice always makes perfect. She's just glad she doesn't have to borrow her dad's Preparation H this time around to soothe the damage.

She looks over and sees Salem comfortably sleeping amongst the bundle of blankets. Ashley leans over and takes a whiff of the bouquet of flowers on her nightstand. A feeling of gratitude sparks her mood for the day. She heads downstairs and hears her parents having light conversation about her. Walking into the sunlit kitchen, Pam sits at the island with her coffee looking through Ashley's old elementary school yearbook. Derrick stands at the stove, flipping pancakes. He's sporting an apron that reads, *Kiss the Cook*. They both notice Ashley walk in.

"Good morning, sweetie," he says, pointing to the stack of chocolate chip pancakes with his trusty spatula in hand.

Ashley smiles. "Morning, Dad."

"You want some coffee?" Pam asks.

"Yes please . . . ow!" Ashley says, wincing as she sits down.

Pam reaches over to grab Ashley a mug.

"Honey, are you okay?" she grabs the pot and pours some coffee into the mug, handing it over to Ashley.

"Thanks. Yeah. I uh, think I slept on my back wrong." She grabs the mug and takes a sip. She loves her coffee black.

"That's what happens when you get older. Things just start hurting for no reason," Derrick says, flipping a pancake midair.

"Nonsense, there's always a reason. You just need to try a different position that's all," Pam says.

Ashley knows she can take that statement in more ways than one.

She takes another sip of her coffee. She curiously walks over and stands next to her mother as the two look at Ashley's yearbook.

"Why are you looking through my yearbook?"

"Oh, just reminiscing on how cute you were. Brings me back," Pam says.

Ashley rolls her eyes.

"Oh! Look how cute you were darling." Pam points out a preschool picture of Ashley. Wearing a purple and white floral dress and sporting a single braided ponytail, Ashley smiles in the picture with two missing incisors.

"*Were?*" Ashley says, slightly offended.

"Oh, I just mean you used to dress so cute and normal . . . and less . . . you know."

Ashley again rolls her eyes.

"Oh, there's Jason." Skinny and pale, Jason grins in the photo. His parted mushroom bowl cut partially covers his eyes, a visual foreshadowing of his present personality. Ashley smiles at the old memories. Life was much simpler back in those days. "I remember he always smelled like grape jelly," she says with a chuckle.

"All you kids were adorable," Pam says.

Ashley scans the yearbook of young faces, most of whom are in school with her now. A few moved away at some point. But one face stands out in particular. She notices a cheesy smile from a mildly freckled kid with strawberry-blond hair. She points him out.

"This kid looks familiar." She traces the photo to the name. Ian Moss.

Pam gets a closer look at the photo. "Derrick, isn't that the kid who attacked the teacher in their class that day?"

"What?" Ashley says, completely shocked. Derrick steps from the stove and gets a closer look.

"Ian Moss. Yeah, I remember. Apparently he had some sort of a mental breakdown or something and tried to attack your teacher with a pair of scissors."

"Oh my God! Are you serious?

"Yeah. I think his mom pulled him out of school after that happened. Wonder whatever happened to that kid. I'm surprised you don't remember that."

"Honey, she was really young, of course she doesn't remember." Ashley's stunned at this newly discovered information. *That has to be him. That has to be the same Ian!* She closes the yearbook and takes hold of it.

"Can I borrow this?" she asks.

"Now who's feeling nostalgic?" Pam says, with a snicker.

Ashley forces a laugh.

The following week at school, Ashley and Jason are seated at their usual lunch table. They have a back-and-forth flirtatious banter going on between them that includes spontaneous bouts of making out. They seem to want to go for round three.

Alex interrupts by taking a seat across from them. "What's up, losers?" he says.

"Not much. Where's Sam?" Ashley asks.

"I think she's in the library doing work for some thesis shit." Alex looks up and notices Ian and Emma walking in the cafeteria together giggling. "You guys see this? Who the fuck is this kid?" Alex says, obviously bothered and jealous. *She's just gonna flirt with other guys in front of me like I'm not supposed to be bothered by it? Typical slut behavior.*

"She's a slut anyway, dude. I wouldn't be surprised if she gives him blue waffle," Jason says, laughing out loud.

"And just like that, I lost my appetite," Ashley says. She glances over and sees Ian standing with Emma in line. With newly discovered information about Ian's past, she can't hold onto this secret much longer. She needs to spill the beans. "Oh my gosh, you guys. I was looking through our elementary school yearbook and found this kid who—"

"Hey guys!" Ian says, walking up to their table.

"What's up, my man. I see you're getting to know Emma a little *better*, huh?" Alex says as he nudges Ian with his elbow.

Ian smiles coyly. "No, we're just friends. We have keyboard class together."

Alex nods his head. He doesn't believe Ian. "How cute. You hear that guys? Keyboard class," Alex says sarcastically as he takes a couple of greasy fries off Jason's tray to eat. "So what's up?" he says, his mouth full.

"Well, I was hoping you guys could hook me up with a little bit of weed," Ian says, sounding a bit embarrassed. It's not like they have any room to judge but this is new territory for Ian. Not only asking for weed but craving a fix. He seems desperate and needy and ashamed of even asking. But it's too late now. It's already out there. Ashley is surprised he smokes. But she knows she can't trust him. She knows who he really is.

Alex and Jason start laughing.

"Man, you smoke weed one time and you're already a pothead. You move fast Ian," Alex says.

They continue joking with Ian by throwing minor digs at him.

"Alright enough. So can you guys help me out or . . ." Alex and Jason look at each other. They like Ian, for the most part. They share a nod.

"Absolutely. In fact, me and Jason were just about to head to the spot in a few," Alex says.

"That's perfect. I'll just go with you guys."

"Hey, are you coming to my party, Ian?" Jason says, right before taking a sip of his Capri-sun.

"Party?"

"Yeah, a New Year's Eve party at my place. You gotta be there, man. It's gonna be fucking dope."

"*Dope*? That's good, right?" Ian asks. The group laughs. This time they're laughing with him.

"Yeah, you definitely gotta be there. Unless Mommy won't let you out too late," Alex says, still picking at Jason's tray of fries.

"I'll be there for sure," Ian exclaims.

Alex nods his head. "Good to know."

The clock seems to tick slower than it usually does, the mind-numbingly painful last moments of class before school's over. Time moves so slow. Like the very last moments of your life draining to a snail's pace before your final rest. Or that moment of realization before the LSD kicks in, gripping the neurons in the brain then shifting to a moment where all reality melts away. Alex's expression shows he would rather die than wait a second longer for the bell to ring. It finally does.

"Finally! *Fuck.*" Hopping from his desk, he darts to the door and heads down the hallway. He turns the corner and sees Samantha at her locker.

"Sam!" he shouts, rushing over. Samantha turns her head and smiles.

"Hey babe." They kiss.

"I'm about to go. You wanna come so we can head to the mall? Then we can get some time alone at my place."

"I would go, but I still need to work on my final. I'm so far behind. I'm just gonna stay here at the library for a while. I can come by your place later."

"But it's Thanksgiving break."

"I know, I know. Please don't hate me. I'll come by later, promise."

"Okay. Don't stay too late."

"I won't. I'll see you later?"

"Okay." He kisses Samantha then heads out the double doors, flooding in cold air and rays of sunlight from the outside. He cuts through the chaos and the noise of the student body as a crowd is gathered around a fight happening a few feet away. The circled crowd cheers on the schoolyard violence.

He beelines it to his Mustang and hops in. Cranking the ignition, the car won't start. Confused, he cranks the ignition several more times. A faint ticking sound can be heard from under the hood. "You gotta be fucking kidding me!" he screams, as he beats his steering wheel with his fists. He turns the ignition a few more times. Still, no action. "Fuck!"

He hops out and begins looking around the parking lot. What a coincidence. He spots Emma heading to her car just a few yards from where he is parked. He heads over, calling out her name. Emma gets to her faded yellow punch-buggy and opens the car door. She turns to the sound of her name. Seeing it's Alex, she rolls her eyes.

"What do you want?" she asks, sounding annoyed already.

"Shit I'm glad to see you. My car won't start. I think it's the battery. Do you have any jumper cables?"

"No. Sorry."

"Well, can you give me a ride? You know where I live. Please? It's Thanksgiving. Give thanks," he pleads.

"Thanksgiving's tomorrow," she says, with an attitude. She looks at her watch, then sighs. Against her better judgment, she gives in. "Fine. Get in."

They both hop inside and drive away. Alex takes in the atmosphere of the punch buggy. It reminds him of some shagged-out hippy ride from the Woodstock era. The front two seats are decorated with rabbit-fur seat covers. A lucky rabbit's foot and a new-car-smell cardboard air freshener the shape of a pine tree hangs from the rearview mirror. The music is faint but can still be heard over the awkward silence of the car ride, punctured only by the music and the road, aside from the creeks and rustic sounds of the vehicle. Gripping the gear, she shifts with ease. Emma has mastered the art of driving stick. Alex notices.

"I've never knew you drove a stick shift."

"I do. Most people don't know how."

"Yeah. I can see you and I don't belong in that category."

Emma turns to look at Alex. She ignores his comment and continues on her annoyingly dissatisfying good deed. She wants a reason to kick

Alex out of the car. He just has to say the right thing. Or the wrong thing, depending how you look at it.

"Are you seeing anyone?" he asks, in a tone that is cautious yet innocently curious.

Emma continues looking forward. "That's none of your business."

"Ok, I'm sorry. My bad. I just saw you and Ian at lunch and thought there might be something going on."

"You know Ian?" Emma says, somewhat surprised.

"Are you kidding me? Ian's my boy. Yeah, we go way the fuck back. How uh, do you two know each other?"

Emma starts shaking her head. She can sense the jealousy and inquisition on Alex's part. She ignores his question. "Ian's cool. And he can sure do a whole hell of a lot better than being friends with you," she says. Her words shoot like darts. Alex takes it as a joke and starts laughing.

"See, that's why I like you, Emma. That sassy, fuck-you-I'm-better-than-you attitude is a real . . . turn on."

Emma slams the breaks, almost sending Alex through the windshield.

"Jesus! Are you trying to kill me?" he shouts.

"We're here. Now get out."

"Okay. Um, you sure you don't want to come in?"

"Bye, Alex," she says, demandingly.

"Fine. I'll see you around?"

"Maybe."

Alex gives her an "Okay," then hops out the car.

Emma speeds off as soon as the passenger door closes.

Alex watches the car disappear.

"Bitch." He walks into his cozy low-income home. The place smells like a bar. He pets his gray and white boxer, Roxy, as she approaches with a wagging tail. He sees his dad sitting in the same recliner in front of the television he sits in all day, every day. Beer in hand, he looks like he hasn't even gotten up to use the bathroom. This is his place of comfort and my God does he love lounging in that recliner for the soul purpose of getting loaded. Jerry Springer is on the television in full display of its trashy and raunchy daytime chaos. Alex's dad, Chris, finally moves by lifting his arm up to finish the rest of his beer. He burps. Chris turns his head when he hears the front door shut.

"Oh, it's you," he says lamentably.

"Jesus, Dad really? It's not even five o'clock yet."

"I had the day off, okay. So quit your bitchin'. You sound like your damn mama."

"Whatever. My car broke down at school. I need a jump."

"Right now?"

"No, we can wait till next year. Yes! Right now! Fuck!" Alex shouts. A part of him almost feels sympathy for his dad as he watches him waddle his way out of the groove he's worn in the recliner. *I hope to God I don't end up like you one day.*

Chris stumbles for a moment as he gets to his feet. "Alright, let me grab my fucking car keys, smart ass." Chris walks off. Roxy sits beside Alex looking up at him, tail wagging. He looks down and pets her.

"Don't worry, I'll get us out of here sooner or later."

Alex puts his keys in the ignition and cranks the vehicle. It roars like it's fresh off the lot. He adjusts the rearview mirror a bit. Admiring himself, he combs his hair back a few times. Brushing off his black leather jacket, he cranks up the radio and drives out of the eerily vacant, low-income landscape. If he is going for the bad boy, motorcycle gang look, he is definitely nailing it. Like an edgier Fonz, with just enough toxicity to keep the ladies intrigued. His MO normally consists of using girls to get what he wants—sex or head. And once he's gotten it, they're usually dumped to the side like a bag of trash. Only the lucky ones get the opportunity to be recycled.

But that is not the case with Samantha. He sees something in her. The fact that he views his relationship with Samantha as a challenge may be the reason he's still around. Or it could be the fact that he hasn't fucked her yet. Spending Thanksgiving with Samantha and her family is nothing new for Alex, but he always feels pressure from her folks. Her dad in particular, who tends to look down on him for reasons Alex is not sure of but assumes it's because of his background and where he resides. They act cordial, nice, and, generous to his face, but Alex knows they disapprove of his relationship with Samantha. He assumes they scold her behind closed doors, questioning why she doesn't dump Alex and go out with someone more like-minded or someone who comes from money or someone who is not biracial. Regardless, he's bringing a bottle of pinot grigio he got from his dad as a peace offering to try and win over the hearts of her parents once again. Not that he cares that much, but it will make the evening easier for him and Samantha. Her little brother Jacob is also unimpressed by Alex. At thirteen years old, even he knows Samantha is too good for Alex.

Alex walks up the steep steps to the upper middle-class home until finally reaching the porch. A set of orange Adirondack chairs with a matching coffee table sit off to the right of the porch. By the door is an empty planter with a scarecrow stuck in the soil. A couple of decorative pumpkins are placed opposite of that. Alex rings the doorbell. He hears someone yell to "get the door." It could have been Samantha or her mother. Samantha opens the door. She is wearing a yellow swing dress with white polka dots, like something out of an old Hollywood movie. She's breathtaking.

"Happy Thanksgiving," Alex says, handing her the bottle of wine. She takes his hand instead.

"Thanks, babe. Come in." They share a quick smooch. Samantha's mother, Sherry, walks down the dimly lit foyer, which is decorated with an expensive looking runner and a showpiece crystal chandelier that has been hand-crafted in a country Alex cannot spell, let alone pronounce. He's just impressed it was delicately shipped to their impressive two-story home without so much as one broken piece. The entire fixture is expensive and took two weeks to make, but Sherry will exaggerate that it took two years to craft, thinking it will add a more valuable impression with guests because of the one-of-a-kind and custom aesthetic it holds. She is uptight and poised and greets Alex in a way that will have one to believe she hails from whatever random country their chandelier was made in. But she's from Indianapolis.

"Happy Thanksgiving, Alex," she says rather coldly.

"Happy Thanksgiving, Mrs. Harvey. My dad wanted me to bring you this bottle of wine." Alex hands over the pinot to Sherry. She looks at the bottle. Alex's dad clearly has cheap taste in wine.

"Oh how thoughtful. Where is your dad? He couldn't make it?"

"No. He'll be visiting my Uncle Earl later tonight, and probably tomorrow as well."

"Well, that sounds nice. Please come in and make yourself at home. I'll be in the kitchen if you need anything." Sherry walks off. Alex removes his leather jacket and places it on the coatrack behind him on the right.

"I never knew you had an Uncle Earl," Samantha says. Alex looks at her, shakes his head, and chuckles.

"Wow," he says, walking off.

"What?" Samantha asks, confused.

The family is gathered around the beautifully decorated sapele mahogany dinner table. The table is laid out with lit candles, a white tablecloth accented with an orange runner, a decorative cornucopia, miniature pumpkins, and of course the feast itself. A beautiful glazed turkey, ham, mashed potatoes, corn, green beans, cranberry sauce, macaroni and cheese, and bottles of wine all litter the already full table for five. Alex and Samantha sit across from one another. Her father, Howard, sits between them at the end of the table. He resembles Sean Connery when he first played James Bond, which makes sense because Howard is in great shape for his age. Sherry sits on the opposite end from her husband. Samantha's sneaky brother Jacob is to her right.

"Honey, we need to bless the food," she says, in a domineering manner. Howard takes a sip of his whiskey, which he drinks neat.

"Okay, everyone, bow your heads," Howard says. Alex is the last to do so. Howard does a short but sweet and meaningful grace for the holiday. They all say "Amen" and dig in the food.

The evening is going better than Alex expected. The conversation flows as the table goes on about topics ranging from television shows, favorite holidays, and current technology. Cringing at the torturous screeching of dial-up internet is a topic the entire room can relate to. Howard describes how his job allows the employees to remain connected to the internet, just so they do not have to endure that obnoxious connection sound. Alex tells a story about how he and his friends joke that dial-up internet sounds like R2-D2 having an orgasm. The joke is a hit. Even Jacob laughs. Sherry still seems a bit cold and unamused. She takes a sip of her pinot grigio instead of laughing.

"So what exactly are your plans after high school Alex?" Sherry asks. *Fuck!* Alex knew this conversation was going to be brought up eventually.

"I plan to work with my dad. Take over the family business someday."

"And what does your dad do, again?" Howard asks.

Samantha can sense the prying of her father's questioning. It's unnoticeable, but she is squirming in her seat. Jacob's eating his food, eyeing the conversation with a devilish grin.

"He's a mechanic. His shop is right off—"

"That's right! Off Park Lake on the southside! Now I remember. That sounds great. So, no college in your future, huh?"

"Maybe. Just not right now. I gotta help out family first."

"That's right. Family first," Howard says, sipping his whiskey. He continues. "I always make sure I put my family first in everything I do." Howard then comes to a moment of realization. "But wait. How is this going to work if you're staying here, and Sam will be off to State, three hours away?" Howard knows what he's doing. His tone is thick with sarcasm, but he knows he's making a valid point, which makes it all the more hilarious to him.

"It means they can't do it anymore," Jacob says, under his breath, but loud enough for them all to hear.

"Do what?" Sherry asks.

"We're not doing anything!" Samantha pleads, hoping they can quickly change the subject and go back to when they were laughing and joking about robot orgasms and weird off-beat shit.

"Hey, I'm rooting for you guys. But the reality is that a long-distance relationship is risky. You two will be living completely different lives. Samantha is going to be around like-minded people her age, and you'll be around . . . cars and old ass-cracks all day," Howard says, bursting into laughter. Jacob follows, while Samantha is appalled by her father's comment.

Sherry disapproves of his joke and quickly scolds him. "Howard, that's enough."

"See, I've got a few jokes of my own. Oh lighten up, Sherry, it's Thanksgiving. But seriously, you guys should think about that. Better to end it now than later." Howard finishes off his whiskey.

Alex laughs with the joke, but he feels deeply embarrassed and quite offended.

After dinner, Samantha walks outside to the front porch to find Alex smoking a cigarette. Cheers can be heard going on inside as the rest of the family are tuned into a traditional Thanksgiving football game. Samantha approaches Alex, who looks bothered.

"I thought you were gonna quit," she says.

Alex turns his head slightly getting a side eye look at Samantha. He takes another drag. "It's not easy to quit with people like your dad around."

"I know. He's an ass. You shouldn't take him seriously, though."

"I wish I didn't. But he's right. What happens when you go to college? You meet another guy. Forget about me. Finally realize you deserve better."

"What? No. We deserve each other. The distance is not that far. We can make this work," Samantha pleads. Alex drops his cigarette and squishes the butt with his shoe. "Now come inside so we can have some pie," she says.

"Nah. I'm okay. Enjoy the rest of your Thanksgiving with your perfect fucking family." Alex makes his way down the steps of the porch.

"So you're just gonna leave like that? Alex!" He ignores her.

Samantha can't believe how he is acting. *Seriously?* She rubs her bare arms in the brittle wind. She brushes her hair behind her ear, watching as Alex hops in his car. She sighs, then heads back inside.

It's a couple of weeks after Thanksgiving break and Lakehurst High is back in session. Samantha taps her pencil on her notepad while unenthusiastically listening to her teacher explain the lesson plan. It's the afternoon, and this class is about to end. Samantha looks up at the clock and sees that the bell should be ringing at any moment. She looks out of the window and sees a huge, repulsive-looking man staring at her from across the street. He notices Samantha and smiles at her, then waves. The school bell rings. Extremely creeped out, Samantha gathers her belongings and rushes to the door.

"Ms. Harvey, can I have a word with you?" she is stopped by her teacher, Mrs. Merril. A very dainty and soft-spoken woman. The type you can see knitting her grandchildren a sweater for the holidays or baking a fresh batch of cookies for the class just because it's a Wednesday. She is not really that type of person, but she does look the part.

"Yes," Samantha says with an exhausted sigh. Her patience runs thin with everything as of late. With Alex, school, and creepy men on her mind, she is not in the mood for small student-teacher talk.

"I just wanted to follow up with you to see if you have chosen anyone to do your thesis on," Mrs. Merril says, stonily.

"I haven't."

"Samantha, you really need to get a jump on this. The midterm is due in two weeks."

"I know. I'll . . . think of something," Samantha says.

"If you're thinking of strong public figures, Hillary Clinton is a great option," Mrs. Merril responds gayly. Samantha ponders that notion, faking a brisk interest.

"Um, no thanks," she says glibly.

"Okay. But if you need help or assistance, I recommend asking any one of the students on the school newsletter. They have a lot of useful and historical information," Mrs. Merril says, tapping her pencil on her desk. Samantha is getting even more annoyed.

"I will do that. Thanks Mrs. Merril." Samantha quickly walks out. She looks down at her watch and notices her next class starts in a little under ten minutes. She has a little time to spare, so why not check to see if anyone on the school paper can help her. She maneuvers through the crowded chaos of the hallway all the way into the next building over. These halls are a little less crowded. Making a sharp turn to the left, she heads up the stairs. At the landing, she heads down the hall to the spacious school newsroom, where the school paper is printed and the morning announcements are filmed. Opening the door, the florescent lights spill into the much darker hallway. A conference table is positioned in the middle of the room. A lounge area is closer to the front, where a television hangs on the wall. A desk holding two computers sits against the opposite wall next to a door labeled, *Red Room*. Brandon walks out of that door.

"Excuse me. Hi," Samantha says, startling Brandon. Nerves shoot through his insides like a glass of prune juice. *This is a pleasant surprise. Why is she here? Play it cool Brandon, play it cool.*

"Hi."

"Sorry to bother you. I'm—"

"Samantha Harvey. I know you."

Samantha is taken aback. She feels a little embarrassed that she does not remember him. He does look familiar to her, but Samantha is horrible with names. "Really?"

"We had world history together back in tenth grade. I remember you did a report on the Berlin Wall. To this day, *scheisse* is the only German word I remember," Brandon says, nervously.

Samantha smiles. "Oh my God. I can't believe you remember that."

"Profanity of any kind tends to stick with me, for some reason."

They share a laugh. Samantha is now getting a better look at Brandon. She's starting to remember.

"So what can I—" Brandon starts to say.

"Brandon, right?" she says, unsure of herself.

Brandon is in awe. She remembers his name. "Yeah," he says, with a smile.

"I remember now. You sat two rows in front of me and you did your report on those Tylenol poisonings, right?"

"Yeah, I just wanted the class to stop taking Tylenol," Brandon says jokingly.

"Well it worked, 'cause trust me, to this day my only headache remedy is Canada Dry and crackers."

Again, they share a laugh. This time, it's a little more flirtatious.

"So . . . what can I help you with?" Brandon says, licking his lips. Doing his best to channel his favorite rapper, LL Cool J.

"Well, speaking of reports, I need a subject for my thesis. I have to write a midterm paper on a person in two weeks and I have no idea who I want to do the report on and . . . I guess I'm just looking for ideas," Samantha says, silently cursing her teacher. She's not afraid to ask for help, but she's now second guessing herself.

Brandon walks closer. "A famous person?"

"Yeah. Well, like a historical figure or something. It's just hard finding someone relatable enough to write a ten-page essay about, you know?"

Brandon laughs. He gets closer. Arm-length close. He leans up against the conference table and crosses his arms. He wants to seem assertive now. He wants to take charge of the conversation. *Women love confidence, or so they say.*

"Well, who do you admire?" he asks, putting Samantha on the spot.

She's drawing a blank. "I don't know."

"There's no one you admire?"

"I admire a lot of people. This is stupid, I'm sorry. I'm sorry to bother you."

"No, you're fine," Brandon says, standing up to further assert himself. "I'll tell you what, why don't we meet after school in the library tomorrow and I can help you out then?"

"Are you sure? I know you're probably busy, so I don't wanna put you out."

"I'll be more than happy to help."

"Okay. That works. I've been going to the library after school anyway, so that's perfect."

"Cool. So is tomorrow at four good?"

"Yeah. Sounds good. I'll see you then," Samantha says, turning around to walk away. She waves to Brandon and utters a soft "bye," then heads out the door.

"Bye," he replies back. He watches her leave, admiring her figure. Smiling, he pleasantly sighs, then heads back into the red room.

The next morning, Ian wakes up to the startling sight of his mother sitting down on the edge of his bed, staring at him. He knows why, but it is still an unsettling way to start his day. She pulls a cupcake from behind her back—white frosting with multicolored sprinkles. There is a single lit candle on top. Katherine starts singing happy birthday to Ian, who sits up, rubbing the crust out of his eyes. He covers his mouth to yawn. It is way too early for celebratory pastries, but the gesture puts a smile on his face. Once Katherine concludes her mediocre singing, she holds the cupcake up to Ian's face.

"Make a wish," she says, excitedly. Ian closes his eyes for a moment, then blows out the candle. Katherine hands him the cupcake. He begins unpeeling the wrapper.

"A cupcake for breakfast?" Ian asks.

"Well I gotta be at work in a few. But I wanted to give you your present now before I leave." Katherine grabs an envelope sitting next to her on the bed. Ian looks confused. He sets his cupcake on the nightstand and takes the envelope, then opens it. He is astounded by what he discovers. He rubs his eyes, adjusting his vision to make sure he is really seeing what he thinks he's seeing. It's a check. For twenty-five thousand dollars.

"Mom! This is a lot of money!"

"I know. It's your college fund, plus a little something your dad left you. Ian, I am so proud of the man you have become." Katherine giggles. "That sounds so weird coming out of my mouth. But I have to remind myself, from here on out, you are now an adult, and you've earned every bit of that money. It's yours to do with whatever you choose."

Ian smiles. He feels an overwhelming sense of love and affection at the moment.

Katherine continues, "And regardless, if you're eighteen or twenty-six or fifty-two, you are still my baby boy. Happy birthday, sweetie." Katherine leans in and gives Ian a kiss on the forehead.

"Thanks, Mom."

"I gotta go okay. I love you." Katherine hops up off the bed, walking out. "Have a good day at school . . . and take your medication."

"Okay," Ian says, still staring at his check. This is the most money he's ever had in his entire life. He places the check in the drawer of his nightstand and gets ready for school.

In the kitchen, Ian is finishing off his cupcake as he washes it down with a glass of milk. He then hears a car horn honking outside. Confused, he opens the front door to find Alex standing by his car in the driveway. He motions for Ian to come over. Jason's in the passenger seat. *Well this is a surprise.* Ian finishes his glass of milk. He walks back to the kitchen and places the glass in the sink. He grabs his bookbag and heads out the door. He stops himself just outside the doorframe.

"Give me one second!" he shouts. He rushes upstairs to his bathroom and shakes a pill out from his medicine bottle. The bottle itself sounds damn near empty. He opens the top and sees two lone pills left inside. Ian pops one, takes a sip from the faucet and swallows. He runs back downstairs and exits the house, locking the door behind him. He checks once more to make sure the door is locked, then walks over to Alex.

"What are you guys doing here?" Ian asks.

"A little birdie told us it was your birthday. Hop in." Alex pushes his seatback forward ushering the birthday boy into the back. The car is foggier than the Mystery Machine. Already in tune with a morning wake n' bake, Jason passes the joint to Ian.

"Happy birthday, dude," he says, coughing plumes of smoke.

Ian grabs the joint. "Thanks." He takes a couple of drags. Alex drives off.

"So how old are we today?" Alex says.

"Eighteen," Ian replies, reacting to the weed in the same manner as Jason.

Alex cheers. "Welcome to the club, man!" Alex says, passing Ian a pint-sized bottle of whiskey. Ian is hesitant but grabs the bottle. *Uh.* With a joint in one hand and a bottle in the other, Ian plays Sophie's choice in deciding which vice to indulge. He takes a swig of the whiskey. His face prunes to a shriveled point. *Jesus, what a wake-up!* He takes another hit off the joint then passes both back to their respective owners. Alex takes a shot while Jason puffs his joint.

"Thanks. Do you guys always get this fucked up on someone's birthday?" Ian asks.

"As far as I'm concerned, it's already the weekend," Alex says, taking another swig of whiskey.

"Where are the girls?"

"Sam's driving her car to school today. But they're not important right now. What is important is you celebrating your birthday today like it's your fucking last." Alex passes the bottle to Ian. In a way, Ian feels this is a rebirth of sorts. The start of a brand-new journey into adulthood.

"To the first of many," he says, holding up the bottle before taking a much longer guzzle.

"That's the spirit!" Alex says. Jason turns the volume up on the radio. Party mode is in full effect for the reckless trio. Ian takes yet another shot of whiskey. At this rate, he'll be trashed by first period.

Once at school, Ian makes his way through the congested halls with the help of his two escorts. In grand, over-the-top fashion, Alex clears the path of students for Ian, so he is able to get to his locker.

"Make room for the birthday boy!" Alex says, triumphantly. Motioning as if Ian is king of Lakehurst, and because so, he must not be bothered by the likes of its peasants crowding the halls. Although Ian is not king, he has made a name for himself by this point. People know him enough to consider him kind, smart, and most important, caring. Several students are wishing him happy birthday as Ian passes them in the hall. Some he knows, some he does not. His state of mind is a bit disoriented by now from the weed and whiskey, but he is able to keep his shit together. He passes Samantha and Ashley.

"We're gonna talk later," Alex says to Samantha on the sly. She rolls her eyes and brushes him off.

"Happy birthday, Ian," she says. Ian smiles and thanks her. Ashley notices him giving Samantha a look that implies Ian wants *her* as a birthday gift. He lit up when he saw her. Ashley's disgusted. She huffs. Samantha turns to her.

"What?"

"He totally wants to have sex with you," Ashley says, in a tone that's part repulsed and part just stating the obvious.

"Oh my God, Ashley. Stop it. He's a nice guy. That's it."

"He's a psycho. My parents told me he tried to stab his second-grade teacher with a pair of scissors."

"What?"

"Yeah. They remembered after seeing his picture in my yearbook. They said his mom pulled him out of school after the incident, and that's why he's been homeschooled this whole time." Samantha thinks Ashley's grasping at straws. Conjuring up a far-fetched story from the past seems pathetic and low, even for her.

"That sounds ridiculous. I'm going to class." Samantha walks away. Ashley's surprised by Samantha's dismissal. She walks the opposite direction.

Ian finally makes it through the crowd to his locker with the assistance of his posse. This is the happiest and most excited he's been since starting school. He finally feels like a part of something. He matters.

"We're outta here, man. See you at lunch?" Alex asks.

"No doubt." Ian high fives Alex and Jason. They make their way down the hall and out of sight. Ian starts grabbing books from his locker. He's approached by Brandon moments later.

"Hey man, happy birthday," Brandon says, with a bit of excitement.

"Thanks, dude."

"So uh . . ." Brandon is trying to talk, but Ian keeps getting distracted by other students passing by, wishing him happy birthday. He engages in small talk with random kids, unknowingly being dismissive toward Brandon. "So, I was wondering if you wanted to spend the night for New Year's Eve. My parents said they'll even let us drink champagne," Brandon mentions, showcasing that bit of information to entice Ian.

"I'd love to, but I'm going to a party New Year's Eve."

"Whose party?"

"Jason's. It's supposed to be fun."

Brandon looks highly upset. His disappointment has reached

a point where it seems all his efforts to try and hang out and be friends with Ian have been slowly slipping away. This is yet another disappointing effort.

"Hey, why don't you come with me?" Ian asks. The invitation is nice, but there is no way in hell Brandon is going to that party, because that's exactly what it will be for him—hell. There's no fun in going to a party hosted by people who don't favor his presence at all.

"Nah . . . I'm fine. I don't like parties," Brandon says, as if he's just come to this epiphany.

Ian closes his locker. The bell rings. "That sucks. Well hey, maybe we'll hang out some other time over the break," Ian says, slowly backing away. He throws up the peace sign and hits Brandon with a nonchalant "later," then lightly jogs down the hall to class.

Brandon shakes his head and sighs. "This fucking guy."

THE Y2K PARTY

CHAPTER 11

I t's New Year's Eve, and through the cold winter air, the upscale suburban streets of Jason's neighborhood are dead. The street itself looks like a vacant ghost town with very few streetlights illuminating the landscape and just a small handful of gigantic neighboring houses with the lights on. Twigs and debris have collected along the curbside down the neighborhood streets. Jason's house sits just about at the end of the neighborhood, secluded from the rest, but still within walking distance to other homeowners. Several cars are lined around the circle of the street, on the driveway, and even on the front lawn. This is where all the noise is located. People are gathered in the street and the porch area of the house conversating, drinking, and smoking cigarettes. It is nearly ten o'clock.

Inside, the place is packed. Loud music plays over the towering speakers located in the living room area, as well as the backyard. From the looks of it, this could be the party to end all parties. After all, everyone is slightly paranoid about all the Y2K rumors. But neither that nor anything else about this night is going to ruin their fun. The whole scene reads like a typical high school party with drugs and booze flowing freely.

The backyard is lined with flood lights on the side of the house. A nice gazebo sits to the left side of the yard where a couple of patrons are making out to the point of almost fucking. An enormous pool takes up the middle portion of the well-manicured lawn. Several floating devices aimlessly jellyfish their way around the inside of the vacant swimming structure. Beach chairs are lined along two sides. More yard stretches out to the right where Jason sits by a huge firepit, which sits near a few charcoal grills and a bar-like brick-layered three-quarter circle that sits about two feet tall. He and several others are enjoying the inferno while passing around several joints and taking tequila shots. Jason takes a nice drag from his joint.

"I'm telling you guys; this shit is real. This is like, the end of the world. It's all been foretold—" Jason is interrupted by a party guest, some stereotypical jock character drinking a beer. His blond cheerleader-type girlfriend sits on his lap.

"Bullshit," he says.

Jason continues. "I'm telling you this shit is real. Bill Gates, uh, the guy who invented fucking computers or whatever . . . he's gonna upload like some fuckin' super virus to the internet and make technology turn against us. The power grid is gonna fry and the whole country is gonna go dark. Then the robots will rise. It's gonna be on some fucking *Terminator* type shit, just watch."

"*T1* or *T2*?" Another party goer asks.

"Fuckin' *Judgment Day*, dude! The end of the fucking world!"

"That sounds fucking retarded! Why would he do that?" The jock asks.

"Because he's fucking rich and evil! The plan is to depopulate the world, so why not have robots do the fuckin' dirty work for him?" The crowd seems to be a bit divided by the banter. Some agree with Jason, but there are quite a few skeptics in the bunch. Jason takes a swig of his beer in the awkward silence. He's not fucked up just yet, but he's well on his way. One party goer from the group stands up and holds his beer to the sky like an award-winning trophy.

"Well, if this is the robot apocalypse, I'm gonna make the most of it," he says. Jason points to the fella because he took the words right out of his mouth. He stands up as well and raises his beer to the air.

"Now that's what I'm talkin' about. To the end of the world!" Jason yells. The rest of the party begins to cheer and continue with their raucous night. The party gets more and more crowded as the night progresses.

Samantha and Ashley are in the kitchen area of the house. The inside of the house is twice as crowded as it is outside. Some people are trying to stay warm, while others are taking full advantage of where the majority of the alcohol is located. Ashley opens the fridge and pulls out two beers, handing one to Samantha. A group is playing quarters on the island in the kitchen. Several rowdy partygoers are on the other side of the kitchen giving a very enthusiastic young man a beer bong. Tube in mouth, they pour two beers down the funnel. The scene is messy. Beer is spilling everywhere but that doesn't stop the continued high jinks. Just as the young man is close to clearing the bong, he removes the tube from his mouth and vomits a combination of beer and stomach acid all over the kitchen floor. Some of the trajectory gets on the enablers as well. The crowd cheers in excitement. Ashley and Samantha are disgusted as they look away.

"Oh, I forgot to tell you, I got into State," Samantha says.

Ashley is thrilled. "What? Oh my God, congrats!" Ashley yells before giving Samantha a hug.

"Thank you." Samantha replies with a sigh of relief. They toast their beers.

"So what about Alex? Are you two still gonna see each other? Because I don't know about you, but I cannot wait to see all the new dick college has to offer once I get out of here."

"Are you breaking up up with Jason?"

"No," Ashley says, in the most nonchalant way possible.

Samantha ponders Ashley's response, then grins as she shakes her head in disappointment. "You are so wrong," she says.

Ashley laughs, then shrugs her shoulders to really emphasize how much she doesn't give a fuck. "Look, I'm entitled to new dick, okay. I want new dick; I deserve new dick. If this wasn't Jason's party, I'd be here trying to find new dick," Ashley utters, pointing her fingers around at the crowd of party goers as if scanning through them. Samantha laughs.

"You laugh now, but new dick is gonna be all over you once you get to State. Then Alex can finally fuck off," Ashley says, taking a sip of her beer.

"That's not gonna happen."

"Why? Because you love Alex?" Ashley replies sarcastically.

"Exactly. We're high-school sweethearts. We'll make it work. We have to," Ashley huffs, then rolls her eyes.

"Speaking of new dick," Ashley says, eyeing the man candy, Trent, that just entered the party. He's the football quarterback. Tall, dark, handsome, and sporting a letterman's jacket, he's the type of guy that can get away with murder because of his status. He is not too bright, but who needs smarts when you can just flirt your way to graduation? Which is exactly why he currently holds a three point one-three GPA. Some even speculate he may have the biggest dick in the school. They're right.

Several party goers are excited to see him, as Trent is welcomed with cheers and high-fives from fellow football players, random individuals he doesn't know, and some awkward introductions from people already drunk. He makes his way over to the kitchen area and notices Ashley and Samantha. The girls smile at Trent, admiring his six-foot hotness. Samantha likes Trent. She thinks he is a genuinely nice guy, but she is not like every other girl, throwing herself at him. Ashley, however, would fuck him at the drop of the Times Square ball if she had the chance. What better way to bring in the new year?

"What's up ladies?" he says exuding swag and finesse. They both greet him with a "hi." "Do you guys know where the beer is?" Ashley seductively walks over to the fridge and grabs a beer bottle. She pops the top and hands it over to Trent, grazing his fingers during the transaction.

"Have I told you about my talents?" Ashley inquires.

"Talents?" he asks, taking a small sip of his beer.

"Yes. I have no gag reflex—" Ashley is immediately interrupted by Samantha, who grabs her by the arm to escort her away.

"Okay, let's go check on the boys. Good seeing you, Trent. Enjoy the party," Samantha says quickly before pulling Ashley outside. Ashley looks back at Trent and starts giving her beer bottle fellatio.

Past the kitchen and down the hall to the left, a secondary party is taking place inside of a lounge area of the house, located just opposite a half bathroom across the hall. This room has the ultimate man-cave aesthetic—red carpet, deer head mounted to the wall, a jukebox, pool table, and lots of football memorabilia from the Indianapolis Colts. This looks to be the members-only portion of the house where only a handful of individuals are lounging around, playing pool, and taking shots. Alex is smoking a cigarette waiting for his turn in a game of pool. He is leaning up against the bar chatting it up with a buddy of his, Luke, who is on the football team. Luke is a dirtbag—rude, short-tempered, cruel, and misogynistic. As a matter of fact, Luke was almost suspended from school after a rumor went around that he sexually assaulted a girl from another school district at a party just like the one he is at now. He was never suspended because it was his word against hers. He plays football, she has a reputation for being promiscuous, case closed.

Luke takes a shot of tequila. Two oversized windows in the lounge have a pretty full view of the backyard. He notices some of the girls at the party are starting to get a little wild and a little drunk.

"I see the ladies are starting to get a little loose now," Luke says excitedly, while rubbing his hands together very dastardly.

"Dude, by midnight they're all gonna be begging to fuck," Alex mentions.

"Good, cause I'm fucking something tonight!" Luke shouts, as he takes another shot. He yells a primal "woo!"

Alex laughs.

"I've been deprived, man. I'm fucking someone tonight and I'm not taking no for an answer, Luke says."

"You know they have a word for that right?"

"Yeah—it's called opportunity," Luke says, pouring up another shot.

Alex continues laughing. "You have issues dude."

"Whatever, man. Just because your girl has a leash on your dick doesn't mean you get to judge me."

"Listen, I am being well taken care of. Trust me," Alex says, putting out his cigarette in a horseshoe shaped ash tray.

"Yeah, if you say so." Luke makes a whip cracking sound with an arm gesture to match.

Alex shakes his head. "I'm getting another beer. You want one?"

"Yeah, bring me one back, stud."

Alex gives a thumbs up, burps, and walks away. Exiting the lounge area, he steps into the hallway and sees Emma walking out of the bathroom. Wearing tight bellbottoms and a Blondie shirt that comes just a couple inches below her breasts, Emma radiates sex appeal. She doesn't notice Alex, but he quickly gets her attention.

"Hey sexy," he says, as he taps the back side of her arm. Emma turns around, holding a beer. Her mood instantly changes when she sees who it is. She rolls her eyes and continues walking.

"Whoa, so you're just gonna ignore me?" Alex says.

"There is nothing for me to say to you. Now please do me a favor and fuck off for the rest of the night okay? Thanks." Emma takes another sip of her beer and walks back into the living room.

Alex looks a bit surprised. He can handle a sassy attitude, but a bitchy one has really got him feeling disrespected, especially at his best friend's party. He and Emma have some unfinished business they need to address, and this party is the perfect opportunity to do so.

Ian walks up to the front porch and takes in the unsupervised craziness. His initial thought was to knock on the front door before he walked in, but that would make no sense, since the front door is wide open and no one would hear his knocks over the loud music anyway, nor would they care. This is his first party party. Not like the one he remembers at age five, where he helped celebrate his mom's work friend's son turning six, where kids played pin-the-tail-on-the-donkey and ate enough ice cream and cake to rot everyone's teeth.

No, this is a high school party like he's seen in the movies, where kids his age are engaging in just about everything associated with the rockstar lifestyle from sex to drugs to alcohol poisoning. There is pressure for Ian to come across as cooler than he is and to not seem so nerdy and awkward. But his nerves are not going anywhere because he is unsure of where he fits in. Looking around, he notices there is an organized chaos to this madness. There do seem to be individual cliques at this party. Possibly intentional. He just cannot seem to really recognize anyone or find anyone he knows. The music gets louder as he gets deeper into the house.

"Yo, Ian!" he hears, barely coming through over the music to his left. He sees a classmate of his, Elliot, a biracial math whiz who sits next to Ian in their calculus and trigonometry class. Their relationship only extends as far as the classroom, but they have great chemistry and as far as Ian is concerned, Elliot just may be the nicest person in the world. He walks over and puts his arm around Ian.

"What's up, Elliot."

"Man, am I so glad to see you. You have to try this, come on." Ian can tell Elliot is a bit drunk. Not just because of his glassy eyes and tipsy grin, but because he smells like a brewery. He leads Ian near the kitchen area where he sees people taking turns attempting to finish a beer bong.

"You want me to do *that*?" Ian says, pointing to the lunacy.

Elliot nods his head violently. "It's really easy, all you have to do is drink. Hey guys, Ian is next!" Elliot shouts.

Ian is unsure about this. He thought he knew what peer pressure meant when he smoked a joint for the first time, but this just seems irresponsible. He does not want to do this, especially in front of all of these people who he may or may not know, but again, he refuses to come across nerdy or awkward. A tall guy holding the beer bong signals for Ian to come over.

Elliot picks up the tube. "So you just put your mouth on this end and drink."

Ian grabs hold of the tube. "Okay," he says plainly.

Ashley and Samantha walk back into the kitchen. Samantha is rubbing her frigid shoulders to warm them up. Ashley stumbles a bit but catches herself. Samantha assists her. "Oh my God, are you okay? Are you drunk?" Samantha says playfully.

"No, it's these fucking heels I swear. I need another drink, to be honest." Ashley takes off her black heels and sets them on the island in the kitchen. She navigates through the crowd to the fridge and grabs herself a beer. Samantha takes notice of the madness happening further down the kitchen.

"Oh my God, is that Ian?" They see him feet away prepared to do a beer bong.

The crowd starts chanting "CHUG, CHUG, CHUG," as Ian puts his mouth to the tube. Two beers are poured down the funnel, quickly flushing down. Ian braces himself then immediately starts drinking once it hits his tongue. The beer is flowing faster than Ian can drink it. His focus is laser sharp as everything else around him seems to fade away. It's just him and the beer bong. The only thing his eyes can focus on are the bubbles from inside the tube. Ashley looks impressed. Samantha looks surprised. Just as Ian feels that he cannot possibly drink anymore beer, he notices suds sliding down the tube. He's finished. Ian stands up and wipes his mouth, then lets out a burp that just about matches the music in volume. The crowd cheers. Ian can do nothing but smile as Elliot holds up his arm letting the party know who the heavyweight champion is. Ian looks over, noticing Samantha and Ashley. He waves. Samantha waves back. Ashley drinks her beer.

"Now, does that look like someone who tried to stab their teacher? Look at him. He's having so much fun." Samantha is happy for Ian and glad to see a vibrant smile on his face.

"IAN!" Emma shouts, rushing to Ian and embracing him with a hug. Ian didn't expect to see Emma but is very glad she is here.

"Emma, hey!"

"Oh my God! We *have* to do a shot together!" She grabs Ian by the hand and heads over to a few bottles of liquor sitting on the kitchen counter. "What are we having?" she says eagerly. There is a glow in her eyes when she looks at Ian. Ian is overwhelmed looking at the various elixirs. And after that beer bong, he knows he's on the fast track to getting fucked up. Before he answers, Emma interrupts. "Wait! How ridiculous was that midterm?"

"Oh, it was totally a waste of time. It's like 'yeah, I've got fingers. I can type.'"

"Right! *So* stupid. And I'm sure by graduation the only thing I'll remember is control-alt-delete." Ian agrees as they laugh together. Emma smiles at Ian, staring for a moment. Ian looks on awkwardly.

"What?" he says with a smile, eyes glassy. Emma snaps herself out of whatever trance she is in and quickly diverts her attention to the alcohol bottles.

"So, what are we drinking?" Ian scans through the skyscrapers of alcohol bottles and decides to go with what he knows. After all, he only just popped his liver's cherry a couple of weeks ago. He points to a bottle of Jack Daniels.

Emma is pleasantly surprised. "Good choice." She grabs the bottle. "Most people usually pick some lame shit they see people drinking in tv shows and movies like vodka or scotch. So fucking basic. But I can tell you have good taste in liquor." Far from the truth. Ian does not even care for alcohol to be honest. The taste is disgusting to him. But he figures he is here to have a good time, and when in Rome and all that.

"I have good taste in a lot of things," he says flirtatiously.

"Is that so?" she says, pouring out the shots and overflowing one of the shot glasses. "Oh shit." They both look around the kitchen for something to dry the spill.

Ian grabs a dish cloth hanging over the sink and cleans the mess.

"Thank you. I'm such a ditz sometimes," Emma proclaims.

"It's cool. Don't worry about it." Ian tosses the rag into the sink as Emma grabs both shots.

She hands one to Ian. "So what are we toasting to?" she says.

Ian thinks for a moment. "To new beginnings. To the start of a bright future for both of us."

"I like that. Cheers." They clink glasses and knock back the shots. The burn slowly creeps down their throats. Ian's face scrunches in disgust. Emma chases her shot with a swig of her wine cooler. She looks around the party, observing the atmosphere. "See any cute girls here?" she asks.

Ian gets flustered. "Uh, I see a few. I do like someone, but she has a boyfriend." Emma is taken aback and surprised to find herself a little disappointed. But deep down she knows their friendship is undeniable.

"Well, I hope it works out. If it's meant to be it'll be. She should feel lucky to be with someone like you."

"You think so?"

"Absolutely Ian! You're a catch and an amazing person. And if she can't see that then she doesn't deserve you!"

Ian's appreciative of Emma's kind words. He's not used to accolades. It feels good to get compliments and affection from someone other than his mom. "Thanks, Emma."

"Anytime," she says, nudging Ian with her shoulder. "You want another shot?" she asks.

Ian sighs. "One more. But only because it's with you," Ian says.

Emma pours two more shots.

Meanwhile, Jason has commanded the attention of the party goers in the backyard. Standing up, he asserts himself as a prophet who has insight into the coming future. He explains that by the year two thousand, Earth will be sent back to the Dark Ages. The billionaires and members of the shadow government have underground bunkers they will be living in as Earth's population consumes itself through disease, famine, and death. Technology will be purposefully shut down by Bill Gates so that his virus upload will allow robots and technological equipment to surveille and finish off the rest of the population, and the shadow government and billionaires can rebuild the world in their image.

Jason's cult-like persuasion has his audience captivated. There may be a few skeptics still in the audience, but Jason's explanation is compelling. The flames from the firepit intensify with the volume in Jason's voice, giving his speech an apocalyptic flare. He tells them that there is only one sure way to stop the coming robot apocalypse.

"We have to destroy our technology. That's the only way. Stop it before it starts." Jason takes off his watch and throws it into the fire. He pulls a pager out of his back pocket and tosses it into the blaze as well. "Who's with me?" he shouts. Surprisingly, the crowd is on board. They cheer on as they begin throwing their watches, pagers, CD players, and Gameboys into the flaming pit. Half of the crowd thoroughly believes Jason, while the other half just think it's cool to emulate the dumb rebellious party shit they see in movies.

This definitely livens up the crowd. More drinks and shots are downed in this shared experience of burning the evil tech. The crowd cheers on as the flames get bigger and bigger. A partygoer grabs one of the lounge chairs from beside the pool and chucks it right into the blaze. The crowd goes wild.

"Yo! Dude! DUDE! WHAT THE FUCK ARE YOU DOING?" Jason yells at the guy.

"Burning the chair," he says, pointing at the inferno. "Woo!"

"No! We're burning watches and technology and shit, not my furniture, you fucking retard!" The other guy looks dumbfounded, ashamed, and embarrassed.

"Oh. My bad. I thought we were just burning shit," he says in a low monotone.

Jason sighs. He points two fingers to his temple and mimes a gunshot.

Walking inside the house from the backyard, Emma yells to a friend that she is grabbing another drink. She stumbles a bit making her way inside. She opens the fridge and sees there are no more beers left. She sighs. She then walks back outside toward the chaos by the firepit.

"Jason! JASON!" she yells, finally getting his attention. "Where's the rest of the beer?"

"There's another fridge in the garage," he says. He turns his attention back to his unruly machine-cleansing ceremony. "No, I saw that, Cassie! Throw that fucking Tamagotchi in there!" Reluctant, Cassie sadly tosses her Tamagotchi pet into the blaze.

Emma shakes her head, walking off. "I gotta get our beers from the garage," Emma yells to her friend. Not knowing where the garage is, she guesses the entrance must be on the opposite side of the kitchen/ living room area. She walks around the staircase in the foyer and discovers some people hanging out in a sunroom on the right side of the house. A hallway goes down that is lined with four doors. Two to the left, one to the right, and one straight down. *One of these doors has to be the garage.* She opens the door to the left. A closet full of linens and throw pillows. She opens the second door next to the previous one. Pitch darkness. She fumbles on the side of the wall for a light switch and flips it on. A steep wooden staircase descends to a concrete slab at the footing. A few cobwebs hang just above the doorway. This is obviously not the garage, and even if it was, Emma has seen plenty of horror movies to know not to go down there otherwise.

"No fucking way." She turns off the light and closes the door. There is a door opposite to the one she closed, but she turns her attention to the door at the end of the hall. She heads down and sees a light switch to the left of the door. She flips it on and opens the door to a well-organized garage loaded with sports equipment, boxes labeled *old shit*, a work bench and wall of tools, a fancy silver Mercedes parked off to the side, and a standard-sized black refrigerator just to the left of the work bench.

Voila.

She heads over to the fridge when suddenly the garage light flickers. Something about this scenario seems awfully familiar to her. She can't quite put her finger on it, but she knows it does not end good. "Just get the beer and get out of here," she tells herself. She opens the fridge and sees two shelves full of beer. Emma grabs as much as she can carry and rushes back to the door. She gets back inside the house and sighs with relief. She closes the door behind her, turns around, and runs into Alex.

Startled, she drops a beer, which shatters instantly. "Jesus! Alex, what the fuck?"

"We're not finished talking."

"Yes, we are. Now move." Emma tries to get by but is blocked.

"I just don't understand why you're acting like such a bitch."

"Because I don't fucking like you, that's why."

"Well this is my best friend's party so if you don't like me being here then you can just fucking leave. Or you can stop this little game you're playing and talk to me."

Emma giggles and mutters the word "game" under her breath to mock Alex. This is certainly the pot calling the kettle black. *He's bothering me, but I'm the one playing games.*

"Isn't your girlfriend here?" she asks shrewdly.

"Yeah. And?"

"And it would be a shame if I told her what we did over the summer. My lips tend to get a bit loose when I've been drinking . . . as I'm sure you know."

Alex goes stiff, his face turning red. He looks worried, but also enraged.

"Now *fuck off!*" she shouts, purposefully bumping his shoulder as she walks pass.

Alex still does not move. He blinks a few times, grinning as he nods his head.

The party continues in full swing. Ian, now feeling the effects of his overindulgence sees Ashley across the kitchen. He drunkenly approaches her, tapping her on the shoulder from behind.

She quickly turns. "Christ, Ian! Creep."

Ian laughs off her insult. "Hey, have you seen Sam anywhere?" he says, slightly slurring his words.

"Sam has a boyfriend, Ian. Okay? So whatever feelings you have for her, you need to let that shit go. Besides, she's not in the business of charity cases these days," Ashley says coldly. Ian's dumbstruck. His inebriation intensifies his confusion. *Where is this coming from?* he thinks.

Ashley continues. "And just so you know, I know what you did. And I promise, before the school year is over, I'm gonna expose you for the psycho that you are. So do me and Sam a favor, and just stay the fuck away from us, okay—creep." Ashley grabs her beer and her heels off the island and storms off. Ian is left speechless.

As the new year approaches, Brandon is once again isolated and bored as he watches a television broadcast of the ball-drop in Times Square from the comfort of his couch. His shirt is covering his nose to block the disgusting smell that's coming from the kitchen. The house reeks. Smelling as if a pig just successfully completed a suicide-bombing mission right in the middle of the household. Tina pops into the living room occasionally from the kitchen to watch the broadcast as well. Marcus is walking around the house talking loudly on the phone with relatives. The volume of his voice rises as the Crown Royal gets lower in his glass.

Tina looks over at Brandon. "Honey, you can put your shirt down. The smell is not that bad."

"We must be smelling different things."

"You're so dramatic. Your friend Ian couldn't come over?" Brandon has to now think of an excuse for Ian. Better to lie about his absence than to express the embarrassment of being blown off.

"No. He's at his grandparents' house." Brandon feels that's a believable enough lie. Regardless, it seems to have worked out for the better because he would feel horrible subjecting Ian to the smell of his house at the moment. "Is this Y2K thing real?" he asks.

"I'm not sure. I guess we're gonna find out soon, huh?" Tina says, walking back into the kitchen. Brandon stares at the television screen zoned out. He is not happy with his lack of a social life. His life is boring. He has no friends. A part of him is comfortable in this lonely state because it is all he knows. He is used to his loneliness by now and any attempts to break that cycle give him anxiety. But the strength in his optimism keeps the wheels turning. Brandon sees a bright future for himself. A new millennium means a new start for everyone, and he knows things will get better for him once he gets to college. But he does yearn for the memories he could be making now, like New Years Eve parties and school dances. He's also thinking of skipping prom just to save himself the embarrassment of not having a date. But having no social life is not nearly as torturous as the assault that is happening to his nose currently.

Back at the party, Alex watches as people continue to rage over the firepit. The beach chair has sent the blaze to new heights and the celebration seems more and more reminiscent of a cult meeting. Jason is egging on Alex to contribute, but he has nothing hi-tech to sacrifice to the fire.

"I told you I don't have anything." He finishes his beer then chooses that as his offering. He pitches the bottle into the blaze and cheers. He picks up a bottle of tequila sitting by his feet.

Samantha storms outside and purposefully beelines her way straight to Alex. She looks furious as she approaches him.

"What's up, babe?" Alex says carelessly.

"I know what you did over the summer," Samantha says menacingly.

"What the hell are you talking abo—" Alex is disrupted by a slap to the face so forceful that it gets the attention of everyone around the firepit. Gasps and "oohs" are the unified reaction. Alex looks confused and stunned. This slap is going to leave a mark.

"Fuck you," she says, teary eyed. The sincerity in her voice cuts deep. She turns around and walks off, then shouts, "Don't fucking call me!"

Everyone is confused but entertained by what just occurred. Alex stares as Samantha walks away. He takes a swig from a nearby bottle of tequila as Jason tries to recenter the attention back to the New Year's ritual.

As Samantha heads for the front door, she accidentally bumps into Ian.

Even in his inebriated state, he notices the distress on her face. "Hey Sam, are you okay?"

"I gotta go. I'm sorry." Samantha walks past Ian out the front door.

He follows her. They get out to the middle of the street, yards away from the front entrance of the house. The cul-de-sac is mostly deserted.

"What happened?" Ian says.

Samantha stops. "I just need to go home, Ian? Okay," she says with tears in her eyes. Ian grabs Samantha by both arms.

"It's going to be okay. I promise." He can sense her pain. He doesn't like to see Samantha like this. There is only one thing he can think to do to make the situation better for the both of them. He leans in and kisses Samantha on the lips.

She backs away. "What are you doing?" she asks.

Ian steps back, ashamed. "Oh. I thought—oh God. I'm so sorry."

Samantha is at a loss for words. She turns around and continues walking toward her car.

"Wait!" Ian shouts.

"What is it now?" Her voice sounds agitated.

"Could you give me a ride home . . . I think—" Ian turns away and vomits in the street.

Samantha's agitation now morphs into a state of nurturing as she realizes Ian is extremely intoxicated. She pats his back as he continues to vomit. "Are you done?" she asks.

Ian stands up, wiping his mouth with his shirt sleeve. He nods his head in acknowledgment. "I think so," he says, spitting to the asphalt.

"Come on. I'll take you home." Samantha guides his drunken steps to her car.

Alex has seen the entire exchange from where he stands on the porch. From this distance the two are just silhouettes in the streetlight, but he knows exactly who they are. His anger has now jumped from furious boyfriend to full-on psychopath. He storms back into the party looking for Emma. All he sees is red. She is nowhere to be found inside. He steps outside and sees her walking back to the house. She sees him standing threateningly by the back entrance.

"I hope you feel good about yourself," he says.

"I do actually," Emma states, with a slight giggle at the end. She continues. "Let's get something clear, okay? You mean nothing to me, Alex. Your entire existence is a waste of perfectly good space. You think you're God's gift to this world, but news flash, you're not. You're a fucking loser who couldn't fuck his way out of a bag of chips. I think I did Samantha a favor actually, because anyone who is willing to put up with your shit deserves a fucking medal of honor or a bullet to the head. You're just a sad excuse for a person who's never gonna amount to shit and you know it. So for the last time, fuck off and stay the fuck out of my life!" Emma shouts, kissing her middle finger.

Alex forcefully grabs her arm before she heads inside. "I swear, from my lips to God's ears, you're gonna fucking regret this," he says.

Emma pulls her arm back. "I'm so scared," she says sarcastically, then heads inside the house.

Alex stands in silence. His mind feels heavy. Everything around him is in slow motion from the party goers to the firepit to the music. Everything seems farther in the distance than it actually is. Alex is standing inside his own personal void. Rage has consumed every aspect of his being.

Ashley rushes over to Jason, who is still entertaining his loyal followers. She tries getting his attention by shouting his name, but to no avail. Like parting the red sea, she commands the crowd to make room as she maneuvers her way through the chaos until she reaches Jason, who's standing on the brick ledge of the short wall.

"JASON!" she shouts, finally getting his attention.

Jason hops off the ledge. "What's up?"

"Where's Samantha?" she asks. Jason looks around.

"I don't know. Maybe she left." Jason looks at Ashley's wrist, spotting a white watch. "Babe, let me see your watch," he demands.

Ashley removes her watch and hands it to him. He checks the time, 11:55 p.m., then chucks the watch into the fire.

"Hey! What the hell, Jason!" Ashley shouts, confused.

"Hey everyone, it's almost time! There's champagne in the kitchen! The countdown's about to start!" Jason yells.

The crowd starts heading to the house.

Ashley pushes Jason in frustration. "What the hell was that?" she asks.

"It's a long story. I'll buy you a new watch, okay? Don't be mad," he says, sweet-talking her. He puts his arm around her shoulders and kisses her on the forehead. The two follow the crowd inside.

At Brandon's house, Tina walks into the living area and giddily serves Brandon and Marcus a glass of champagne. Brandon's glass is half-full while Marcus's is to the rim. He is already quite drunk, which is why Brandon would rather switch glasses. Tina walks in with her glass and sits on the couch next to Marcus.

"Oh! It's almost time," Tina says excitedly.

"The year two thousand. Wow, in a way this is a once-in-a-lifetime event. Who would've thought we as people would make it this far?" Marcus questions. His words are clear, but slow and punchy. He spills a bit of his champagne midsentence.

"Careful, honey—the couch," Tina admonishes.

"I got this," he says, a bit snarky, feeling as though Tina is trying to baby him.

"Well apparently this is how far we're gonna get," Brandon says. He begins thinking, *what if the world actually does end at midnight? Would I be happy with my life so far? Fuck no! If the world ended now that would really fucking suck.*

Tina turns to her pride and joy. "What's your New Year's resolution?" she asks.

Brandon has a moment of realization as his answer dawns on him at that very second. "Fortune favors the bold, right?"

"That's what they say," Tina says.

"Then that's my resolution. To be bolder," Brandon says.

Tina smiles. "I like that," she says, taking a sip of her champagne. She looks at the television. "Oh! Here we go!" The countdown starts. The crowds cheer as they count the seconds until the illuminated ball slowly drops. Nine . . . eight . . . seven . . .

Jason's party is nearly elbow-to-elbow as everyone crowds the inside of the house. A television in the living room is broadcasting the ball drop. Six . . . five . . . four . . . the entire party counts down with the television. Jason stands behind Ashley with his arms wrapped around her as they stare at the screen, counting down as well.

"THREE . . . TWO . . . ONE—HAPPY NEW YEAR!" The crowd yells.

Jason and Ashley celebrate with a kiss. Other party goers begin chugging their champagne or whatever liquor they have in hand. Elliot opens a bottle of champagne, spraying the crowd, a christening to signify the start of the after party. Emma and a few other girls shield themselves from the projectile bubbly.

Emma sips her champagne daintily while talking with a good friend of hers, Stacy, a red-headed cheerleader and fellow hater of the other girls on the team. They go on about the politics and gossip of the cheerleading squad. How they hypocritically preach about the sanctity of sisterhood and the integrity of cheerleading but deliberately shun those who are not on their hierarchy of squad importance. Emma's reputation precedes her with the school and her cheerleading squad. They look at her as a loose and promiscuous girl, when in reality she has only hooked up with two people at school and regrets one of those hookups. Furthermore, it's worth noting that Emma knows about a secret rendezvous between the cheer captain Amber and her second in command, Amy.

One day after cheer practice, Emma had been walking back to the girls' locker room to retrieve the house keys she had forgotten in her locker. Upon walking in, she had seen Amber sitting naked on one of the benches between the row of lockers while Amy was on her knees in front of her helping herself to an afternoon snack. When the girls noticed Emma, they were completely horrified. Ashamed, they had rushed to put their clothes back on, begging Emma not to mention to anyone what she had just witnessed. Amber explains that they would be the laughingstock of the school and that their reputations would be ruined if anyone found out about their extracurricular activities. Emma laid down the law very simply.

"Fine. But under one condition—a permanent position on the squad," she had demanded.

"Well it depends on wh—" Emma had quickly cut Amber off.

"This is not negotiable! Unless you want the school to find out what big dykes their star cheerleaders are."

Amy interjected. "Deal!"

Amber had looked at Amy in concern as they mumbled something to one another.

"Good," Emma had said, walking to her locker, located on the next aisle. She had shouted to them, "And please wait until I'm gone before you two start carpet munching each other again!"

Emma had not spoken of their secret since. Her blackmailing has paid off thus far. As she drinks her champagne, Emma is beginning to feel slightly more drunk than she thinks she should be. Her vision starts to blur. She tries to focus on her conversation with Stacy, but her concentration is slowly fading.

"Yeah, screw both of them. It doesn't matter anyway because come graduation, my ass is on the first thing out of here," she says.

"You're moving?" Stacy says shockingly.

"Hells yes. I'm leaving this dump and moving back to Florida, and I cannot fucking wait." In her drunkenness, Emma stumbles back a little. She assures Stacy that she is fine and continues sipping her champagne. Stacy explains that she will be attending a local college after graduation but wishes she could go to Florida with Emma instead. "You would love it," Emma says. As she finishes her champagne, she stops herself for a moment and looks at the bottom of the glass to see what looks like remnants of a crushed pill.

Her stumbles become more apparent as she can barely stand. She tries to speak but her words are slurred and unrecognizable. "Some—in my glass—" Stacy does her best to hold Emma up and not let her hit the floor. She takes her champagne glass and sets it on the kitchen counter.

"Oh my God! Emma, are you okay? she asks. Emma tries pointing to her champagne glass but can just barely move her limbs. A lifeless doll. A mannequin without structure.

Stacy tries getting the attention of someone to help her but is unsuccessful. She positions Emma over the kitchen counter just to transfer most of her weight. She spots Jason walking past. "Jason, oh my God. I need your help. I think Emma is passed out." Jason leans over to try and get a look at Emma's face, but it's buried in the tiles of the counter.

"Emma? Are you alright? You fucked up?" He looks at Stacy. "Wow, she is fucked up."

"I know. You gotta do something," Stacy requests.

Jason ponders. "I'll tell you what. I've got a guest bedroom upstairs. Help me take her there." Stacy nods. They get on each side of Emma and assist her through the party. Slight groans and moans from Emma indicate she is in and out of consciousness.

Jason peeps the watch on Emma's wrist. "Didn't she burn her watch like everyone else?" he asks Stacy.

"What?"

"WHY DO YOU HAVE A WATCH?" he yells into Emma's ear. No response. They make their way up the stairs. The walls are lined with family portraits.

As they get to the landing, Jason points to the first door on the left. "It's right there."

Stacy opens the door and turns on the light. The room is spacious and plain but accented with a lovely buttercream-colored comforter and matching curtains. The room's atmosphere is bare and a bit sporty. Jason and Stacy plop Emma on the fluffy queen-sized bed. Her body nearly sinks into the comforter. They both sigh.

"Are you gonna stay here with her?" he asks.

"No, I'm going back to the party. She's fine." Stacy leaves.

Jason, feeling awkward, begins hearing Emma snoring. "Um, stay here until you feel better, I guess. There's a mini fridge over there with water and Dunkaroos inside. Help yourself." Her response is louder snores. "Cool," he says to himself. He then turns off the light, closes the door, and returns to his party.

During the trip back, Samantha and Ian are subjected to a somewhat awkward ride home. Faint music plays over the radio station. Prince sings about parting like it's 1999. Ian has the window down a quarter of the way just to feel the fresh air. Maybe it will sober him up a bit. He is afraid to speak. He wants to apologize again but figures Samantha will get more annoyed. So instead he periodically looks back at her like a scared puppy dog, hoping she opens the door to conversation.

"What?" she says.

"I just want to apologize—"

"Ian, you've apologized. It's okay, I'm not mad . . . and considering the night I had, I'm actually quite flattered."

"What happened?"

"I don't want to talk about it."

"Oh my God . . . *please* don't tell Alex what I did. He will fucking kill me!" Ian pleads.

Samantha sees the fright in his eyes. *He looks really scared.* Samantha is starting to see Alex in a whole new light. He is shaping out to be a person who she does not recognize anymore. *Has he always been like this? Did this behavior just start? Or did I just not see it?* She sympathizes with Ian and resents Alex. "I won't. I promise. Besides, you don't have to worry about me even talking to him for a while."

Now Ian figures Alex must have upset her at some point during the party. He wants to console her, but even he knows it is way too soon for him to be attempting any romantic moves after his kiss-and-hurl stunt back at the party.

The awkward silence continues before Samantha finally speaks. "So, was this your first official high school party?"

"Yeah, and I had fun . . . for the most part. Until I didn't."

"Why do you say that?"

"Because I made a fool of myself and puked all over the street." Samantha starts giggling.

Ian is happy to see a smile on her face. It seems like she's feeling better. As does he. "You saw it. You were there," Ian says, laughing about it.

"Yeah, but why am I just finding out you're a beer-chugging pro?"

Ian laughs bashfully. "I'm no pro. Again, may I remind you of the horror scene that was me puking back there? That wouldn't have happened if I was high."

Samantha is surprised. "I didn't know you smoked. What else are you hiding from me Ian Moss?" Samantha says jokingly.

Ian takes it literally. He's getting nervous. "Nothing."

"Let's see, you're smoking weed, chugging beer, and kissing random girls at parties. Sounds to me you've crammed four years of public school into one night."

Wow, she's right. He laughs at her joke.

Samantha doesn't think her joke was that funny, but Ian's laugh is infectious. Peeping down at the radio, she catches the time. 12:02 a.m. "Oh my God! Happy New Year!" she says.

"Happy New Year, Sam." He is surprised yet very happy he got to spend this time with Samantha, even after embarrassing himself. He figures everything must happen for a reason. Or at least that's what they say.

Moments later, Samantha pulls up to Ian's house. This is her first time seeing his house and she likes the design. It's modest but classy, and it seems to be a perfect fit for Ian, given his personality.

"Well, this is it," he says.

"You have a nice house."

"Thank you. And thank you for the ride. I don't think I would have lasted much longer at that party."

"Yeah, no doubt." They share a laugh.

Ian's got something on his mind. It must involve Samantha the way he's curiously staring at her. Samantha figures Ian may be trying to make a move on her, again. "What?" she says intriguingly.

Ian musters up his courage. "I wanted to ask you something but—"

"Ask me what?" Samantha genuinely wants to know.

"Do you have a tattoo?" Ian asks. That's not the question Samantha was expecting, but it is a welcomed relief.

"No, I don't. But I want one, though. Maybe somewhere on my hip."

"I figured," Ian says with a smile as he exits the vehicle.

Samantha doesn't know what he means by that. She brushes it off. "Well, goodnight," she says awkwardly.

"Goodnight, Sam," he says, closing the car door.

"And make sure you drink plenty of water before you go to bed," she says, offering her experienced, motherly advice.

Ian turns, giving Samantha a thumbs up. "Will do," he says.

Samantha smiles. She drives off as Ian reaches the front door.

Jason, returning to the party, walks into the living area where most of the party guests are. He puts a joint behind his ear and grabs a full bottle of champagne, then starts chugging. The night has turned down a bit but there are still a handful of drunk and rowdy individuals making sure the party goes on. Jason walks over to Ashley, who is talking to a friend of hers. Jason leans in on their conversation. Ashley turns around. She smells Jason before she sees him. A mixture of weed and liquor gives him that late-night bar smell. Luckily for Jason, Ashley likes it.

"Where do you keep finding bottles of champagne? Does your rich-ass family have like an unlimited supply or something?" she asks him.

Jason is about to answer but is interrupted by a party guest, a guy who is clearly drunk, wearing a two-piece nylon sweatsuit. Half of his chest is exposed. He gets Jason's attention but stumbles on his words and his feet. "Hey! You said the world was going to end and we're still fucking here!"

Other members of the party take notice to this fact as well because it is clearly past midnight, and the new year has begun without a hitch.

"Yeah, dude, you made me throw my favorite Ninja Turtles watch in the fire," says another party guest.

The nylon suit drunk then gets the party to rally behind his cause. "Boo this dude!"

The party starts booing Jason and throwing crushed beer cans at him. Ashley and her friend laugh as they quickly move out of the way. Jason tries explaining himself but is unheard over all the boos as he attempts to karate chop a few of the cans being thrown at him. He hits a few, but there are way too many to not get hit himself.

Half of the party is starting to leave. Jason tries to get everyone to stay by turning the music up louder. "Come on guys, don't leave! Fine! More weed for me then!" Jason grabs the joint from behind his ear and sparks it up. The majority of the guests make their exit.

Upstairs, the guest bedroom door slowly creaks open. A silhouetted figure stands in the frame of the door, watching Emma passed out on the bed, lying on her side. He enters the room and closes the door behind him. The room is completely silent except for the slight snores coming from Emma. The figure walks up to the bed. He runs his fingers up Emma's leg until he reaches her hip. The figure pulls her shoulder so she's now lying on her back. The snores stop. Emma, barely conscious, flutters her eyes, only seeing pitch darkness. She senses a presence in the room with her but is unsure whether she is dreaming or not. The figure then hops on the bed, straddling Emma. He unbuttons her pants, slowly removing them. Emma feels helpless. She is unsure what is happening. Her mind is foggy. This may all be a dream. But the weight on top of her feels very real. She cannot move. She cannot speak. The figure then removes her shirt, struggling with the last arm. Emma, now in her bra and underwear, passes out completely. The figure removes her underwear and proceeds to penetrate her. She groans at the sensation. The figure presses his hand against her mouth.

"Shut up," he whispers in Emma's ear. The voice is menacing. Emma feels the hotness from his breath as he continues to assault her. Her body lays stiff, as if she were dead. She floats between flashes of awareness and a dream-like state. At moments, she can feel the weight of the thrusts from her assailant while subconsciously reliving a memory of her and her dad fishing off of a pier near a beach. She can feel the sun on her skin. The smell of salt water and marine life fills her nostrils. Seagulls chirp above as her dad assists in tossing the fishing line. She then feels the pressure from her attacker's hand against her mouth. She tries to talk but it only manifests as low hums. The line between fantasy and reality is blurred. The ordeal lasts about ten minutes. The figure slowly gets off the bed and pulls up his pants. He picks up Emma's underwear and slides them back onto her lower half. She squirms on the bed in an effort to get more comfortable. A flash illuminates the room followed by the transactional sound of a polaroid camera. A second flash soon follows. The figure stands over the bed watching Emma, breathing deeply. He soon exits the room.

The next morning, Emma wakes up to the sound of birds chirping. She is disoriented, confused, and looks a total mess. She has no idea where she is. She shockingly discovers her clothes are missing. And even though she does not remember how or why she ended up in this situation, she does know that she passed out with her clothes on. She fears the worst. She is not completely sure, but she assumes she has been sexually assaulted in some way, which becomes evident once she notices dried semen in her underwear. *Is that . . . ?* She doesn't feel pain anywhere except for a drilling headache that just won't go away.

She manages to get enough energy to sit up in bed and try to collect herself both physically and mentally. She looks down and sees her pants and shirt on the floor. *Maybe I got hot and took my clothes off.* She wants to believe that, but her gut tells her otherwise. Because if that's what transpired, then why does she feel ashamed? Embarrassed? Dreading that walk of shame out of wherever the hell she is. Angry at herself for getting so drunk. Emma glances at her watch. 7:47 a.m. She puts on her pants and shirt and stumbles over to an antique mirror hanging on the wall. She looks worse than she thought. Her hair is disheveled, her eyes are puffy and red. There are tiny red bruises located on each side of her mouth. *I need to get the hell out of here now.* She grabs her shoes and opens the door to the bedroom to complete silence. Emma looks down the hall, seeing and hearing nothing. The upstairs to the house is absolutely spotless. She tiptoes her way down the stairs hoping it does not make a noticeable sound. Almost at the bottom of the landing, she sees the downstairs area is trashed. Empty bottles, smashed cans, and cigarette butts all litter the floor. There is an odd odor in the air as well, but Emma has no interest trying to figure out what it is. Her only concern is getting out of this house and back home to take a shower. And as much as she does not want to believe anything happened to her last night or even tolerate the idea, she senses something is not right. Emma puts on her shoes before stepping off the stairs, tiptoeing her way around the bottles and cans on the floor. She notices a couple of people are outside passed out by the now extinguished firepit. A few others are sprawled on the furniture and floor of the living area asleep. She quickly passes through the foyer and heads out the front door. She lightly closes it behind her and begins to step off the porch when she hears a familiar voice.

"Looks like you had fun last night." Emma turns to find Alex sitting in a chair smoking a cigarette. *Did he do something to me last night? Why would he say that? What does he know?* She feels betrayal, anger, fear, and repulsion on the inside. As she stares at Alex, her face is blank with a subtle hint of sadness. If what she's thinking is valid, Emma is in complete disbelief that Alex would go to such great lengths to not only spite her, but to violate her as well. Her body is slightly trembling. She can barely focus on breathing. There's a huge lump in her throat. She quickly heads down the steps of the porch, hops into her car, and drives off. Alex grins. He chuckles to himself, then takes another drag of his cigarette.

CHAPTER 12

It is the start of the millennium and school is back in session. Students crowd the hallways greeting and catching up with friends they haven't seen over the break. The morale and energy of the student body is pulsing. Lakehurst is definitely in the Tiger spirit, and it shows. Especially for the seniors who are now grasping the scope that graduation is only a couple of months away. Brandon is rummaging around inside of his locker trying to better organize his space.

His resolution was to be bolder and that certainly is true when it comes to his wardrobe. Brandon is a modest and low-key type of person who plays his strengths when it comes to what he wears. His clothes are not completely outdated, but there has always been a lack of style, which doesn't bother him since he has no passion for fashion and doesn't strive to look cool for the acceptance of others. His outfits usually consist of plain T-shirts and jeans, or something a bit nerdier. But as of now, his style has definitely upgraded. New Jordan sneakers, Girbaud jeans, and a yellow plaid Sean John shirt give the illusion that Brandon must be the coolest kid in school. He's not. But he would most likely win a contest for looking the most like "Hip-hop Urkel." He just wanted to try something different. It must be working because he has gotten a couple of compliments throughout the day. The one that meant the most so far was from football QB, Trent. Brandon was surprised Trent noticed him walking down the hall.

"Yo, Brandon, nice Jordans!" Trent had said, as they fist bumped each other. Brandon thanked him, walking away with the biggest grin on his face. It was a great feeling, but Brandon is not letting compliments and nicer clothes distract him from what's really important, and that is graduating. The plan is to graduate and attend State in the fall to pursue his dreams of becoming a journalist and he is going to make sure that happens.

"Yo, what's up dude? Nice clothes!" Ian says excitedly. It feels as though he hasn't seen Brandon all break and that's because he hasn't. Which is why he is so excited to see him and catch up from where they left off.

Brandon doesn't show the slightest bit of excitement to see Ian. He gets one look at him then turns his head back into his locker.

"What's wrong with you?" Ian asks.

"Me? Nothing. Sorry if I don't seem more thrilled to see sometimey friends," he says with a deep cut of sarcasm.

Ian is confused by the attitude. "Sometimey? What do you mean by that?"

"I'm guessing your *posse* doesn't want to hang out anymore, huh? Is that why you're here?" Brandon asks.

"Oh I see. That's what this is about? You're jealous?"

"I have no reason to be jealous of you or your crackhead friends," Brandon explains.

"And you're jealous because they wanna hang out with me and not you. I'm going to parties, having fun and you're just lonely and miserable at home with no fucking friends, so yeah, I'd say you're very fucking jealous."

Brandon shakes his head. "Whatever, man."

"You think changing your clothes is going to help you make more friends? The school year's almost over dude. Sorry, but you're about four years too late for that."

"You think I care? Because I don't. But I'll tell you what, don't come crying back to me when your new 'friends' stop hanging out with you when they find out you're a fucking crazy schizo."

Wow. That cut Ian deep. He trusted Brandon with really private information and now he's using it to weaponize Ian's mental illness against him. Ian thinks Brandon really hit below the belt with that one.

"You know what, I don't need to hang out with you anymore anyway. So fuck you," Ian says passionately, walking backward from the situation.

"Fuck you." Brandon says.

"No fuck you."

"Fuck you!"

"Fuck you, dude!"

"FUCK YOU!"

"No seriously, like fuck you."

"I don't give a fuck if you're serious, fuck you!" Brandon says, slamming his locker shut.

"Fuck you!"

"Fuck you!"

Ian, walking back slowly, throws both middle fingers up. Brandon turns to walk away then notices sheets of white paper littered all throughout the hallway. Some are stuck on lockers and walls, but most are scattered on the floor. Seems the entire student body is now reacting to what they see on the pages. Shocks, gasps, and laughs erupt in student unison. A couple of teachers have caught wind of what is going on and are trying their best to instruct students to ignore what they see and go to class. Brandon and Ian are both confused. Brandon looks down at the pages scattered by his feet. He bends over and picks up a page. Ian looks to his right and spots a page pinned to a bulletin board. It reads: *FOR A SLUTTY GOOD TIME, CALL 219-555-7392.* Underneath the headline is a bleak yet revealing photo of Emma spread out on a bed in her bra and underwear.

"Holy shit," Brandon says as he looks around the halls. These pages are spread all over the school.

Unaware of the chaos in the halls of campus, Emma is in the restroom applying lip balm in the mirror. Her mood is uneasy. The uneasiness turns to paranoia as several girls enter and exit the bathroom laughing at her. Emma never considered herself to be a popular student, but she feels her reputation is hindering her from enjoying her final year of high school. The outsider trait she possesses does provide a "fuck these bitches" mentality, but something is obviously not right. She is not one to get picked on or sit back and take any disrespect from anybody. She ignores the snickers and mumbling from her peers and focuses on evenly distributing the lip balm to her full set of lips.

"Looks like you're ready to blow the rest of the school, huh?" one dark-haired girl says. Emma turns her head with a threatening look on her face.

"What the fuck did you just say?"

The girl and her two followers giggle to one another as they exit the bathroom. Emma looks at herself in the mirror and huffs angrily. She drops her lip balm in her clutch purse and storms out of the bathroom. She is greeted by what seems like the entire student body looking at her and laughing. They are spewing rude, vulgar, and repulsive insults at her. One student runs by and showers the explicit flyers all over Emma. Disorientation kicks in for her. The confusion is overwhelming.

Am I dreaming?

She bends over and picks up a flyer. To her surprise, she is mortified. Tears well up in her eyes as she looks around. She is the circus freak of the school. A shunned member for society's amusement. If they had it their way, Emma should bare a bold red S on her shirt for *slut*.

"SHUT UP!" she screams at the crowd. Her efforts do nothing. She zig-zags her way down the hall ripping flyers off the walls. The ridicule continues. Her humiliation is fuel to their fire. Harsh insults and paper balls fly at Emma from every direction. She is surrounded by shame. The feeling proves to be too much for her to handle. Emma screams at the top of her lungs. She then rushes down the hall in hysterics. Unbeknownst to her, she passes Alex and Jason who are standing off to the side. Jason is laughing wildly at a flyer as Alex watches her run by with a smirk on his face. The school bell rings.

After school hours, Brandon and Samantha sit at a table in the school's library. It is almost dead quiet as few students are present. Brandon and Samantha sit a far distance from the entrance to the library, where the librarian sits behind her desk flipping through a salacious tabloid print. Behind the two are a wall of windows that overlook a line of desks with computers stretching all the way to the other side of the library where aisles of bookshelves stand. To their right are several aisles of bookshelves that come parallel to a far-off section of tables and chairs. So far, their conversation seems to be going very well as they laugh and high-five each other as they talk. Samantha expresses to Brandon how much she appreciated his assistance in helping her find such a great historical figure to do her midterm on—Princess Diana. Samantha was surprised she hadn't thought of her before. Samantha admires her deeply and feels she shares some similar traits with her. She got a B+ on her midterm and cannot thank Brandon enough for his help. He is appreciative, but now he figures that since her midterm is done, there will be no need for him to be around anymore. That dark cloud of insecurity begins to loom over him.

"So, I guess my work here is done then," he says.

"Well, no. That was my midterm. I'm still gonna need help for the final. That is, if you don't mind."

Brandon does mind—a little. He also doesn't mind because Samantha is hot, and they seem to be forming a real connection as of late. Worst case scenario, he gets his ass kicked by Alex on a regular day-to-day basis. Best case scenario, Samantha dumps Alex and gets with Brandon instead. After all, they are both going to the same college in the fall, which is great for Brandon because now the anxiety of loneliness seems to be fading away slowly each time he hangs out with Samantha.

"No, not at all. I've actually been looking for reasons to stay after school longer anyway," Brandon says with a smile.

Samantha picks up on his joke. "You think you're so funny, don't you?" she asks. Brandon shrugs his shoulders. "Speaking of which, tomorrow can we meet at lunch instead? I'm taking a tour of State after school."

"Yeah, that's fine. A tour huh? You're gonna love it. Beautiful campus," Brandon says.

"I'm so excited. It's good to know I'll have a friend when I get there."

"Likewise. High school is lonely enough. College will be a fresh start for me."

"For the both of us."

They lock eyes for a moment.

"Cheers to that," Brandon says, holding up his pencil.

Samantha smiles. She clicks her pencil against his then laughs. "You're such a nerd," she says flirtatiously.

"Did you see those flyers in the hall earlier today?" Brandon asks.

"Oh my God, yes. That was horrible. It's crazy to think anyone would do such a thing. She must be horrified." The two continue to chat and gossip about the outrageous situation for a period of time. So much so that it's distracting them from their studies. But it's fair to say they've been distracting each other this whole time.

The next morning, just before dawn, an alarm clock rings to awaken a woman asleep in her bed. It's a nice queen size, but she sleeps alone. Moaning as she turns over, she reaches out and turns on the lamp sitting on her nightstand. 6:15 a.m. She slaps off the alarm. This woman, Debra, is a hardworking thirty-six-year-old with dark brown hair but looks older than she actually is. Maybe it's because she's just waking up. Maybe she has lived a stressful life or maybe her biological clock is moving faster than what she expected. Her life has been stressful. Getting divorced from her husband, Jamie, was not an easy thing to get through. But she managed, and because of the divorce, decided to pack her bags and move from Florida to her home state of Indiana to be closer to her family. There is no malice or bad blood between Debra and her ex-husband, but she is glad to be out of that marriage. These days she finds thrills in going to work and having girls' nights every weekend, or every other day for that matter. Getting drunk with people she can relate to has always taken the edge off. Debra is the manager of a hole-in-the-wall beauty salon called *Beauty Salon*. She loves the beauty shop but hates the name—so boring. She believes the previous owner purposefully named it that in an attempt at being funny. If not, it just shows their lack of creativity in her eyes. Debra sits up in bed and stretches. She slides her house slippers on and walks over to open the blinds to her bedroom windows. It's a dark and gloomy Wednesday. She shuffles out of her bedroom, which leads to the kitchen. The house is dead silent. Only the ticking of a clock can be heard in the living room area as she walks through the house. She hits the answering machine as she heads up the creaking hardwood stairs, holding the railing for support with each step.

"You have eighty-nine new messages. "Hello Ms. Debra, this is Sasha . . ." a properly vanilla voice says over the machine. "I just wanted to confirm my hair appointment for this weekend. Give me a call back when you can. Bye." *BEEEEP* "Yes, I was calling about that blowjob . . ." Several snickers can be heard throughout the message. "Just wanted to know how much you charge, SLUT!" the immature voice of a taunting teen yells. *BEEEEP* "Hey slut!" a cheerfully upbeat female says. "Just wanted to know what it feels like to be the town whore!" The messages go on and one, each more vulgar, disgusting, and vile than the next.

Debra is still so drowsy that the soundtrack of insults coming from her answering machine doesn't register with her as she heads up the stairs. At the landing, there are four doors along the hallway. Her daughter's bedroom door is ajar. Debra serves as her daughter's personal wake up call because she hates the sound of alarm clocks.

"Emma, time to get up," Debra says, opening the bedroom door. But Emma is not in her bedroom. Her bed has not been made and the room is far from tidy. Debra looks down the hallway and sees the bathroom light shining from underneath the door. She slowly approaches at a zombie's pace. She knocks on the door. "Emma, are you getting ready?" There is no answer. Looking down she sees what looks like a pool of motor oil coming from underneath the door seeping into the hardwood as it dries. Debra gasps. "Oh my God."

She's starting to panic. She starts fiercely banging on the door calling Emma's name but is met by silence. "Emma, open the door, okay? Emma!" Debra throws herself against the door and it flies open. Debra falls inside, falling in a puddle of fresh blood. Emma's body is slumped on the toilet, leaning against the bathroom sink. Two deep lacerations run across her wrists. The wounds leaking slowly. Her body is pale and her vacant eyes stare directly into Debra's. A razor sits on the floor between the toilet and the tub, barely visible in the pool of red.

"Emma!" Debra screams as she scrambles to get to Emma, slipping in the thick blood. She sits on the edge of the tub and pulls her daughter closer to her. Emma's dead weight causes the two to fall back into the tub. "Come on baby, wake up . . . wake up, Emma," Debra pleads, lightly tapping Emma's face, praying for a response. Devastated, she cradles her daughter. The crushing feeling of reality sets in, the dreadful feeling that every parent fears more than anything. Gasping for breath through her sobs, Debra rocks Emma's lifeless body as the voices of demoralizing insults continue to echo from the answering machine downstairs.

THE LAST SEMESTER

CHAPTER 13

The sun has finally risen, but the ominous skies hide it from the morning. Just as there is a momentary break in the sky and it seems like sunlight might shine through, more clouds cover up the blemish. Ian, who is already fully dressed and ready for school sits by his window overlooking his neighborhood. He woke up extra early and got ready for the sole purpose to wake n' bake. *I might as well smoke since I'm waiting on the bus.* Ian casually takes hits from his joint. He makes sure he blows the smoke out of the window, so Katherine doesn't smell the burning herb. A part of Ian is actually curious to know how she would react if she found out he was smoking weed. After all, the purpose of enrolling in public school was to gain some real-world insight on the high school experience. And as cliché as it may sound, drinking and smoking is not only a part of that process, but culturally relevant as well. Who knows, she may encourage Ian to experiment with drugs and anything else he fancies.

But revealing something so potentially damaging to his character will have to wait until he is at least out of the house. Ian is now feeling the euphoric effects of the joint. His mind whirls at a thousand miles a minute. He begins to wonder how distraught Emma must feel after that stunt was pulled at school yesterday. *What asshole would think to do something like that?* He wishes he knew who it was, not to confront that person but to tell Emma, so she can handle the situation how she sees fit. But for right now he figures it's best to be a supportive and sympathetic friend to Emma.

Feels like I'm floating. I wonder what's for lunch today. His mind wanders. Ian coughs a few times after a couple drags. He hears a knock at the door.

"Oh shit." In a panic, Ian throws the joint out the window. He tries to muffle his coughs but is unsuccessful.

"Ian, I'm on my way to work, okay?" Katherine yells, her voice muffled from the other side. She tries to turn the doorknob. "Ian, why's the door locked?"

"Mom, I'm getting dressed!" he yells, coughing a few more times as he fans lingering smoke out the window.

"Okay, sorry. Don't forget to take your medication."

"I just did," he says slyly.

"Okay. Have a good day at school. Love you." Ian sighs. He looks at his clock. The bus is scheduled to arrive in ten minutes. *I wonder if Dr. Price smokes weed.* Ian blankly stares out the window. He sees Katherine hop into her Lexus sedan and drive off. "I'm really high right now," he says surprisingly.

Alex, on his way to school, looks intent. Hand gripped tight on the wheel, he drives in silence. Jason's in the passenger seat, flipping through radio stations. Alex has not seen or spoken to Samantha since the New Year's Eve party. He knows she's mad at him for what Emma revealed, but she doesn't know that Alex knows about her secret moonlight kiss with Ian. He's just as upset as she is—even more so. Jason says something to Alex through the high volume of the music, but Alex ignores him. There's a lot going on in his head at the moment. He's plotting. Mapping out a solid plan of action. Jason then mentions the prank that was pulled on Emma yesterday. Even he is unaware of who's responsible, but in his view, nothing that hilariously epic has happened at Lakehurst since Paula fell off the top of the cheerleader pyramid during lasts year's homecoming game and broke her leg in three places in front of the entire town.

"Seriously dude, that was the funniest shit. I wanna shake the hand of whoever pulled that genius prank off," Jason says.

Alex grins. "I'm going to need your help today," Alex says. Jason's a bit taken aback. This seems a bit out of character for Alex. He's never needed Jason's help with anything unless he needs a ride somewhere, and that's only if his Mustang is out of commission or getting a tune up.

"Help with what?" Jason asks. They pull into the school parking lot. The sharp, frigid air keeps the vast lot deserted for the most part, a few students are hotboxing in their cars with the heat on. The two hop out of the vehicle. Alex throws his signature leather jacket on.

"So you got it?" he asks Jason.

"Absolutely. Dude, I wish I would've known. I would've kicked his ass myself. How long—" Jason cuts himself off as he sees Samantha's silver sedan pull into the parking lot. "There's Sam." Alex turns around, threateningly. He's been waiting for the opportunity to confront Samantha for some time now, and today is the day. "I'll catch up with you later. Don't forget," he tells Jason.

"Yeah, yeah I got it," Jason says. He notices Ashley by Samantha's car and signals her to come to him as he walks toward the school building.

"I gotta go, but I'll see you at lunch?" Ashley asks Samantha.

"I got some stuff to do at lunch," Samantha says apologetically.

"Ugh—whatever. I'll catch you later." Ashley blows Samantha a kiss. She turns her head and sees Alex approaching. She quickly turns to Samantha, giving her the heads up. "Dipshit alert," she says. As she makes her way past Alex, she doesn't say a word. Just a menacing expression that mirrors Alex's as well. She approaches Jason and gives him a kiss. She noticed something off about Alex as she looks back at the parking lot. A part of her is even slightly worried about Samantha. Distracted by Jason, she heads with him toward the school. Alex steps in front of Samantha from behind a parked car, his hands in his pockets.

"I need to talk to you," he demands. Samantha is not in the mood to entertain anything he has to say.

"Too bad, because I have nothing to say to you," she says, adjusting the strap on her messenger bag.

"Oh, I think you do," Alex says, nodding his head.

"Do I now?"

"Yeah. You know, I think it's funny that you overreact about my situation, then turn around and do the exact same thing."

"What the hell are you talking about?"

"So you're gonna make me say it? Fine. I saw you tongue-fucking Ian at the party." She wants to deny it, but she doesn't have a quick enough rebuttal.

"No, that's not what happened, Alex. He kissed—" Her explanation is cut short by Alex's outburst.

"It doesn't matter! Okay? You're a fucking hypocrite! And a slut. But don't worry, your little homeschooled side piece is getting what's coming to him." Samantha doesn't know what to make of that last statement. She looks confused, but also apologetic.

"Alex, you don't know what you're talking about, okay? That night—"

"Save it, alright? I'm done." Alex walks off.

"What do you mean? What are you gonna do?" Samantha pleads.

"No! See this is the part where I get to dramatically walk away and leave you on a cliffhanger. Don't follow me!" he shouts, walking away.

"What?" Samantha says, confused and a bit stunned. She stands alone in the desolate parking lot trying to figure out what the hell Alex is talking about.

An uneasy feeling seems to be following Ian the moment he makes his way down the crowded halls. It's a creepy feeling, like the Grim Reaper is stalking him, lurking behind the faces of oblivious students making their way to class or leering at him from a distance. Even more so, everyone in the hall looks ominous. They seem to be conspiring, isolating Ian, making him feel like the butt of the joke. Paranoia soon follows. Ian tries his best to point blame at the fact that he is high, but the feeling seems much heavier, frightening almost, as he straddles the fence between haze and reality.

Just be cool. You're cool.

As if things couldn't get more out of tune, he notices Brandon making his way down the hallway toward him.

Should I say something or just ignore him?

Brandon looks to be on a mission. His face is determined and focused on whatever matter he has on his mind. As they cross paths, Brandon looks directly over at Ian and without hesitation, mouths the words "fuck you" to his face.

Did that just happen?

Now Ian is wondering if Brandon had just passed him without even looking his direction. The paranoia seems to be evolving into hallucinations. That thought alone is causing Ian's anxiety levels to rise above normal.

You're fine.

He walks over to a nearby water fountain and takes a long drink. He takes in a deep breath, slowly exhaling.

Finally.

A moment of Zen. The chatter and noise around him cease to exist. He is in his own world. A safe bubble that abruptly bursts with the screeching of the school intercom. Principal Owens clears his throat before speaking into the mic.

"Good morning, Lakehurst." His voice is somber. Ian notices that time seems to have stopped at this moment. The hall is silent. No movement from anyone or anything in sight. Everything seems frozen in time. "It is with great sorrow that I have to report that a student of Lakehurst, Emma Parsons, was found dead this morning from an apparent suicide." Students react to the shocking news with chatter and gasps. Some even feel guilty at this point for participating in what they could only assume was the triggering event to her suicide.

Principal Owens continues. "The school will be holding a memorial service in honor of Ms. Parsons tomorrow at ten-thirty in the gymnasium. We ask that you keep the family and friends of Ms. Parsons in your thoughts and prayers, and if there are students who need to speak to someone or provide any information, the guidance counselor will be extending operating hours to five o' clock. And, as always, my office door is open. At this time I ask that you now join me in a moment of silence."

Ian is in disbelief. *I must still be tripping.* He turns to a fellow student next to him. "Did I just hear that?" Ian asks.

The student tells Ian to "shhh", as he bows his head. As uneasy as Ian's day has been going, it just got a whole hell of a lot more uneasy.

This can't be happening. He slowly walks toward his locker in the stillness of the hallway. Ian's the only one moving in a sea of comatose bodies, all with their heads bowed. He gets to his locker, bowing his head up against the metal. Moments later, a hand grabs Ian's shoulder. Startled, he jumps back. He sees it's Jason, who greets Ian with a "S'up dude?" The school bell rings as chatter and student traffic resume through the halls.

"Oh, what's up Jason? Dude, did you just hear the announcement? I can't believe it," Ian says, pointing to the intercom on the ceiling.

"Yeah, yeah, real sad shit," Jason says carelessly. He places his arm over Ian's shoulder. "Listen, me and Alex are headed to the spot. You up to smoke?" Ian is speechless. A part of him is still in shock from the news he just heard. And given his state of mind right now, smoking more weed is not the answer to his instability. He attempts to deviate. "I don't know, I should really get to class—"

"Oh come on, dude, it won't take long. I got some new shit from my guy that you have to try."

Against his better judgment, Ian gives in. "Okay. But I gotta be quick," he says, earnestly.

"Yeah, dude, of course," Jason says, escorting him through the halls. The journey still seems uneasy for Ian. A part of him feels as though he is being taken to his execution, but that could just be his paranoia.

"Is Alex meeting us there?" Ian asks timidly.

"Yeah. I think he's already there." They make their way across the campus, heading to the gymnasium. As they go through the side entrance, Ian notices one of the ceiling lights flickering. Jason follows behind as Ian leads the way through the locker room. Dripping water from the shower heads echoes. As he reaches the vacant storage area, he sees nothing.

Where is Alex?

He turns to question Jason but is struck by a punch to the face. Ian falls back and hits the ground, a sharp sting in his mouth. He checks his lip and sees blood on his finger. Terrified, he looks up to see Alex standing over him looking enraged—psychotic even. Ian's lip is quivering. Not from the impact, from fear. Alex snorts a few times, wiping a white powdery substance from his flared nostrils.

"I've wanted to do that since I first saw this pussy," he tells Jason, who's standing by laughing.

Ian scrambles away from Alex. He is petrified, in disbelief that something like this is happening to him. Ian feels like an ant under the magnifying glass of Alex's rage. He's shaken with terror and flinches at every movement Alex makes.

Alex then leans over to get a good look at Ian. "You look surprised. What? You didn't think I would find out about you kissing Sam?"

"I—I—"

"I think he's about to shit his pants, dude," Jason says, ending his words with a chuckle.

"I saw you," Alex says, towering over Ian. Leaning down in front of his face. "This is how close you two were, right?" Alex strikes Ian in the face once more, this time causing a nosebleed. He grabs Ian's shirt and pulls him closer. "Right?" Alex says angrily, punching Ian again across the face.

"Please . . . I'm sorry . . ." Ian pleads, trying his best to enunciate his words. The pain is unlike anything he's experienced before. His face feels like it's on fire. Tears and drops of blood fall onto his shirt. Jason mocks Ian's pleas.

"Yeah, everyone's always sorry when they get caught," Alex says, lighting up a cigarette. He exhales. "No need to be sorry. Next time just don't get caught." Alex takes a long drag then flicks the cigarette against the brick wall. He walks over and kicks Ian in the stomach then follows it with a kick to the face.

Ian cowers in the fetal position. He hopes this will block any more blows or at least ease his pain. The school bell rings.

"Fucking pussy. Stay the fuck away from my girl!" Alex yells. He spits on Ian just to add insult to injury. "Let's get the fuck outta here," he tells Jason. The two leave as Ian squirms on the concrete floor, crying and bleeding. This was Ian's first physical altercation, and the feeling is overwhelming. In his dizzying state, Ian hears his dad's voice. It's coming from up above. Or maybe from inside his head.

"Aw, it's okay, buddy. It's just a little boo-boo. I'll go get you a Band-Aid." Ian opens his eyes, staring up at the ceiling. He sees a small crack begin to fissure, splitting the ceiling in half. The sound is thunderous. The motion is violent. Ian gets himself up and rushes out of the storage area, pass the locker room, and down the hallway of the gymnasium. He bursts through the double doors, welcomed by the bright sunlight. The sun may be out, but the temperature remains frigid. Ian continues running. Through the courtyard, past the student parking lot, then off campus, he does not stop. The only comfort he needs right now is his bedroom, a place where he can feel safe.

The cooling temperature enhances the discoloration on Ian's face. His bloody nose has turned red. His busted lip has turned purple. His left eye has turned black. Tears continue to stream down his face with a mixture of mucus and blood that's beginning to dry. He hates Alex. Not just for the physical torment, but for allowing him to destroy Ian's first high school experience. All his efforts to make this the best year possible have just gone in vain within minutes. Tired, he pauses for a moment to wipe the blood from his nose. He can see his breath in the freezing temperature. Alone on a deserted street, Ian screams at the top of his lungs.

Moments later, Ian gets to his neighborhood. He is drained. With no more energy left to run, he walks defeatedly the rest of the way until he reaches his house. Oddly, he spots his mom's and Dr. Price's cars parked in the driveway. Ian knows something does not seem right. He walks inside the house and closes the door behind him. He hears nothing at first, then some mumbling and shuffling coming from Katherine's bedroom. Ian gets to the door and puts his ear against it. He hears Katherine. She sounds like she's giving orders or demanding something. Dr. Price's voice is too muffled to make out what he is saying. Ian then turns the knob and pushes the door open. He sees his mom bent over in the doggy position as Dr. Price thrusts from behind. Katherine screams when she sees Ian and quickly covers herself up.

"What the hell is this?" Ian shouts furiously.

"Ian! What are you doing here?" Katherine says, covering herself up as she sits back on the bed next to Dr. Price, who looks very awkward at the moment. She notices Ian's face is beaten and bloody. "Oh my God, baby! What happened to your face?" she asks.

"What the fuck is this? Why are you fucking my therapist? And you," he says, looking at Dr. Price, "isn't this a conflict of interest? You fucking my mom?" Ian yells.

"Well . . . technically no. It would be a conflict of interest if *you* and I were fucking . . . not to mention illegal . . . wait, how old are you?" Dr. Price asks.

"This is insane," Ian says to himself. He begins feeling dizzy and a bit nauseous.

"Ian, sweetie. I am so sorry. This was not supposed to happen," Katherine pleads, trying her best to ease the situation. It's not working. Suddenly, a sharp headache overcomes Ian. He cringes from the pain but only for a moment. The headache quickly goes away. Katherine is talking to him, but he's unable to concentrate on what she is saying.

"I can't—" Ian says to himself. Images begin flashing through his mind—his violent attack, he and Emma at the New Year's party, the storage-room ceiling, which continues to fissure and pulse violently. The sharp headache returns.

"If it makes you feel better Ian, we can talk about this incident at our next scheduled session. I think I have you down for this Saturday," Dr. Price says.

Ian doesn't say a word. Still cringing from his headache, he simply turns around and walks away.

Katherine calls out his name. She is embarrassed and distraught. She wants to comfort Ian, but she must get dressed first. Ian walks to his bedroom. The headache goes away but his nausea increases. He doesn't feel right. He rushes to the bathroom and vomits in the sink.

He looks at himself in the mirror. "What is happening with me?" he says, breathing heavily. He rinses out his mouth then slowly walks to his bedroom. He feels numb. The pressures and stresses of the day are too much for him to process. His expression is blank and zombielike. He grabs a bag from his closet and throws a few clothes inside. He opens his nightstand drawer and grabs his birthday check and puts it in his bag, then heads downstairs. He notices Dr. Price's car keys on the living room coffee table. He picks them up and looks at them closely. A silver heart-shaped keychain is attached with a photo of Dr. Price and his wife. Ian puts the keys in his pocket. He then walks over to the keyring by the kitchen door and grabs Katherine's car keys as well, then heads out the door, leaving it open.

He hops in Katherine's Lexus, throws his bag in the passenger seat, and cranks up the car. A memory flashes of Ian as a child, sitting on his dad's lap and wiggling the car steering wheel. Ray had pointed out all the simple car mechanisms like the radio, gears, and the windshield wiper switch.

Ian shakes his head and huffs as he puts the car in reverse. Katherine and Dr. Price hear tires screech outside. They look at one another, perplexed. Katherine finishes getting dressed. She rushes to the window and sees Ian driving away.

"He stole my car! Oh shit, what do I do? I should call the police, right?" she asks Dr. Price, hoping for reassurance.

"Relax. I know Ian is in a rebellious state right now. It's best we just give him time to cool down and we'll have a talk with him when he gets back."

"Ian doesn't know how to drive!" Katherine exclaims. Dr. Price looks out the window.

"Well I don't see your car out there, so he must've learned somehow," Dr. Price adds.

Katherine scowls at him stone-faced. "Leave," she demands.

CHAPTER 14

Ian's mind is at full throttle—for sure faster than he's currently driving. Even with his lack of experience, he seems to have the hang of it. He cautiously stays in the slow lane for safe measure. Regardless, driving properly is the last thing on Ian's mind. Unknowingly, he drives through a stop sign, but luckily no other cars are around. His grip is tight on the steering wheel to the point his hands are sweating and his palms are turning red. Ian glances in the rearview mirror, taking note of the imperfections on his face. He takes his sleeve and wipes the remaining blood from his nose. His licks the blood from his swollen lip, then spits a few times out the window. A melancholic rock song plays over the radio station. Ian is unfamiliar with it, but the tone seems to be an appropriate soundtrack to his madness. He shuts off the radio. He feels Dr. Price's car keys poking his leg through his left pocket. Ian pulls out the keys and throws them out the window.

"FUUUUCCKKK!" he yells, beating the steering wheel with his fists. He floors the gas and swerves the car over to an open strip mall parking lot and parks. He continues beating the steering wheel and even aims a few blows at the dashboard as well, screaming until his lungs give out. He has no idea what to do. He's lost. Ian just wants the physical and emotional pain to go away. He also wants things to go back to normal, back to before he had been diagnosed with the lifelong curse of schizophrenia. Back to the way things were before Brandon was pissed at him. Before Emma killed herself. Before he caught his mom doing doggy style. As the car continues to run, Ian sits in silence, almost in a trance.

"Hey, buddy!" a voice says.

Ian quickly turns around to the familiar sound as he yelps. He is shocked to see his father, Ray, sitting in the back seat of the car.

"Dad?" Ian knows this must be a hallucination. The feeling is overwhelming and scary.

"In the flesh . . . well, you know. How've you been? You don't look so good, son. Are you okay?" Ray asks, exuding the loving father role Ian has been missing in his life for so long.

"Why are you here?" Ian asks.

Ray pauses. He then chuckles. "Well you're having problems dealing with this meltdown of yours, so I'm here to offer some help—unlike that shady quack who's fucking your mom right now."

Ian is still in disbelief of what is happening. But he knows he's too far gone at this point. With his back against the steering wheel, his eyes are fixated on Ray. Ian's on guard. For safe measure he keeps his right hand on the car door handle.

"Ian, I'm not going to hurt you, okay? Like I said, I'm here to help—offer advice. I've been through what you're going through," Ray says calmly.

Ian relaxes a little. "I—I guess you're right."

"Absolutely. Our disease is hereditary after all. I have firsthand experience with this."

Ian knows how crazy this situation seems, but he's feeling quite relieved. He could use some fatherly advice from a man he sorely misses. It feels good to finally share commonalities with someone.

"Right. So uh . . . what should I do?" Ian asks.

"Kill yourself."

"What? Uh, that wasn't the answer I was expecting." Ian proclaims, already feeling defeated. He was hoping there would be a few more options left before contemplating that last resort.

"Yeah, take it from me . . ." Ray says, slightly turning in his seat to expose the gunshot wound through the back of his head. The meaty gap is grotesque, revealing brain tissue and clots of blood that drip onto the back seat. The wound looks fresh. "That was the only option I had, and the only option you'll have."

"I can't do that," Ian replies.

Ray sighs. "Listen son, we are talking about a disease in the brain, okay. You think today was bad for you? Life gets harder as you grow older. And given the cards we've been dealt, that's a recipe for disaster. A ticking timebomb. And eventually the bomb will explode." Ian looks inquisitively at Ray as he continues. "Ian, this is something you're going to be living with for the rest of your life. So just end it now and stop torturing yourself," he concludes casually.

"No. I have medication that helps me deal with shit like this," Ian says, remembering that he had forgotten to take his medication this morning.

"Yeah, I can see it's doing you wonders right now." Ray's becoming frustrated. He scratches the back of his head, then continues. "Ian, look at me okay . . ." Ray points to himself with both index fingers, his right hand now covered in blood. "This is your future, alright. Just accept it. You're gonna end up just like me."

Ian knows this is not fatherly advice. He knows what Ray did was wrong, selfish, and gutless. And now he's encouraging him to follow the same path.

"Wow. Even my therapist gives better advice than you. You said I'm gonna end up like you? No I won't. Because I'm not a fucking coward. I'm gonna do something about my problems, you'll see. So fuck you!" Ian shouts.

"Oh, fuck me, huh? Okay, so what the fuck are you gonna do about it then, hotshot? You're gonna get a gun, go to school, and fucking shoot everybody?" Ray asks sardonically.

Ian looks out the driver's side window and sees a giant yellow banner atop a plain white building in the strip mall parking lot. Bold orange letters read: *GUN SHOP & RANGE*. If this is not a sign, then Ian doesn't know what is.

"That's exactly what I'm gonna do," Ian says, grabbing his backpack from the passenger seat.

"Yeah, okay, Rambo . . . good luck with that," Ray says.

"I don't know who that is—" Ian says, exiting the car and slamming the door shut. This gun shop seems to be the answer to Ian's problems. So much so that a ray of sunshine peaks through the dense clouds and shines a beacon of light on it. Ian is now convinced this is exactly what he is supposed to do. And regardless of what happens afterward, he is determined to make sure he finishes the hit list.

The sun brightens up the sky as the clouds start to part. His tunnel vision is focused on the entrance to the gun shop, intensifying as he inches closer to the door. A rushing sound like television static hisses in his head. He grabs the handle and enters the building. The static noise stops. He now hears the soft elevator music projecting from the warehouse speakers. The atmosphere is calm. Several hunting displays are showcased throughout the elongated front entrance. There are only two other customers inside browsing. Ian looks to his right to see a clerk standing behind a long glass counter filled with ammo, firearms, and knives. The selection of guns on the wall behind the clerk grow bigger in size the further down you go.

Ian walks up to the clerk and reads his nametag—Carl, a stocky White man with a beer gut, a red bowl haircut, and a red bushy mustache to match. He and Ian are nearly the same height. Carl is polishing a boldly shiny, onyx-colored Glock 19. He places the weapon in the glass display case and diverts his attention to Ian. Immediately, Carl is suspicious of him, not from his distraught appearance but because of his young-looking face.

"I need guns," Ian demands.

"Whoa, whoa, slow down there, young buck. Now, I need to see some proper identification," Carl says in a deeply rooted country accent.

Ian hesitates for a moment. He reaches into his pocket and pulls out his Lakehurst student ID card and sets it on the counter. Still suspicious, Carl picks it up. Ian's smiling photo is centered below. Carl searches for a birthdate, then hands the card back to Ian. "How old are you?" Carl questions.

"I just turned eighteen."

"Okay, that'll do."

"Cool," Ian says, as he stuffs it back into his pocket.

Carl looks at Ian with an intimidating expression on his face. "Now before we get you a gun, I need to ask you some very important questions. And don't lie because I would know. Now, have you ever been convicted of a felony, or have you been convicted of a misdemeanor in the past five years?"

Ian simply replies, "No."

"Alright . . ." Carl is now flipping through a worker's manual. He forgot the other question he was going to ask. "Ah, okay. Here we go—do you now, or have you ever suffered from a mental health issue or illness?"

Ian ponders for a moment. "Uh, no?"

Carl closes the work manual and tosses it behind him. "Alright, what kinda gun do you want?"

Ian looks through the glass counter at the variety of weaponry. *Ninja stars, cool.* He's like a kid in a deadly candy store. Any weapon seems to be at his disposal. Ian then focuses his attention on the assault rifles hanging on the wall behind Carl. One rifle stands out from the rest.

"I like that one," Ian says, pointing. Carl turns around.

"Ah, that's an AR-15 there. Really good military-style weapon. Semi-automatic. Great for combat use." Carl takes the rifle off of the wall. He explains the workings and history of the weapon, nothing too in-depth, then holds the gun out toward Ian. "Here, see if it's a good fit for you," Carl says.

The feeling is unlike anything Ian has experienced before. He feels like a total badass—powerful, invincible, like he could conquer the world one bullet at a time. His handling of the weapon seems second nature to him. Carl notices and assumes Ian must have more experience with weapons than he originally thought. The grin on Ian's face is off-putting.

Ian plays out the scenario in his head. First, he'll kill Alex, then Jason, then Ashley. He disregards the advice given to him by Ray. Ian figures if anything, he'd rather have a shootout with the police instead of the whole cliché mass murder/suicide thing. That trend is so nineties.

"I also want that gun you were polishing earlier, too," Ian says, nodding his head toward the gun in the case.

"This Glock here? Sure, but I gotta tell you, that AR is a thousand bucks alone. Plus this Glock here is four fifty-nine. I'm assuming you also want bullets, right?"

"Bullets don't come with it?" Ian asks.

Carl starts to laugh. "No sir, which means you need to make every shot count, cause you're paying for it," Carl says, continuing his laughter.

"Well, yeah, I want bullets," Ian says nonchalantly, enamored with his new toy.

Carl's doing the math in his head, but he seems to be having trouble. He pulls a calculator out from inside the counter for better accuracy. "Okay, I'll tell you what, I'll sell you the AR, the Glock, and a box of hollow points for the Glock, and in return I'll add a free ammo cartridge for the AR."

"For how much?" Ian replies, diverting his attention back to Carl.

"I'll let it all go for eighteen-fifty. How's that sound?" Carl asks.

Ian sets the gun down on the counter and pauses for a moment to think.

"You take checks?" he asks.

"Yes we do," Carl says with a smile.

"Perfect." Ian looks down into the glass counter and sees a leg holster for a gun. He points down to it. "Throw in that holster, too."

"Yes sir," Carl replies, getting Ian's arsenal together. The transaction goes smoothly.

Ian stands in full combat mode. The holster is secured to his leg with his Glock 19 at the ready. His AR-15 is strapped to his back. Carl puts his ammo in a plastic smiley face bag, the type you normally see at Chinese restaurants, and hands it over to Ian. "There you go my friend. It was a pleasure doing business with you. Just don't cause any problems with your new toys, alright?" Carl says jokingly.

Ian smiles. "These toys are problem *solvers*, not starters."

Carl lets out a booming laugh. "I know that's right!" Carl shouts. "Happy hunting, Ian!"

Ian thanks Carl and heads out the store. Casually strolling through the parking lot, his tunnel vision has returned and is even worse than before. Ian doesn't even stop for oncoming cars. He ignores the outside noise and makes a beeline to Katherine's sedan. Once inside, he takes a deep breath and cranks up the car. He looks down and turns on the radio. Enjoying the tune, Ian nods along to the music as he drives. He is now ready to live, "La Vida Loca."

Back at the house, Dr. Price is frantically searching the house for his car keys. Katherine trails behind him but is confused as to what he is looking for. She is too busy explaining to him that their sexcapades must come to a complete halt, indefinitely. She sounds annoyed and frustrated. She makes her way into the living room area where Dr. Price has begun searching under couches, the coffee table, the inside of a couple candy dishes on top of the mantel, and just about every other nook and cranny in the space.

"Why are you still here?" Katherine asks.

"Um, earth to terrible mother. I'm looking for my car keys . . . I swear I put them—" He pauses and turns to Katherine. "You don't think Ian took my car keys, do you?"

"No, he took mine."

"I put them right here on this coffee table when I got here."

"They must be somewhere. Oh, and I think this goes without saying, but you will no longer be Ian's psychotherapist from here on out."

"I figured," Dr. Price says, getting to his feet after checking under the large couch. Positioned next to Katherine, he glares at her with arrogance. "And just so you know, your cancellation will have to be in person and you have to fill out some paperwork explaining why you've decided to get treatment elsewhere," he explains, like a spiteful child getting the last laugh.

"I'll be there first thing tomorrow morning," she adds.

"Good."

"Great."

"Fantastic," he says.

"Splendid."

"I can't fucking wait—" The front door opens, interrupting their immature banter. Ian walks in, guns strapped to him like the Terminator. Katherine is shocked. Dr. Price is frozen. They both stare at Ian like a deer in headlights. Dr. Price immediately draws his attention to the AR-15 in Ian's hands.

Katherine calls out to him. "Ian, sweetie, where were you?" Ian doesn't reply.

Dr. Price looks terrified. He tries to ease the tension. "Hey Ian, where'd you get that *sweet* gun? Maybe we can go hunting sometime, yeah?"

Ian says nothing but raises his gun and points it at Dr. Price.

"Whoa, whoa, whoa, whoa, Ian! Hear me out, okay? I'm sorry, alright, I'm very, very, sorry, okay?" Dr. Price pleads, hands in the air. Dr. Price slows his breathing in attempt to reduce his copious sweating. He continues. "You know, it's kind of a funny story, I—" Without warning, the left side of Dr. Price's head explodes in brain matter and red mist. His body quickly drops to the floor.

Katherine screams at the top of her lungs. Twice now, she has been the witness of gun violence in her own home. She is shaking uncontrollably. Her face is covered in red specs and chunks of tissue. Blood streams out of the bullet hole in Dr. Price's skull, pooling onto the carpet.

Ian now turns his attention to Katherine. She's crying and pleading for her life. Katherine looks at him, tears continuing to stream down her face.

Ian stares. He lowers the gun to his side. "I'm so disappointed in you." Ian walks out of the house, slamming the door behind him.

CHAPTER 15

The student body of Lakehurst is buzzing over the news that was shared earlier this morning. Everyone is talking during lunchtime about the suicide of Emma Parsons. Regardless of her reputation or how people felt about her personally, the incident is garnering relatively mixed thoughts. Each clique and group has their own opinions and theories about what really happened and why. Some are upset and feel bad about the ridicule Emma had endured, especially what had happened yesterday. Some feel it is karma for the way Emma carried herself and that something like this was bound to occur in her future at some point. Some don't care at all and find the situation somewhat humorous. Jason is straddling the seat of the lunch table with Ashley sitting next to him. She's eating a tray full of grapes. Jason picks through her tray as well, while drinking a Mountain Dew. They go on about their own theories and assumptions on Emma's suicide.

"Do you know how she did it?" Jason asks.

"Well, Tanya Fielders sits next to me in Algebra, and you know her dad is a cop. Apparently, he was called to the scene. She told me her mom found her in the bathroom, sitting on the toilet with her wrists slit open."

"Oh shit," Jason replies, surprised.

"Yeah. She said when he got there, there was so much blood on the bathroom floor, that it was leaking through the ceiling below. Gnarly shit."

"Yeah, no doubt. I didn't expect that from her. She seemed fine at my party," Jason says.

Ashley eats a couple more grapes, then takes a sip of her Diet Coke. She's thinking. "You don't think . . . Alex had anything to do with it do you?"

Jason's stunned she asked that question. Jason knows Alex is capable of a lot of things—drug use, bullying, beating up supposed friends. But aiding in someone's suicide would be crossing the line, even for Alex. He is not even sure how someone could aid another person into ending their own life, but Alex wouldn't do something that extreme . . . he thinks.

"No. That's crazy. Why would he do that?"

"Because he cheated on Sam with her. Did you know about that?"

Jason plays coy. He knows nothing about nothing. That's his story and he's sticking to it. "No. When did that happen?"

"Last summer. Sam found out at your party. That's why she left."

"Wow. That's news to me," Jason says casually, taking a sip of his Dew.

"I'm just saying, he's being really shady lately. More so than before. Like he's hiding something."

"I'll say. He beat up Ian this morning in the smoke spot."

Ashley is shocked. Even though she never really liked Ian, she knows he didn't deserve to get physically assaulted in the way Jason is describing to her.

"Oh my God. I mean, the kid was creepy and all, and I never really cared for him, but I don't think he deserved that. But that's my point. You need to keep an eye on Alex 'cause he's clearly disturbed."

Jason appreciates Ashley's concerns, but he is not at all worried about Alex or his actions. He is his own person and a true friend to Alex, so he feels it's time to switch the topic of conversation from high school drama.

"How's Salem doing?" Ashley's face lights up at the sound of her cat's name. You would think she had given birth to Salem by the way she cares for and nurtures him. He is her favorite thing right now. In fact, Jason and Salem are competing for the number one spot.

"Salem is doing just fine. My mom complains but fuck her." Ashley takes another sip of her soda.

Jason laughs and tells Ashley that's one of the reasons why he loves her—she's an outspoken hottie with a Daria-like attitude. Not to mention her amazing breasts. He pulls her closer to him and kisses the side of her neck. Their PDA is short-lived once Alex takes a seat at the table. Ashley's demeanor changes instantly. Her face is stone cold. Jason greets his friend as they fist bump one another.

"Sup Jason? What's up Ash?" Alex says.

Ashley doesn't respond. Instead, she turns toward Jason. "I gotta go. I suddenly got a headache. I'll see you after school?"

"Yeah, of course." They share a kiss. Ashley grabs her tray and walks away from the table.

Alex is confused. *Why is she acting like such a bitch? Must be because of Sam.* "What's up with her?" he asks Jason.

Jason sighs. "She thinks you had something to do with Emma's suicide."

Alex starts laughing. "What? She does realize how ridiculous that sounds, right?"

"She only said it 'cause she knows you two hooked up last year."

"Yeah, okay. And what kind of Jedi mind-control power do I have to make her fucking kill herself? That's crazy," Alex says, chuckling at his statement.

Jason shrugs his shoulders, takes another sip of Mountain Dew, then burps.

Brandon and Samantha are browsing through shelves and shelves of books in the library. Their conversation flows naturally as they discuss their favorite books, favorite movies, and celebrity crushes.

Samantha has a thing for Ryan Phillipe, while Brandon has always had a crush on Halle Berry. They find several informational books on history and the life and times of Princess Diana. Brandon picks out some of the books and the two discuss whether they think each one will be beneficial to Samantha's final or not. She decides to add Queen Elizabeth II to the equation to beef up the length of her final paper. Holding four books in hand, Brandon leads the way to a computer station. They pull up two chairs next to one another and take their seats. They surf the internet, finding a bunch more useful info on the Princess of Wales, the Queen, and everything in between.

As Samantha takes notes, Brandon takes note of her leg bumping occasionally into his during their study time. It seems intentional. He is beginning to get aroused. Brandon places his left arm across his lap. *Is she trying to get me hard on purpose? Just relax. Baseball, right? Isn't that what people think of? Wait, what am I supposed to think of? I don't know anything about baseball.* He takes a look around the library. Quite a few students are inside. A sudden uneasy feeling comes over Brandon. The library is quiet. He knows as well as anybody that libraries are supposed to be quiet, but this seems different. It's unnerving. Like a calm before the storm.

"Are you okay?" Samantha asks.

"Yeah, I was just thinking. Maybe we could go see a movie together sometime. You know, to celebrate all the hard work you've done," Brandon says nervously.

Samantha laughs. "You mean all the work that *we've* done. And I'd love to," Samantha says smiling.

"Then it's a date," Brandon exclaims.

Samantha likes the sound of that idea. The bell rings.

"Well, I'll let you get to class. I'll stay here and do some more studying," she says.

"You're not going to class?" Brandon asks.

"My next class is what this project is for, so I'm just being proactive." Samantha smiles.

"Well, I know for sure I can afford to miss a day of home ec," Brandon says, hoping to persuade encouragement from Samantha to stay.

Samantha looks pleasantly surprised. "Can you bake?"

"Hell yeah! I can make you a German chocolate cake to die for." They both laugh.

"One of these days, I'm going to call your bluff," Samantha adds.

"Please do. That way you'll know I'm not lying."

Touché, Samantha thinks. She only assumes this means their budding relationship is far from over. Brandon makes her optimistic about the future and what's to come. "That's great. Well, let's get studying, then," Samantha says, moving to a table in the center of the library.

A good portion of students exit the library and head back to class. The library is now about a third full. Brandon then remembers the treat he had stashed in his bookbag earlier today. He reaches in the front pocket and pulls out a Kit-Kat bar. Hiding it from the librarian, he holds it under the table, showing it to Samantha. She looks down, surprised. Chocolate is her weakness. The two each break off a piece and enjoy.

CHAPTER 16

The afternoon sun gleams from its highest point in the sky. Katherine's car pulls into the student parking lot of Lakehurst High. Ian parks the car erratically in a spot closest to the overhead walkway that leads through the campus maze. He pauses for a moment, staring out the windshield. He looks possessed. Ian has no second guesses about what he is about to undertake. This was an event that was bound to happen. The right cocktail of trauma, betrayal, and physical pain has manifested its way into rage.

He steps out of the car, which is left running, and walks around to the open trunk. A small handful of students smoking cigarettes in the parking lot glance over and take notice.

"Yo, who is that?" one of them says. The rest of the group is just as confused as to the identity of this individual. They simply watch as Ian takes the leg holster out of the trunk and straps it to his thigh. He pulls the Glock 19 from the trunk and slides it into the holster. Ian's face is emotionless. His tactical and robotic movements indicate a person who's on a clear mission. He then pulls the AR-15 from the trunk and slings the strap over his shoulder. Ian slams the trunk, handling the assault weapon with positive control. He's ready for action. The parking lot crew witnesses this set up and cannot believe what they are seeing. In disbelief, they gawk as Ian begins walking toward an entrance to the school.

Lunch has just ended, and classes have resumed, so the landscape of the school is bare, desolate, and quiet. Ian looks to his left. He doesn't see or hears anyone. He looks to his right and sees a squirrel digging under a bush. Ian contemplates shooting the squirrel, but he restrains himself and continues moving forward. He reaches the entrance to the building where his homeroom class is located, which is the first door to the left. Ashley and Ian share the same homeroom, but she won't be there because homeroom has already come and gone. He begins deliberating what class she should be in right now. Ian hadn't thought this part through enough. He cannot keep up with anyone's schedule except his own, really. He knows that Samantha should be in World History and Brandon should be in Home Ec. He then remembers Jason has chemistry at this time but is drawing a blank when it comes to Ashley and Alex.

Ian grabs hold of the door handle and enters the building. Looking down the hall, he notices three students walking from the opposite end of the hall, and one of them is Ashley. She looks down the hall upon hearing the door open. The sun creates a glare in her vision. She can't quite make out who it is until the door shuts behind them, eliminating the glare. She sees Ian, holding a rifle-style weapon.

Ashley freezes.

Ian continues walking toward her. He and Ashley lock eyes.

"Ian?" she says softly. Her voice quivers. She's fearful. Ian raises his gun, taking aim. Ashley's eyes bulge as she quickly turns around to escape the blast. She doesn't get far. Ian fires off a round. The bullet hits the back of Ashley's left calf. A chuck of her leg explodes from the shot, causing her to fall to the floor. The alarming gunshot sound echoes through the building hall. The other two students scream and run out of sight down the corridor. Ashley's screams and cries travel through the hall, echoing with agony. She tries squirming away by dragging herself, leaving a trail of blood on the vinyl flooring. Ashley screams for help, but no one is coming to the rescue. She watches in horror as Ian inches his way closer and closer to her. He gets a good look at her leg. It looks as if an animal has torn her calf completely off. Blood quickly trails from the wound. Once Ashley realizes Ian is close, she gives up trying to escape. She turns on her back, getting a clear view of Ian's demented expression. She just hopes that her pleas and cries are enough to be granted some form of mercy.

Ian looks at her, for what he knows will be the final time. He takes aim and fires another round into Ashley's chest, killing her instantly. He slowly takes in a deep breath, then slowly exhales. "I knew you never liked me," he says. An electrifying feeling of satisfaction takes over. Some weight has been lifted. He hears his watch beeping and looks down at the face. It's 12:40 p.m. Time for a smoke.

As usual, Alex and Jason are at the smoke spot passing a joint back and forth. They have been chatting about all the drama that has been happening lately, particularly on Alex's account. Alex reflects on the beating he gave to Ian earlier and expresses to Jason how he feels a little bad by how things went down but is by no means sorry for what he did. He feels he's been disrespected by someone he trusted and for that, Ian needed to be taught a lesson. He needed to let Ian know who the Alpha is and that he is someone not to be fucked with. He isn't even that mad at the fact that Ian likes Samantha, he's just angry that he had to go behind his back and pull a move on her without thinking Alex would find out—a blatant lack of respect. Alex then expresses his take on Emma's suicide, stating she obviously had issues percolating from previous traumas in her life if she had been so willing to kill herself because of an exposed naked picture of her. But he notes that he wasn't surprised.

"Emma's always been a fucking drama queen," he says.

Jason agrees and passes the joint back to Alex. "So, what's up with you and Sam?" Jason asks.

Alex takes a drag and exhales quickly. "Dude, I don't know what the fuck's up with her. I'm honestly done. Plus I think she's been hanging around that nerdy Black kid, Brandon, behind my back. So as far as I'm concerned, she can go fuck herself."

Jason glances down at his watch as Alex offers him the joint again. "Nah, dude. I gotta get to class. Mrs. Conner said this is literally the last time I can be late. I'll catch you later though, dude." Jason fist bumps Alex, then leaves the storage area.

Alex takes a couple more drags then looks down at the joint.

"This is some really good weed," he says, exhaling. Moments later he hears mumbling coming from down the hall to the side exit of the gymnasium. One of the voices sounds like Jason. Alex eavesdrops. *Maybe Coach caught him.* Alex then hears what sounds like whimpering. An ear-shattering bang explodes the quiet atmosphere of the vacant gymnasium. Alex nearly jumps out of his skin at the loud bang, dropping the joint to the floor. Part of him wants to think maybe someone's pulling a firework prank in the building. But a major part of him thinks it is very possible that what he heard was a gunshot.

At that moment, Principal Owens is on his office computer illegally downloading music onto his hard drive. He doesn't feel bad about it. He knows thousands of people are doing the exact same thing. His office phone starts to ring. He doesn't answer. It rings again. Again, no answer. Moments later, Heather bursts through his office door. Principal Owens is startled. He straightens himself up and clears his computer screen. By his reaction, Heather thinks he may have been watching porn, but what she needs to say is more pressing than trying to figure out what the principal was doing.

"Jesus, Heather, do you knock?"

"Why are you not answering your phone? I just got a ton of calls and reports from teachers that say we have an active shooter on campus!" Heather says frantically.

"What?"

"He's already killed a student, sir!"

Principal Owens is in shock. He never thought something like this could happen at a school that he was in charge of. The feeling is strange and overwhelming for him, but he has trained for this. He instructs Heather to lock down the entrances to the office and to call the police. Principal Owens immediately removes his blazer and grabs the mic to the PA system.

"Attention students, faculty, and staff. Code red! I repeat, code red! This is not a drill. Active shooter on the premises. Lockdown has commenced. Code red! I repeat, code red!" Principal Owens puts the mic down on his desk. He's flustered. Agitated. Dumbfounded at the fact that this is actually happening. "Fuck!" He screams, unaware he still has a hot mic.

In the library, the gray-haired librarian, Ms. Gibson, is instructing students to hide underneath the tables and to be as quiet as possible. Ms. Gibson is in a panic. She has never dealt with a situation like this in all her twenty-plus years as an educator. Her mind is a bit frazzled, but she instinctively does her best as guardian to these kids because now she knows that she is the one responsible for the safety of them all. Not to mention, protecting her own life as well. She rushes to the front double doors of the library and locks them from the inside. She turns off all the lights and tells the students once more to be quiet and to stay where they are. Ms. Gibson hides underneath her desk. She dials 911 and waits to be answered. Her breathing is heavy. She tries holding the phone steady to her ear, but her shaking won't allow it.

Samantha and Brandon are hidden under the same table. Samantha's bulging eyes stare at the double doors, hoping the unknown assailant doesn't try to enter. Her fear and anxiety are at an all-time high. Her claustrophobia sets in and her mind becomes frantic. *What if he comes in here? We're trapped. Just sitting ducks waiting to be picked off.*

Samantha's experienced this familiar feeling before. As a kid she had attended Camp Forest Lake every summer back when her family lived in Connecticut. At age six, a couple of kids tricked Samantha by telling her that the camp counselors kept a big stash of candy in the office basement. They had escorted Samantha to the vacant office shack, pointing inside to a closet where the candy was supposed to be located. Samantha had opened the closet door only to realize that it had stairs in it that led down to a basement area. Two of the campers had pushed Samantha down the stairs onto the concrete floor. Scratched and bruised, she had tried to scramble back up the steps, but the kids slammed the door shut and placed a chair underneath the handle. The basement air smelled moldy and thick. Samantha was trapped in total darkness except for the beams of light shining through a couple of grimy windows that lined the basement at ground level outside. She made her way back down the steps and tried to get to a window but was too short to reach them. She began hearing chanting noises. The sounds seemed to be coming from a young girl, deep in the darkest part of the basement. The language was not English. Terrified, Samantha rushed back up the stairs and pounded on the door, crying for help. She had screamed until her throat was sore. She stayed in the pitch-black, musty room for hours as her cries went unheard. Eventually, the door swung open and Samantha ran into the arms of one of the counselors, who consoled her. The experience traumatized her so much that she left camp and never returned. She had felt so helpless and trapped.

That same terrible feeling has returned. As a tear falls down her face, she quickly wipes it away, hoping Brandon didn't notice. He turns to look at Samantha. She looks frightened.

"Hey, we're gonna be okay," he says softly.

"Is this really happening? This doesn't seem real."

Brandon grabs hold of Samantha's hand and squeezes. "We're gonna be fine. I promise."

Samantha pauses for a moment. She takes a deep breath and slowly exhales. She looks at Brandon and nods. His grip is beginning to calm her down.

Alex, standing alone in the storage area doesn't move a muscle. He's just finished hearing the principal's announcement and is sure he is in the clutches of the shooter. He is afraid to peek down into the locker room. He slowly takes a step forward, then another, then another. He wants to call out Jason's name but knows if anyone's out there, Alex is giving them verbal coordinates to his location. He takes another step. At the entryway of the locker room, Alex slowly attempts to watch for suspicious activity. He gets a peek into the desolate locker room, seeing nothing out of the ordinary. Attempting to sneak out to safety, Alex is blocked as Ian pops from around the corner. Startled, Alex yelps and falls back inside the storage room. He crawls back, noticing the striking appearance of Ian's face, his tactical get up, and most of all, his high-powered rifle.

Ian slowly approaches Alex. "I knew you'd be here. It's like you never left," Ian says ominously. Alex sobs. He unknowingly backs himself into a corner of the storage room. Ian stops. He notices the fear in Alex's eyes and gives him a look of perplexity. "What's wrong? You didn't think I was capable of something like this? Neither did I. I guess you knocked some sense into me, right?" Ian asks.

Alex pleads. Snot and spit project when he speaks. "Please, please, Ian. I'm sorry, okay. I'm so, so, sorry . . . you can have Samantha! Just please let me go, PLEASE."

Ian looks annoyed. He then chuckles at Alex's begging. "Everyone's always sorry when they get caught." Ian aims his gun at Alex's face.

Alex is frozen with terror. He knows this is the end.

Ian takes one shot from a five-foot distance away. The result is extreme. Alex's head bursts like a water balloon. The spewing blood and ruptured tissue splatter on the cement wall behind him, the remains slowly trailing down. Half of Alex's head is gone. His lifeless body slumps over to the wall on his right.

"Wow, I was *not* expecting that," Ian says to himself, surprised by the graphic results. He wipes the blood spatter off his face as he stares at Alex, getting one last look at his defaced corpse. "Serves you right, dead fuck." Ian spits on Alex's body, adding insult to death, then simply walks away.

He steps outside into the oppressing brightness of the sun. He doesn't hear or see a soul in sight. Unsure of what to do next, Ian figures he'll head to the building closest to him. He walks into complete silence. The hall is lined with classrooms to the left and right. Ian starts checking doors, curious if one is unlocked. He is unsuccessful. He continues nonchalantly walking down the hall, checking doors.

He's getting bored. *This is getting boring. Where the fuck are the police? Why haven't they gotten here yet?* By this point, Ian was expecting that he would be involved in an epic shootout with the police, but no action of any kind is happening. He then notices a vending machine off to the left side of the hall. Each row is filled with chips, candy, and sweet pastry snacks lined at the bottom. Ian knows exactly what he wants. He pulls a stack of bills from his pocket. Hundreds, fifties, twenties, fives. He finally gets to single bills and grabs a dollar. Placing the rest of the stash in his pocket, Ian inserts the bill and punches *C8*, on the keypad. The spiral divider rotates until a Snickers bar falls to the bottom. Ian grabs his candy bar. A satisfying look comes over his face.

"Hey!" a voice shouts. Ian's expression quickly shifts back to a menacing glare. He sees Mr. Sadler, his human bio teacher, standing about a fifteen-foot distance from him. Mr. Sadler, dressed in khakis, a navy-blue button-up shirt (which is tucked in), and loafers, slowly approaches him. Ian puts his Snickers bar in his pocket.

"Ian, right?" Mr. Sadler asks. Ian instinctively points his gun. Mr. Sadler stops, raising his hands as a form of surrender. "It's okay, it's fine. I'm just here to ask why you are doing this?"

Ian doesn't respond. He just stares.

Mr. Sadler continues. "I know high school can be hell sometimes, but this is not the way to go about it. Life doesn't end after high school, Ian. You have plenty of time to be who you want to—" Mr. Sadler's interrupted by a gunshot. Flinching, he's not even aware that he's been hit. With both hands still raised, he looks over to his left hand, which is now only a thumb and a partial index finger. Everything else is gone. Blood gushes from his wound. He screams in agony, shocked to see what's left of his hand. "Oh my God!" he yells.

"Now, unless you want the next one to go through your skull, I suggest you shut the fuck up and GET THE FUCK OUT OF MY WAY!" Ian screams.

Mr. Sadler, now applying pressure to his left wrist, takes Ian's advice. He tries running back down the hall he came, slipping on his blood in the process. He gets away and rushes back to his classroom. He bangs on the door, screaming to be let in. A student unlocks the door and lets him in. The class full of students are stunned when they see his hand. Mr. Sadler turns the lock and falls to the ground with his back against the door. He's in shock. Sweating, bloody, and crying from pain.

"That kid is fucking insane!" he says to the class, as some students try to find first aid materials to help.

Back in the library, students are reacting to the sound of the gunshot moments earlier. Their panic is causing unnecessary noise. Ms. Gibson, with phone in hand, is motioning for students to be quiet and to stay hidden under the tables. She expresses to the operator that the gunshots sound very close and that they should hurry and get to the school as soon as possible. As calm as she is trying to present herself in front of the students, it's not working. She looks and sounds just as terrified, if not more. Samantha covers her mouth in shock at the sound of the gunshot. Brandon squeezes her hand harder in an attempt to focus her attention on him instead of the chaos outside the library. As Ms. Gibson stays on the line, the operator asks if all entrances to the library are locked.

"Yes, the main entrance is locked as well as—oh my God." Ms. Gibson realizes there is a second entrance into the library from the librarian's office, which then leads to the building hallway. She drops the phone. She rises to a crouch and walks from behind the desk. She quietly tells the students that she has to retrieve something from her office and for them to stay quiet and to not move. She obviously doesn't want to tell them the truth, that her carelessness could cost them their lives, but if she can lock that office exit to the hall, everything should be okay. She makes her way through the library to the far-right side that leads down a corridor to the office. Her mission is simple and sneaky. She gets down the corridor to the office and opens the door, only to find Ian standing in front of her with his gun pointed directly at her head. She sees the side door to the office is wide open, exposing the building hallway.

"Turn around and go back inside," he says. Ms. Gibson trembles in fear. She agrees and slowly turns around and walks back toward the library, with Ian following behind, his gun pointed at her back. The students see Ms. Gibson return, looking distraught and frightened. They then see Ian appear behind her from around the corner. The students scream, gasp, and cower in place. There is nothing they can do now.

"Thanks for leaving that door unlocked. I was starting to get bored out there," Ian says.

One student speaks out. "Thanks a lot, Ms. Gibson."

"Alright, everybody out from under the tables, or wherever you're hiding, and have a seat right here!" Ian points to the open floor area of the library. Students carefully crawl from underneath the tables. Some students appear from behind bookshelves and join the group. Ian tells Ms. Gibson to join the rest of the students and have a seat on the floor. As the floor area begins filling up with the students, Ian notices

Brandon and Samantha appear from underneath a table together. He's confused. He had no idea they even knew each other.

"Brandon? Sam? What are you two doing here?" he asks.

Brandon and Samantha don't know what to say. They look at each other, then back to Ian, speechless. They see his face is bruised and bloody. They then take note of the dangerously scary weapon in his hands. Samantha wants to help Ian and question him about what happened, but the terror of seeing him in this distressed manner, clutching a weapon renders her stunned.

"Well, I'm glad you're both here," Ian says. "You get to witness the beginning of a brand-new Ian. It feels like I've been baptized, a fresh start to a new and exciting journey. Plus this thing is so much fun to shoot." Ian points the AR in the air and pulls the trigger.

The library of students gasps and flinch at the clicking sound of the trigger.

"What the fuck?" Ian says, confused. He pulls the trigger several more times, but nothing happens. He takes the ammo cartridge out of the gun and sees it's empty. He realizes that Carl shortchanged him on ammo. "Goddammit Carl! What the fuck!"

Ian removes the gun strap and throws the AR-15 to the ground. He then pulls out his Glock. "Luckily I have a backup." Ian points the gun in the air and fires off a round.

The group screams. The manic grin on Ian's face is horrifying. Gunfire seems to arouse him in a way. Samantha looks as if she is on the verge of having a panic attack. Ian then focuses his attention on Brandon. "Pretty cool huh?" he asks.

Brandon nods his head. "Yeah, that's pretty cool," Brandon says, voice cracking. The realization that he might die today is finally sinking in. Worst of all, he'll feel as though he has broken his promise to Samantha that everything will be okay. He now knows, regardless of what happens, everything will not be okay.

Ian looks anxious, constantly looking through the skinny rectangular windows on the library doors for any suspecting cops or

SWAT team members trying to gain access to the library.

"Are these fuckers tailgating or something? Why is no one coming here to help?" Ian demands, unknowingly pointing his Glock in the direction of one terrified student. He begins ferociously shaking his head while mouthing the words, "I don't know, I don't know," hoping to God Ian points his gun elsewhere. Ian rolls his eyes and sighs. He takes another look out the window, then focuses his attention back to his hostages.

"Both of you, stand up," Ian orders, pointing at Brandon and Samantha. They both stand. "What was that thing you said to me the other day? Something about me being a *sometimey* friend. Right?" Ian nonchalantly waves his Glock as he's talking.

Now Brandon looks like he's on the verge of a panic attack. Beads of sweat appear on his forehead. *Oh my God, he's gonna shoot me.*

"I guess everyone is seeing what a crazy schizo I am now." Ian smiles. He looks over at Samantha and notices the frightened look on her face. He wants her to feel comfortable and wants to assure her that she will be fine. "Hi Sam," Ian says cheerfully.

"Hi Ian," Samantha responds, the lump in her throat making the words sound like a croak.

"I just want to say that I appreciate everything you've done for me, and I want to tell you in person that I am not going to shoot you." Samantha is somewhat relieved. Her inhales and exhales sound sporadic as if she's scared to breathe.

Both she and Brandon stand completely still.

"I do want to ask you a question, though." Samantha is fearful of what he may ask. Her mind wonders through all sorts of scenarios. *What if he asks me to kill Brandon? Maybe he wants to know where Alex is.* "Will you go out with me?" Ian asks in a soft and sweet tone.

Samantha doesn't immediately respond. She has to build up the courage to even speak at this moment. She dry swallows, then speaks.

"Um, that's sweet Ian. But, um . . . I have a boyfriend," she says, her voice like a fragile branch on the verge of snapping off a tree limb with just the slightest gust of wind.

"Alex, yeah. Well, you don't have to worry about him anymore, 'cause he's dead," Ian says plainly.

Samantha's eyes enlarge. "What?" she cries out.

"Yeah, I shot him in the face like ten minutes ago," he says carelessly.

"Oh my God." Samantha covers her mouth with both hands. She is in absolute shock.

"No, no this is good. He's out of the picture so we can finally have a relationship." The optimism in Ian's voice shows just how out of touch with reality Ian is. Samantha just stares at him.

"Why are you doing this?" Brandon says. He figures if he is going to die today, he needs a good explanation as to why. He knows it obviously has something to do with Ian's current mental state, and whatever happened to his face, but he just wants to know how they all got here. What was the straw that broke the camel's back?

Ian lowers his gun. "Because I'm a fool. I tricked myself into thinking everyone had my best interests at heart. I'm so gullible. I let my guard down for the first time and I get stabbed in the back, multiple times. You see, you don't get it. You don't know what it's like to be discriminated against. To be ostracized, bullied. To be hated just because of what you are. Well I've decided to take back control," Ian declares.

Brandon looks puzzled. He looks over at Samantha, who's as pale as a ghost. "Is he being serious?" Brandon asks.

Samantha doesn't respond.

"What?" Ian asks, gripping his Glock tighter.

Wow, Brandon thinks to himself.

"Nigga, I'm *Black!*" Brandon shouts. "I think I know better than *anyone* here what it means to feel discriminated against," he says, looking around the library of White faces. "I honestly don't think *you* know what it means to be discriminated against," Brandon protests frustratingly.

Samantha looks at Brandon, fearful for his outburst, but admiring his courage. She sees a brave soul in Brandon but thinks to herself, *Does he have a death wish?*

Ian walks up and points his gun in Brandon's face.

Samantha gasps.

"Does it feel like this?" Ian asks.

Brandon's now realizing the riskiness of his outburst. He quickly agrees. "Yep, I'd say it feels exactly like this. One hundred percent. Sorry for talking," Brandon says timidly as he cowers.

"I thought so." Ian puts the gun down. He, along with the rest of the library, hears the faint sounds of sirens coming from outside the building. They unify in optimism and a shared sense of rescue. The group gets antsy thinking help should arrive through those double doors at any minute. "Alright everyone, calm down. This isn't over." Ian proclaims.

"But it can be," Brandon says. He positions himself in a space of comfort. He doesn't act threatened or scared, but rather concerned and supportive. He steps a little closer toward Ian, who's nearest to the library entrance. "Ian, I understand what it's like to be different. And bullied. And feeling oppressed. The important thing is to hold your head high and . . . to be yourself. You're my friend, Ian, and I care about you. I don't want things to end this way. You can stop this right now and no one else has to get hurt."

Ian doesn't immediately respond. A moment goes by where he hears the encouragement of his father telling him to kill himself. He then remembers that this journey is not about giving up. This is a journey of revenge. And it must end epically. Ian steps closer to Brandon.

"I'm afraid it's too late. No going back now," he tells Brandon, in a rather depressing tone. Ian spots one of the students attempting to escape in his peripheral vision. He quickly aims his Glock at the young freshman, who stops in his tracks. "Hey! Get the fuck back!" Ian yells. The freshman pleads to Ian as he slowly backs away, retreating with the rest of the group. Ian is moments from pulling the trigger.

Brandon sees this as his opportunity and rushes Ian, grabbing hold of the Glock as they wrestle for it. Ian has the majority of the grip, but his hold is slipping away. He pulls the trigger, distorting both of their senses. The rest of the group screams and cowers under the tables. The bullet pierces through a row of books lined on a shelf. The fight continues to the floor. Their struggle seems to be even on both ends. Brandon is on top of Ian, but it is unclear who has positive control over the weapon. Suddenly, a shot is fired. Both Ian and Brandon freeze, staring into each other's eyes.

"Brandon!" Samantha cries out. Brandon backs off of Ian, crawling away as he's pointing the gun. Ian has been shot in the abdomen. He clutches his midsection as he cries out.

Samantha helps Brandon up to his feet. He looks traumatized from the ordeal. His body is stiff as he continues pointing the gun.

"You shot me, dude! Ow, this fucking hurts!" Ian screams out.

"Everybody out!" Brandon yells to the crowd.

Ms. Gibson immediately stands up, guiding the students out of the library. Everyone disperses in a speedy manner with Ms. Gibson trailing behind, leaving the main three in the library alone. Brandon looks at the gun in his hand and is repulsed. He tosses it away, far from where Ian lays.

"I should've bought a bulletproof vest," Ian says to himself, clutching his stomach.

Samantha grabs Brandon by the hand. They stare at each other, either mesmerized or stunned. They embrace with a tearful hug, solidifying an unbreakable bond they'll share for the rest of their lives.

"Hey! You guys, help me please!" Ian shouts, squirming on the ground as he's holding his stomach. The blood flow is pretty rapid. It won't be long before the carpet is soaked. He continues begging as Brandon and Samantha slowly approach.

Ian takes his bloody hand, extending it toward Brandon. The pitiful look on his face is apologetic. "Guys, help me please. Brandon, dude help! I'm dying," Ian begs, extending his hand out further.

Brandon stares, emotionless. He then leans over, extending his hand, bypassing Ian's reach, to grab the Snickers bar sticking out of Ian's pocket.

"I have a bit of a sweet tooth," he numbly tells Samantha. Samantha, wiping away tears, nods her head. Brandon slips the candy in his pocket. Samantha, still holding his hand, guides Brandon as they exit the library.

"I was gonna eat that. So you both are just gonna leave me here? Please, I'm sorry alright! Just help me!" There is no response. "You guys are fucking assholes!" Ian cries. He then hears snickering coming from his right. He looks over to see Ray leaning up against the front desk with a box of Cracker Jacks in his hands.

"See, I knew this wouldn't work," Ray says amusingly, continuing his laughter.

"Fuck off, Dad," Ian weakly utters, coughing up blood.

CHAPTER 19

Four months later, Samantha is standing in the mirror, applying just a tad of makeup. She fully embraces her natural look, but this occasion requires a little embellishment. A touch of blush, some mascara, and peach-flavored lip gloss. Her plush bedroom is scattered with stuffed animals, floral-print furniture pieces, and a white cloud of a comforter. A small portable television sits on top of a stack of textbooks on the corner of Samantha's dresser, angled toward her.

Her focus is on her makeup application, but she is listening attentively to the television as a news segment is covering the shooting event that took place at Lakehurst High months prior. The reporter, Sue Chin, recaps the incident with added detail. She explains how Ian purchased the weapons he used to carry out the violent act. Standing in front of the same gun shop, protesters are circling the property with picket signs and chanting for gun control and for the establishment to be shut down.

"Reports show that eighteen-year-old Ian Moss used a military style AR-15 assault rifle to carry out the heinous act that took the lives of three students and injured one teacher. Alex Castillo, Jason Cunningham, and Ashley Campbell tragically lost their lives. Authorities add that an additional shooting took place before Ian Moss came to Lakehurst High. They had received a 911 call from his mother after Ian shot and killed his therapist, Dr. Andrew Price, bringing the death toll to four victims."

Samantha turns her head toward the screen. She shakes her head, then looks back at the mirror to apply more mascara.

Sue continues. "The carnage ended with Ian Moss getting shot in the abdomen by a fellow classmate, Brandon Scott, who authorities are calling a local hero. I've been told by reports that Ian Moss is recovering and will be set to go on trial within the next couple of weeks, where sources say it is likely he will plea not guilty by reason of insanity. Protesters here are calling for actions to be taken to prevent tragedies like this from happening again. I'm here with gun shop owner Carl who says guns are not the problem." Sue walks over to Carl, who is standing off near the entrance of his gun shop. He looks pissed, but eager to put in his two cents on the situation. "Carl, what do you make of these protestors who say we need more regulations on guns?"

"Guns are not the problem here. It's crazy people who get guns that are the problem!" Carl says, looking into the camera.

"The suspect, who is said to suffer from a mental disability, purchased his weapon here." The mic goes back to Carl.

"Legally! He purchased his weapon legally. He showed me proper identification—"

"His school ID," Sue adds.

"He passed the questionnaire—"

"By lying," Sue also adds.

"It is not my responsibility to know what people do when they leave my store!"

"But it is your responsibility to use good judgment on who should and who shouldn't have access to a gun, am I right?" Sue says in a snarky way.

Carl feels he's being pressed on a matter that he has no control over. "You know what I think, I think this is all some false flag tactic so that the government can take away our gun rights! Using the media to spread misinformation to get everyone to go out and protest against their own (bleep) rights, which is retarded to me. But I'll tell you what—" Carl grabs Sue's hand and pulls the microphone closer to his mouth. "Come on down to Guns and Range today and get fifty percent off all guns and ammo if you come and punch one of these (bleep) sissy protesting sons of (bleep) right in the (bleep) mouth!" Carl says into the camera. Sue pulls her arm back as Carl turns around and gives the protesting crowd the bird.

The crowd boos him.

Samantha looks over and notices a small heart-shaped gold necklace hanging on the side of her vanity mirror. She picks it up and admires it. It was a gift from Alex. Samantha then reminisces about their first date. Alex had been so sweet then. They were so innocent. So much had happened and Alex had changed into someone she didn't recognize by the end. But he hadn't deserved what happened to him. She decides she would rather remember the good times.

She takes the necklace off the mirror and places it around her neck. Sherry walks into Samantha's room and notices the news segment. The reporter is trying her best to get word about the upcoming trial from Katherine, who hides her face from the cameras and jumps into the back seat of her lawyer's car. Sherry turns the television off thinking it will upset Samantha.

"You really don't need to be watching that right now," she says concerningly.

"Mom, it's fine." Sherry pauses for a moment to admire her daughter. Dabbing gloss on her lips, she notices her mom staring at her in the mirror. She turns around in her graduation gown, confused. "What?" Samantha asks.

Sherry smiles. "I'm just so proud of you, honey. And I'm so glad you're here." Samantha smiles. Sherry reaches her arms out as the two embrace in a tight hug. "You are so brave, and smart, and beautiful, and I couldn't be happier or prouder to call you my daughter." Sherry brushes Samantha's hair behind her ear.

Samantha again smiles. "Thanks, Mom."

Sherry gives Samantha a supportive kiss on the forehead. "Now hurry up because we have to get there fifteen minutes early," Sherry says as she exits the room.

Samantha brushes her gown, removing lint and some slight

wrinkles. She sprays some perfume on her neck, then stares into the mirror. She cannot believe the day is finally here. After everything that she has been through, Samantha feels she deserves this sense of accomplishment and strength. She is truly proud of herself. She grabs the matching cap to her gown and heads out of the bedroom.

At Brandon's house that morning, Marcus and Tina sit waiting in the living area. Marcus sits in the single recliner reading the latest issue of the *Lakehurst Journal*. Tina is perched on the adjacent couch tuned into the same news segment detailing the shooting incident. The sun bleeds brightly through the open blinds. Tina looks very attentive, anxious even, as her foot bounces off her crossed leg. Sue Chin explains that Ian will most likely plead the insanity defense, news Tina is not at all pleased to hear as she shakes her head at the television.

"Not surprising. All he's gonna get is a slap on the wrist. They need to fry his skinny White ass!" she yells at the screen.

Marcus is in his own world until he sees Brandon in his cap and gown coming down the stairs.

"There's the man of the hour," he says. Tina turns her head and is overcome with emotion, almost to the verge of tears. She rushes to her pride and joy as Marcus takes his time ascending from the comfort of his recliner.

"Oh, my baby is so handsome," she says, brushing off his gown and adjusting his cap.

"Mom, stop." Brandon replies, pushing her arms away.

"I'm just so proud of my baby." Tina gives one final squeeze of his hands. "Oh, let me grab the camera," she says, trailing off. Marcus takes a gander at his son, admiring his studious persona.

"Are you ready?" he asks. Brandon takes in a deep breath and sighs.

"I think so."

Later that day, crowds of people are gathered in front of the gymnasium as the graduation celebration is about to commence. Families and friends are taking pictures and hugging one another. The sun captures the spirit of the occasion, shining brighter than usual at this time of morning.

Brandon and Samantha spot each other from a distance. They approach one other, stopping parallel to the main entrance of the gymnasium. They are the only two who exist at this moment. Nobody else is around. They don't speak right away. They just smile and stare into each other's eyes.

Samantha breaks the silence. "You're wearing contacts," she says surprisingly.

Brandon blushes. "Yeah, I figured I'd give it another shot."

Samantha's smitten. She finds Brandon even more attractive without glasses. He looks mature and very handsome in his graduation gown. "You're like a local celebrity now," she says. Brandon looks around at the crowd of people.

"It's bittersweet. I'm grateful and appreciative, but I don't want the rest of my life to be about being a school shooting survivor, you know?"

"But you're not a survivor, you're a hero," Samantha says gracefully. Brandon tilts his head down and smirks. He's bashful.

Samantha grabs both of his hands. They lock eyes. "*My* hero," she says with a smile. They share an intimate kiss.

Brandon's a bit calmer and more relaxed after his smooch.

"Are you ready?" she asks.

"As ready as I'll ever be," he says, trying to hype himself up. They walk hand-in-hand toward the ceremony.

Inside the gymnasium, family, friends, teachers, and graduating students crowd the large space. Three metal chairs are set up on stage. A dark wooden podium sits in the center. The crowd is uproarious with small talk, handshakes, and encounters between family, friends, and school staff. People make their way to their seats, or whatever seat they can find to get a better view as they take polaroid pictures and film moments with their camcorders. Brandon makes his way to his seat on stage. Next to him is Wendy Toreleski, Lakehurst's valedictorian. Just feet from the stage are the row of seats for the graduating class. Everyone is getting comfortable and preparing for the ceremony to start.

Brandon takes notice of Samantha sitting in the second row to the right. She smiles and waves to him. He looks nervous as hell. Light beads of sweat form on his forehead. He's cracking his knuckles and his right leg nervously bobs up and down rapidly.

Wendy notices his nerves. "It's okay to be nervous. My method is reaching the audience. Once they understand how I feel, I get more comfortable," she says.

"That's good advice . . . thank you," Brandon says, trying to collect himself.

"Don't mention it," she responds.

Principal Owens walks onto the stage thinking the podium is already equipped with a microphone. It's not. He turns his attention to one of the AV students and shrugs his shoulders, then makes a hand gesture that indicates he needs a microphone asap. The student quickly rushes to another fellow AV student who hands him a microphone. He then passes it to Principal Owens, who takes in a deep breath as he puts the microphone in the holder attached to the podium. He speaks into the mic and it reverberates throughout the entire gymnasium.

"Let's hear it for the class of two thousand!" he yells as he begins clapping. The entire auditorium follows with claps and cheers. Their collective uproar shakes the windows. Principal Owens then motions for everyone to take a seat. "Okay, settle down. Now, before we get to the graduation ceremony, we want to honor a very special student who bravely fought against adversity in what is to be remembered as Lakehurst's darkest hour. Not only did he manage to disarm the suspect, but he also saved sixteen lives that day, including his own. Words cannot begin to describe how proud and honored we are to have a student like him graduating from Lakehurst. Not only will he be accepting the first diploma issued, we also would like to honor him with the Lakehurst Silver Hero award for his bravery . . ."

Principal Owens holds up an encased silver medal. The lanyard attached is made up of the school colors—orange, white, and navy blue. A tag below the medal reads: *To honor, Brandon Scott, for his strength and bravery.*

"Ladies and gentlemen, and Lakehurst graduates, Brandon Scott," Principal Owens concludes. The auditorium goes insane. Emotions are a bit high for Brandon, who is having a minor panic attack at the moment. Principal Owens is encouraging him to stand and accept his award.

Wendy gives him a nudge. "Go ahead," she says.

Brandon stands up and slowly walks toward the podium, his heart pounding harder and faster with each step closer.

Principal Owens hands Brandon his diploma and his medal, then shakes his hand. Tina is in the audience taking pictures and cheering her son on. She's the loudest in the room. Principal Owens backs away and takes his seat to the right of the stage. The crowd begins to simmer down. Brandon gets a good look at his medal. The silver is smooth and shiny enough to see his reflection. He looks at the audience, who are anticipating his speech.

One student yells out. "Speech!" Half the auditorium laughs. Brandon takes a deep breath. At this point, you can hear a pin drop in the building. Samantha knows Brandon's nerves are getting the best of him and silently encourages him to speak.

"Hi—" Brandon says, taken aback by the screeching of the microphone. More awkward silence follows. He takes another deep breath in, then continues. "Um . . . some of you probably didn't know me before this happened. Some of you probably did and some of you probably even bullied me. I was never popular, and I didn't have many friends . . . but Ian was my friend. He was sick, and I knew this. I never thought he would do what he did, but in doing so he taught me a valuable lesson of acceptance and friendship. But I won't let this incident dictate me from living the rest of my life. We're graduating in a new millennium. I mean, how cool is that? A new period in history. A new era. And instead of dwelling on the past, I intend to look toward the future. Because I know the future is bright. It's bright for all of us. Because we're here, right now, in this moment, together. Life is just beginning for us." Brandon takes another quick glance at his award. "And I'm truly honored and thankful to be receiving this," he says, holding up his medal. "And even though I didn't know them well, I want to dedicate this award to the victims, and to you, Mr. Sadler, wherever you are"

Samantha wipes her teary eyes.

Standing near the back of the gymnasium, Mr. Sadler gives Brandon a bandaged two-finger wave. Brandon turns to look at Principal Owens, who seems to be holding back tears. "I think I'm done," Brandon says. He turns back to the audience. "Thank you," he concludes.

The auditorium erupts into cheers and applause. Brandon stares out, amazed by the love and respect he's receiving. He glances over at Samantha, who blows him a kiss. Brandon sends back a wink, realizing in that moment how truly grateful he is to be alive.

EPILOGUE

A bright November morning shines over the vast campus of Indiana State University. Several college students make their way to their next destination, as Brandon journeys through the busying morning. The campus is a barren gray landscape of melted snow and dead grass. Brandon provides the only splash of color in the otherwise cold and depressing atmosphere. Sporting a desert sand peacoat and a red and white plaid scarf, he's clearly unbothered by the outside elements. His focus is not on the weather or his surroundings either way, but on the casual conversation he's having on his new Nokia cellphone. It's a device that may seem exciting to own for most people, but it's just a bare necessity for Brandon. It's a phone with no cord, nothing too special. Besides chatting with Samantha from time to time, the majority of his cellphone use is attributed to the exhilarating rush he gets from playing the game *Snake*.

"I'm already packed . . . well you did say you were gonna drive . . . Sam, it's Thanksgiving, not a job interview," Brandon assures as he casually strolls through the campus courtyard. He pulls a pair of keys from his pocket as he enters a brick building. The foyer to the hall is beautifully adorned in Christmas decorations—faux snow sprayed on the widows, garland around a staircase railing, tinsel strung along the walls, and a gold and silver seven-foot Christmas tree. Footsteps and chatter from the student body echo through the hall.

"Fine, I'll drive. Are we still meeting for lunch? Okay, I'll see you in a bit. Love you too." Brandon kisses his end of the phone then hangs up.

He reaches an offset U-section of the hall, as he's surrounded by little brass mailboxes. Brandon walks over to his mailbox, number 329. Upon opening the tiny brass door, he sees a few envelopes inside. Flipping through, he sees a letter from his mom, a school newsletter that details the campus schedule until the new year, and a letter from Westchester State Hospital. It says it's from Ian Moss. Brandon is stunned. He momentarily stares at the envelope, frozen. His mind is racing. He looks up, now alert to his surroundings. Not a soul is in sight. He closes his mailbox door, then slowly opens the letter from Ian.

Dear Brandon,

How's it going? First off, I want to let you know that this is not a manifesto, and to also congratulate you on graduating. I envy your current college experience, which I'm sure is wonderful. I know I am the last person you want to hear from, but my therapist, Mrs. Sellers, tells me that this letter will be the much needed "closure" I need to move forward. Plus, I think you of all people deserve an explanation as to why I did what I did and what led up to it.

As you know, I have schizophrenia. When I was young, my dad killed himself, right in front of me. I know, right? That really messed me up. To this day, I'm not sure if that was the catalyst to my mental decline or if it was already in me, but my life has been a mental struggle since that day. But for many years afterward, I was doing great. Therapy was great. I felt great. And I know this sounds cliché, but coming to Lakehurst really did feel like the first day of the rest of my life. I was optimistic, excited, and anxious to finally experience what kids my age should.

I will admit it was a bit of a rough start—until that day we sat beside each other on the bus. That day I just knew I had a friend, a best friend who I felt comfortable around. Someone who made me not feel so alone. You gave me hope and optimism even when things didn't seem right with me. I just want you to know that my intention was never to hurt you. And if I could change the way things happened I would do so in a heartbeat.

I used poor judgment. I trusted the wrong people and it backfired on me (no pun intended). I was not in the right headspace those days leading up to the shooting and self-medicating with weed didn't help my case either. You have to understand that all of this was new to me. Not to use that as an excuse for what I did because looking back I am disgusted with myself for the way I handled things. So much so that my guilt and shame led me to wishing that I could have traded places with Alex or Jason. In that moment of regret I truly felt like my dad's son. Thinking that all of my problems could go away with just one bullet, unaware of the irony at the time because that's the reason I'm stuck here in the first place. But trust me, I have had a lot of time to reflect about what happened while I was recovering from my gunshot wound.

Which reminds me, I'm curious to know how you felt about shooting me. I know I deserved a lot worse, but I just want to know, did it freak you out? Did you like it? Will that stain of pulling the trigger haunt you for the rest of your life? I know it will for me. But I'm getting better at dealing with it. One day at a time.

But in all honesty, this place I'm in now is not that bad. I get to eat and watch whatever I want. My therapy sessions go without a hitch every time. Mrs. Sellers has got to be the best therapist I have ever had. She reminds me of old school Oprah, you know, back when she was fat. Just a truly generous soul with stellar advice. She has even helped me to continue with my schooling, so I'm on the fast track to graduating in the spring. I can't wait!

I'll wrap this up because lunch is being served soon. Meatball subs and strawberry cheesecake. My favorite. But I want you to know that I hold no resentment toward you at all, Brandon. You did the right thing and because of that I am exactly where I deserve to be. I'm content where I am because my actions proved that I am not quite ready to be the outstanding citizen I so yearn to become. But a step toward achieving that goal of modern sovereignty comes from admitting one's past mistakes and asking for forgiveness. I hope I am worthy of that forgiveness. This would be the part that I wish you the best and all but having known you I already know you are going to do great things in this world with or without my blessing.

Take care of yourself, Brandon, and happy holidays. Hope to hear from you soon.

Your friend,
Ian

Stunned, Brandon pauses as he stares at the last three words, *Your friend, Ian.* This revelation is a moment of disbelief for Brandon. He is not sure how he feels about this letter or its contents. A part of him feels as though he really didn't get the explanation he wanted out of it. But the other part feels as though he got just what he needed. Brandon is then startled by the ringtone on his cellphone, a cheesy digital chime that almost sounds like a Christmas carol.

"Hello? Yeah, I'm on my way now," he says, letter in hand. Looking around the hall, he doesn't see anyone. He continues his phone conversation as he makes his way toward the front entrance. Brandon crumples up the letter and envelope and tosses it in a nearby trash bin as he walks through the double doors.

ACKNOWLEDGMENTS

First, I would like to thank my good friend Kelvin, who was the first person to read the rough manuscript of this novel. Seems you already knew the direction and tone that I was going for with this book from the first line you read. But I thank you for taking the time to not only read my novel, but to offer constructive criticism as well. It was much needed.

Next, I would like to say thanks to my editor, Becky Hilliker. With your expertise and guidance, you have taken this story to new heights and places that I have not even imagined. This story shaped itself to be what it is because of the hard work and suggestions you provided. Collaborating with you on this story was the best possible outcome to get it to where it needed to be, and I sincerely thank you for that.

Also, a big shoutout and a thanks to my cover and layout designer, Lauren Sheldon. When you presented the book cover to me it honestly felt like you pulled the cover concept straight out of my head. I could not have imagined a better design. Seeing the layout for the first time damn near brought me to tears, and I thank you for all of your hard work and dedication to this project. It warms my heart to know that when people pick up a copy of this book, the first thing they are seeing is your hard work displayed on the cover. Again, thank you from the bottom of my heart.

Furthermore, to Mr. John Koehler and the rest of the Koehler

Books team, I would just like to give a huge thank you for providing me the platform and the opportunity for the world to read my weird little story. This has been a dream of mine for quite some time, and I thank you all for making this possible and giving me the chance to live out this dream of being a published author. You all have shown me the ropes and guided me along this process and have taught me so much. Words alone cannot describe how thankful I am for all of this.

But last and certainly not least, I want to thank my biggest supporter—my mom. I think it goes without saying that without you, none of this would be possible. Not only have you been a great mother to me, but you've also encouraged me to follow my dreams and to never give up. And for that, I truly feel blessed to have a mother like you in my life. This one's for you mom. Love you.